Warden of Greyrock

BOOK THREE

Warden of Greyrock
THE WARLOCKS OF TALVERDIN

K.V. Johansen

ORCA BOOK PUBLISHERS

Library and Archives Canada Cataloguing in Publication
Johansen, K. V. (Krista V.), 1968-
Warden of Greyrock / written by K.V. Johansen.

(The warlocks of Talverdin ; bk. 3)

ISBN 978-1-55469-005-3

I. Title. II. Series: Johansen, K. V. (Krista V.), 1968- . Warlocks of Talverdin; bk. 3.

PS8569.O2676W37 2009   jC813'.54   C2008-907211-1

Summary: In this third volume of the Warlocks of Talverdin series,
Maurey must make an impossible choice while Annot, Baroness of
Oakhold, fights for freedom; should either fail, Talverdin will fall.

First published in the United States 2009
Library of Congress Control Number: 2008940627

Orca Book Publishers gratefully acknowledges the support for its publishing programs pro-
vided by the following agencies: the Government of Canada through the Book Publishing
Industry Development Program and the Canada Council for the Arts, and the Province of
British Columbia through the BC Arts Council and the Book Publishing Tax Credit.

Cover artwork by Cathy Maclean

ORCA BOOK PUBLISHERS
PO Box 5626, STN. B
VICTORIA, BC CANADA
V8R 6S4

ORCA BOOK PUBLISHERS
PO Box 468
CUSTER, WA USA
98240-0468

www.orcabook.com
Printed and bound in Canada.
Printed on 100% recycled paper.
12 11 10 09 • 4 3 2 1

To the memory of Pippin (1995-2007).
We shall not look upon his like again.

CONTENTS

PART ONE

PART TWO

PART THREE

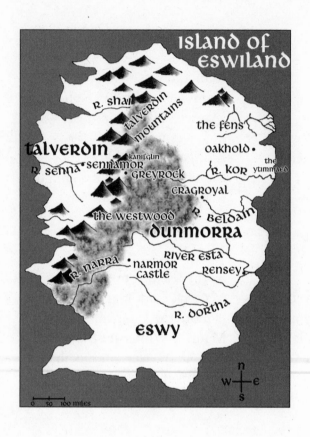

ISLAND OF ESWILAND

R. Shail

talverdin mountains

the fens

talverdin

oakhold

kanifglin · sennamor

R. senna

the yummaed

· GREYROCK

R. KOR

CRAGROYAL

R. BELDAIN

the westwood

ðunmorra

RIVER ESTA

R. NARRA

· NARMOR CASTLE

RENSEY

R. DORTHA

ESWY

N
W ✛ E
S

0   50   100 miles

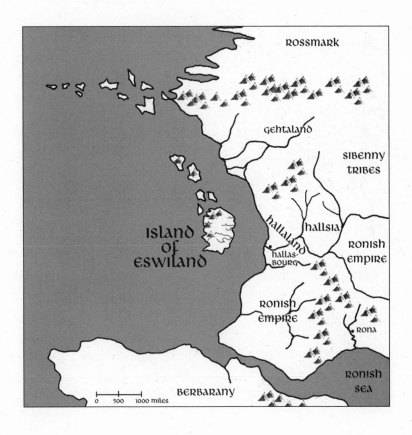

PART ONE

✴ PROLOGUE ✴

KANIFGLIN

Here follows the history of the conspiracy of the Yehillon against the peace between humans and Nightwalkers, written by the Warden of Greyrock:

A silver-haired girl ran towards a dark plume of smoke. She had been hunting hares on the mountainside and supper dangled from her hand. The girl dodged through the copse of pines that sheltered the cottage and the sheep sheds and the two wind-bent apple trees, and the hare dropped, forgotten. The cottage was a bonfire, and as she stared, the roof fell in with a roar and a fountain of sparks.

She shouted for her grandfather and ran again.

Two strangers stood looking up the length of the long narrow valley to where the peaks closed in, all ravines and scree and high snows. They turned, hearing her cry. An elderly man lay a little distance from them, dead. An axe was by his hand, and his dogs lay near him.

The girl had a bow in her hand, a quiver on her back. Quicker than thought, she shot one man, striking him in the throat. She wounded the second in the shoulder. He ran to his horse, abandoning his dead comrade. The girl fell to her knees, which is how her sister, returning frantic from distant pastures too late to help, found her.

They were free peasants, masters of their own valley and the high pastures, with no lord over them but the Warden of Greyrock and their king. They were not loved in the nearest village, Kanifglinfoot down under the forest eaves. They had a reputation for being strange, hiding secrets. The reeve of the village and the steward of the Warden of Greyrock coveted their valley and their flocks. Besides, the Warden who had governed the western part of the forest since the old king's day was not known for justice to the poor. The sisters were alone in the world with no one to protect them or even speak a good word for them. They had murdered a stranger, a foreigner, perhaps a wealthy man's servant, judging by his good leather armor and his weapons. They knew whose side the Warden and the magistrates of Greyrock Town would take, when they were brought before him for judgement.

So, alone, they buried their grandfather and the faithful dogs. Alone, they said the prayers to Genehar, whom most humans called Geneh, the Great Power of life and death. Alone, they sang songs in a language that made no sense even to them, but it was what they had been taught to do.

And then they left. They disappeared into the Westwood. It was spring, and through the summer they lived, hunting, robbing villages in the night and occassionally holding up lone travelers on the king's highway. Once they crept into the camp of the king himself as he traveled to Greyrock Town to appoint a new Warden of Greyrock, his own notorious half-brother Maurey, who was also a prince of Talverdin, a warlock only half human. They knew nothing of the reason for the king's journey and the hope it should have given them for justice. They simply stole what they could carry, and shortly thereafter, they took prisoner a ragged girl on a fine horse, a Talverdine horse. The girl claimed to be a minstrel, but she was Eleanor, Crown Princess of Eswy, bride-to-be of King Dugald of Dunmorra, and she escaped them, which is how they thought the king and the new Warden of Greyrock learned of them, and began hunting.

But they were hunted not because they robbed the king of a basket of provisions and a hound puppy, not because they stole a purse from a Nightwalker lord's horse and took a princess prisoner. They were hunted because a human witch, a lord of the Fens, dreamed of them and saw their grandfather's murder in his visions.

He saw the tattoo on the hand of the man they killed, the body they dragged to the ditch about the yard for the brambles to cover.

Seven concentric circles around a central boss, each joined to the next by a single line.

The symbol of the Yehillon.

All the latter part of the summer, the new Warden's scouts sought the sisters in the Westwood, while the fate of kingdoms was settled elsewhere, and treason unmasked and war averted. Always, the girls avoided capture. They were wary and cunning as foxes; they were witches though they hardly knew the word, and there were supposed to be no witches on the island of Eswiland except among the Fenlanders of the northeast. But while they were hunted, to find out what they knew about the man they had killed and what secrets they had guarded in Kanifglin that the man marked with the Yehillon symbol had wanted, Maurey of Greyrock put other plans into effect. He feared that, for the safety of Talverdin and the peace between humans and Nightwalkers, he could not afford to wait.

An autumn wind carried the bite of snow down Kanifglin's narrow valley though in the Westwood not all the leaves had fallen yet. Serrey and his sister Arromna had followed a little-used track up from the forest, passing the human village of Kanifglinfoot by night, safely hidden in the halfworld, where humans could neither see nor hear them, nor know if a Nightwalker walked right through them. Maurey'lana had been made Warden of Greyrock by his human brother a few months before. The people of his lands should be growing used to seeing the white-skinned, black-haired, black-eyed folk of his household, but still…it was not so long ago that warlocks, as humans called all Nightwalkers whether they were magic-talented Makers or not, were burnt alive in philosopher's fire whenever they were captured in the human kingdoms of Eswy and Dunmorra. Times were changing, but Serrey and Arromna did not want to test how much. Humans, especially northerners with their translucent raw-chicken-meat skins and eerie pale eyes, were not creatures either of them felt very comfortable with yet, though they had met many in Greyrock Castle while consulting ancient maps with Maurey'lana.

Besides, the prince wanted to keep their mission secret.

Maps of Dunmorra did not show the Kanifglin valley at all. It was not the sort of place that would be put on maps, just a long steep valley rising like a gash into the mountains, narrowing to nothing along a stony streambed, disappearing into cliffs. Nobody had ever lived here except one family of shepherds. The burnt ruins of their farmstead were at the lower end of the valley, just blackened stone and two apple trees heavy with fruit now, russet and golden-green, and the grave of the old man. Even with all his magic, Maurey'lana, the greatest Maker—or warlock, humans would say—in generations, could not find the granddaughters. Or rather, every time he thought he had found them, the girls seemed to know, and they slipped away to a new lair before they could be taken. Maurey'lana would catch them in the end, Serrey was sure of that. And when he did, perhaps the prince would learn the secret hidden by this valley. Now that he saw it, Serrey had no doubt but that it did hide secrets.

Two miles above the farmstead, where the head of the glen narrowed to nothing but a gash, a scar of scree and fallen slabs with a trickle of water at the bottom, a ruin stood on a spur of the mountainside, a hollow shell no more than head-high. The foundation showed that the ruin had been a round building of massively thick walls. It was surrounded by a circular green bank, with a gap that had no doubt once been a gateway in the rampart. Serrey waited while his sister, who had lingered longer, climbed back down to the bed of the stream from exploring those ruins.

"It's definitely a watchtower," said Arromna, "or it was once, long ago. And a watchtower, generally, has something to watch other than a dead-end valley."

Serrey nodded. There was no sign that there had ever been a village here, no humps and bumps beneath the sheep-cropped turf. What had the tower been watching then?

The prince feared it had watched some secondary pass through the mountains, some way long forgotten between Talverdin and Dunmorra, connecting what had once been provinces of the great Nightwalker kingdom of Eswiland, before Bloody Hallow came from the mainland five centuries before to slaughter Nightwalkers, claiming he was doing the will of the Powers. And Maurey'lana feared that the enemies of Talverdin— the people who would gladly send every Nightwalker, even bedridden grandmothers and babes in arms, to the fire if only they could find a way into the hidden kingdom—had somehow learned of Kanifglin and come seeking that forgotten pass.

"Dreams," the captain of rangers had said when Aljess'den, the captain of the prince's guard and a distant cousin of Serrey and Arromna, had asked for scouts to be sent to Greyrock. "Human nonsense." So he had sent Serrey and Arromna, the youngest and least experienced of his rangers. He could not quite refuse the prince, who despite being half human was the queen's own nephew and next heir to the crown after her own children.

The task of the rangers had always been to guard the mountain border between the Nightwalkers' hidden kingdom of Talverdin and the humans in Dunmorra and Eswy, who would invade and slaughter them all if they could. Every human knew that the Greyrock Pass, the only route into Talverdin, was guarded by deadly spells, warlocks' magic, and that the rock-bound coast was the same. Armies vanished in the Greyrock; armadas sank or were smashed to pieces in freak storms on the jagged western coast. Humans believed that the Talverdin Mountains were an impassible barrier, even more dangerous than the Greyrock Pass, and Talverdin's safety lay in their continuing to believe so. The truth was, no ancient spells protected the mountains, only the treacherous terrain. Every now and then human hunters or gold-seekers lost themselves and rarely, very rarely, found a way through to the west. The rangers saw to it that that did not happen very often.

Serrey and Arromna had looked at ancient Talverdine maps, as well as the useless old human ones, with the prince. There were certainly no passes but the Greyrock marked on their own maps. But one of them, a faithful copy of the oldest of all, showed Kanifglin and the tower, marked even then as ruins, and that also made it seem as if it had once been important, for what did one small valley in the human kingdom matter, among so many unmarked? It might not be impossible, for the mountain-skilled, to hunt a way through to the northwest from Kanifglin, angling towards the headwaters of the River Senna in the East Quartering province of Talverdin. Arromna thought so, and she had an instinct for such things.

And that was what they were here to test, before true winter sealed the land.

"I've had a nasty thought," Arromna said. "What if these Yehillon humans came back last summer? One escaped the witch-girls, or that's what the other witch saw in his vision. What if they're already in there, somewhere"—she tilted her chin at the looming peaks—"waiting for us?"

"If we can't hide from a handful of humans and make sure they disappear into the mountains for good, we aren't fit to be called rangers," Serrey said cheerfully.

"Elder brothers are supposed to be more reassuring than that," Arromna grumbled. "Why don't you tell me there's no chance humans could possibly have gone into the mountains without the Warden knowing, even if he was away half the summer stopping that rebellion in Eswy?" And under her breath she added, "Besides, what if there's more than a handful?"

But she followed Serrey when he strode forward, leaping from one flat slab of rock along the autumn-shrunken streambed to the next. It was, after all, an adventure, which was why she had joined the rangers. And the mountains were in her blood. If she and Serrey found and mapped a new pass, or a forgotten pass, they would be remembered in the annals of the rangers forever. Unless of course the humans calling themselves the Yehillon had found it first and were even now preparing an invasion, or lying in wait to ambush two young Nightwalker scouts, in which case the rangers and everyone else would all be dead soon enough and there would be no one to remember.

✳ CHAPTER ONE ✳

KORBY: DEAD END IN RONA

Here continues the narrative of the Moss'avver,
as set down at the command of the Warden of Greyrock by
Mathilda, Clerk of Asta College at the University of Cragroyal:

Master Arvol was dead. There was no doubt about it. I've seen enough dead people in my life to know that men with a whacking great knife stuck between their shoulder blades do not wake up and gasp out any useful last words, like, for instance, "Look out behind you."

I knew someone was there though. I'd known when I broke the door down, hearing Master Arvol's sudden cry and the harsh gasping that ended almost as soon as it had begun. I'd felt the life, the light of his mind, flicker and fade, and I'd felt the heart-pounding heat of his killer's nerves, that mix of terror and urgency that said this was no practiced Ronish assassin or warrior used to fighting for his life—not that stabbing an overweight scholar in the back was exactly a warrior's fair and honest fight anyway. It was murder—nasty, dirty and simple.

The young Hallalander had come here to Arvol's dingy little room on the upper floor of the tenement building to meet him. Arvol had opened the door and offered him a cup of wine "before we get down to business"; I'd heard that much from where I lurked behind the door to my own room across the landing, before Arvol had shut them in. No matter, I'd thought. I would whip up to the flat roof where the women dried their laundry and, by lying along the eaves over Arvol's window, be able to hear everything they said. But the murderer hadn't wasted any time. I'd only set my foot on the first rung of the ladder to the roof when Arvol cried out.

Now I moved as if I hadn't seen the killer standing frozen in the shadows to the right of the door, stepping further into the room as if about to kneel down by the fallen man to check for a pulse or turn him over. That gave the terrified youngster— all right, so he was hardly any younger than me, in years at least—his chance. If he had tried to flee out the door behind me I would have followed him as he bolted for home, to find out who sent him, but panic had boiled up into elation and fierce, personal hatred. He recognized me, just as I had him—blond, brown-eyed, soft-featured—one of the Hallalanders who had attacked my lord and me in the Hallasbourg library last spring. He swung at the back of my head with the first weapon that met his hand: a heavy earthenware water jug. At least he had the sense not to shout, but you can't sneak up on a witch. We walk in a sickening sea of other people's emotions. Anyhow, I heard him move. I caught his arm and bashed it against the edge of the door. He dropped the jug with a crash. It broke. So did his wrist. With a whimper, he fell to his knees in the spreading flood, but still he didn't cry out, and the next moment he had lurched back up, a narrow boot knife in his other hand.

He almost took me by surprise. I caught the knife just in time, before he could plunge it into his own ribs.

"Fool," I muttered and held him against the wall a moment, feeling my way into his scrabbling, terrified, animal emotions. Fury, terror, relief that he was still alive after all, howling misery— it's a shameful thing to see anyone so—deeper, deeper...there. Hand on his head, I shoved him into sleep, nice and gentle. As he slumped against me, I lowered him to the floor, closing the door. No one had come to investigate Arvol's dying cry. It was almost noon and the fried-fish shop five storeys down on the ground floor was a roar of customers shouting for attention at the street-front counter, the mistress of the place hollering at her daughters in the kitchen.

"So, my lad, what did Arvol have that they sent you to kill him for, I wonder?"

I searched the young man's purse and checked his jerkin and doublet for hidden pockets. He was carrying quite a lot of money and another little blade in his hem, but that was it. And yes, the boy was wearing an amulet, a fine enamelled disc, silver and red. His comrade, whom I'd killed, had worn something similar, and in a vision I'd seen another dead man with the same design tattooed on his hand. I had come to know that pattern well: a series of concentric circles, each joined to the next by a short line placed, apparently randomly, between each ring. *The symbol of the Yehillon* was what Master Arvol had labelled it in the coded notes my lord and I had stolen from him the past spring. What it meant I still didn't know, but I was suddenly a lot closer to finding out.

Master Arvol lay in a puddle of blood. In reaching for winecups from a book-laden shelf, he had turned his back on the boy. I didn't think much of Arvol, but I pitied him then, and I would cheerfully have finished off his killer if that wouldn't have made me just as wicked, murdering a helpless man. Besides, the boy was going to be very useful, whether he liked it or not.

Nothing in Arvol's purse but a few coins; nothing in the wide sleeves of his black master's gown. The exiled scholar had been supporting himself by selling the books he had stolen from the library of Hallasbourg University, once he had finished with them for his own research. We still didn't know what he had been looking for. Something that would give him a weapon against the Nightwalkers, we feared.

Last spring, humans, this boy among them, had ambushed my lord and me from the halfworld, and no human should be able to enter that shadowy colorless layer of the world without a Nightwalker to take them. Their weapons had been painted with some alchemical brew that burned through flesh like acid.

They had probably been watching Arvol themselves when we attracted their attention by spying on him. They had recognized Maurey as a Nightwalker and tried to kill him. Not so surprising in itself; lots of people loathed and feared the Nightwalkers. But why had they been watching Arvol? I was starting to think that it was because the thing Arvol had been hunting through all those old books was not some recipe for nasty poisons, but the secrets of the Yehillon itself. And the Yehillon was something to do with this folk, who all wore its symbol.

When I had finished searching Master Arvol, I turned to the little table he had obviously used as a writing desk. For Arvol, it was remarkably tidy. No mess of unwashed dishes, no heaps of papers and apple cores and sticky wine cups. Had he wanted to impress his visitor and look like a real scholar, not a miserable drunkard? There was only one book…and a letter.

The writing was not Arvol's. I scanned over the usual sort of flowery greetings. It was from a Master Labienus—that was the bookseller he sold his stolen texts to. Once he was through greeting his most noble, honorable and gracious friend, whose wisdom outshone that of the ancient sages—and it took him a paragraph to do that—Labienus got down to business. He could perhaps find a buyer for the item they had discussed. It was, as Master Arvol knew, an unusual text. Though it had little value, being badly damaged and difficult to read and what little that could be read seemed to be a fanciful children's tale rather than any useful work of history, a princely patron of his to whom he had mentioned it might find it worth a few pounds. This nobleman had asked that his librarian be allowed to examine the volume late in the morning tomorrow, the second of Theyin-month…Well, that was today, and I knew all about that.

Was the book so valuable that this nobleman was going to murder to get his hands on it without paying? Scholars can be pretty greedy about books, but still, that seemed unlikely. And the boy had been ready to kill himself to avoid capture. I didn't think the aristocracy of Rona commanded that kind of loyalty. Not from their librarians.

The book on the table was old, the leather of its binding black and cracked. The spine was broken, the sewn-together folds of parchment—quires, they're called—were loose and falling out. I leafed through it carefully. I had trouble reading the old style of writing, and the language was Old Ronish. I didn't have time to do more than glance over it, but I could make out that the first two-thirds of this book was a history of the end of the first Ronish empire almost a thousand years before, a time of civil wars and foreign invasions and general nastiness. Most of the rest of it, copied by a different scribe in a different hand, was the life of some emperor or other. And then—ah. The very last section, just eight pages, was different again. It had been in a fire, for one thing, and was scorched. The red-inked title was—what? *Iarakulanar and Iahillalana* sounded like a schoolboy's tongue twister, but it was the only thing that wasn't definitely history and so might be "a fanciful children's tale."

My stomach lurched and I felt hot with excitement. It wasn't any change in the headache-clamor of all the minds in the building and the street below, which I'd sort of gotten used to ignoring, the way you do an ache that can't be eased. I might be slow at dead languages, but I can get by in Talverdine, the language of the Nightwalkers.

What we translate as "Prince Maurey" is actually Maurey'*lana*—the honorific comes last. So even though the book was in Old Ronish, I'd read *Iarakulanar and Iahillalana* as though they were Talverdine. I'd thought "the Iaraku princes and Prince Iahilla" without even thinking, if you see what I mean.

Languages are always changing their sounds, sprouting new bits and dropping old ones. Maybe I'd been hanging around with bookish sorts too long, that I could excited about that kind of thing, but it looked to me like you could take "Iahilla'lana" and get "Yehill-lon" out of it.

I'd have bet my favorite horse and my sister's jewels, if she had any, that Arvol had jumped to the same conclusion. He'd been trying to find out about the Yehillon a lot longer than I had, and he had a better education.

I broke the last thread holding in that quire of pages and tucked it down the front of my shirt next to my skin, beneath doublet and jerkin. Then I took the book and the letter and went back to the sleeping murderer. I set his wrist and splinted it with a couple of slats from the bedframe, then tied both arms together across his chest.

"Up you get," I said cheerfully, speaking Ronish with what everyone but me thinks is a horrible accent. I hauled him to his feet, waking him up as I did so.

He mewled with pain and then clamped his lips tight. The wrist was starting to throb. I knew. I could feel it.

"Don't worry about the book, I'll look after it." I waved it at him. "We're going to cross the landing to my room so's I can pack up my things. And while I pack, you can tell me all about the Yehillon and this nobleman who likes old books."

He didn't intend to tell me anything, and his hatred was going to give him strength. It was making me feel quite sick. Seen close to, his face, softer, younger, was that of the blond brown-eyed man I had dropped dead with a thrown dagger during the fight in the library.

"Was he your brother?" I asked, not teasing him now.

"This fat fool?" he burst out in disdain. His Ronish accent was far better than mine.

"No, when you ambushed us in the Hallasbourg library last spring."

"The man you killed? Yes, he was my brother. And you left my other brother a cripple. And your warlock killed my cousin." He shut his teeth on the words as though he had given too much away.

I bit my own tongue on a snarky comment about a jolly family outing. I wasn't going to apologize for killing a man who was trying to kill me and my lord, but I could forgive the boy wanting revenge. I shut Arvol's door carefully. The splinters around the lock didn't show in the perpetual night of the landing. He probably wouldn't be found until the next day, when the coming week's rent was due. And of course, once the corpse was discovered, the big Fenlander with the scarred face and the red braids was the most obvious suspicious character around.

Depending on what I learned that afternoon, I hoped I might be well on my way out of Rona by then. I hate cities. Too many people.

I sat the young Hallalander down on the floor, his ankles tied together with his own linen neckcloth, while I packed up my few belongings and changed to more practical clothing than fashionable doublet and hose: leather trousers and a brigandine lined with horn plates. I strapped on my greatsword and long dagger, even if they did make me look like some nobleman's barbarian mercenary. My prisoner might have people looking for him. I left *Iarakulanar* and *Iahillalana* inside my shirt. Not the best place to carry around old parchment pages, especially ones with charred and crumbling edges, but it was out of the boy's sight.

"What's your name?" I asked, squatting down by him.

Sullen hatred, and fear too, was all I got from him. Fine. I could make him talk. Maurey, who is my lord by my own choice and oath and blood, and Dugald, who is my lord by right of being my king whether we Fenlanders like it or not, would both have my head if I did anything too nasty. Being a Fenlander witch, I didn't need to.

I tried first to simply strengthen in his mind that urge we all have to please other people, to like and be liked, to trust. With a lot of people, that would have been enough. Like an innocent child or someone who'd had over much to drink, they'd have said things that better sense would have told them they should keep quiet. It didn't work on this lad. He hated me too much to betray secrets so easily. I do admit he had reason. I could maybe have forced my way deeper into his mind, found the checks we all use to stop ourselves babbling out our secrets and pulled down those barriers by force. He'd have told me whatever I asked then, but the Powers alone know what that might have done to his mind. Mind and soul are a lot slower to heal than the body. Every child in the Fens who shows a talent for witchery gets told how terrible a sin it is to do damage to another's mind, how folk have been killed by a witch tearing at them this way and how, more often than not, the witch's mind and soul are shattered along with the victim's. Not that one in a few hundred is ever born strong enough to do such a thing.

I took the easy way and simply began to stoke his fear into outright terror. Influencing someone's emotions isn't the same as attacking the actual fabric of his mind, but still, it isn't a trick most witches can do. Most of us just feel the emotions of those close by, and dream true dreams, and work little magics of the will, able to call up flames or frost, or tame wild animals to our hand. Me, I'm one of the strongest. My sister is another, and it's actually a trick of hers. I learnt it by being its prime victim. She was a dreadful bully when we were children, viciously jealous of the spoilt little heir to the chieftaincy, but she's not so bad now we're grown up. (She says it's me who's improved.) To tell the truth, I couldn't do without her.

Anyway, I simply made the boy terrified of me, building up the fear that was already there, till he was nearly sick with it.

My cousin Annot claims this is just as wrong as beating him

or taking red-hot pokers to him, or maybe even worse: turning someone's own mind against him. I don't know. I've never dared ask Maurey what he thinks about it, for fear of what he might say.

"Now," I said, squatting down by the Hallalander. He flinched away. "I don't have a lot of time. I want to know who you are, who sent you here and why. For starters."

I'm not proud of having done this, but the way I saw it, it had to be done. And he was alive and unharmed at the end of it, and not so shamed and debased as he might have been. So.

He trembled like a dog in a thunderstorm.

"Tell me what I need to know and I'll set you free," I said. "We're both warriors, in our way. I give you my word, by the Yerku and Fescor: help me and I won't harm you." The Yerku, the twin patrons of warriors, and Fescor, the escort of the shades of the dead, were not the most comforting Lesser Powers to invoke under the circumstances. I didn't intend them to be.

He wanted badly to believe me, but he was convinced all the same that I was going to butcher him here, just as he had butchered Master Arvol. Yet he had to hope.

"So who are you?" I asked.

"Gerhardt," he said. His teeth chattered. "Son of Count Gerhardt of Maasvill."

"Maasvill's in Hallaland?"

"Yes."

"Any relation to Lady Katerina, the lady-in-waiting to the Dunmorran queen?"

"You touch her and I'll kill you!" Gerhardt screamed. I clamped a hand over his mouth.

"She's in no danger if she serves her mistress honestly," I said. "But she does have a problem with that, doesn't she? What is she to you?"

"My sister's daughter and—"

"Is she really? Sure she's not your sweetheart? You're about the same age." I didn't really disbelieve him; I just wanted more detail. The more I knew about this murderous family, the better.

"No! Her mother is my sister. Katerina's my niece, my kin. I grew up with her as a sister, and if you harm her I'll—"

"She'd better keep faith with her lady then, hadn't she?"

But Gerhardt had confirmed what we already believed. Lady Katerina had not only betrayed Eleanor once, but twice over. She had worked for the traitor Sawfield and for these Yehillon people. And she was in Cragroyal right now, free at the court of the king, because Eleanor, too good-hearted for her own safety, wanted to trust her.

Dugald ought to be sleeping in armor.

"Is she going to harm the king?" I asked. That was more important than anything else I could learn, even about the Yehillon.

Gerhardt shook his head violently, eyes wide. "No. No! Don't hurt her. Katerina just reports on the warlocks when they come to the court, that's all. She warns us what they're doing in Dunmorra. Don't hurt her! In her last letter she said she wouldn't spy on the queen again; she wouldn't report on her, just the warlocks. She said she wouldn't even try to make the queen see how evil they were anymore. The prince was furious."

Not all Nightwalkers were warlocks, but I decided against giving him a lecture. "What prince?"

"*The* prince," he said. "Alberick."

"Prince of where?"

"*Our* prince," he whispered. "Chosen by the High Circle. The one who's been born to finally purify the world of the warlocks. At last."

"What do you mean?" I took a guess. "The Yehillon. He's the Yehillon?" Amidst Gerhardt's fear there was contempt for my stupidity. "No, you're the Yehillon, all of you. A clan? A religious sect?"

He actually tried to scrabble to his feet, a surge of mindless panic making him run. I pulled him back down. "I want an answer. What's the Yehillon?"

"H-holy," he stammered. "Sacred trust. From the Powers. We have to get rid of the Nightwalkers. They don't belong here. They're wrong, they shouldn't be here. We have to get rid of them. You wouldn't understand, you filthy warlock-lover, you *wallachim*! We pass on the trust, mother to daughter, father to son, through the years. We keep the light alive! We're blessed with the Lesser Gift. Prince Miron almost succeeded in Good King Hallow's day, but even he didn't have the Great Gift. Alberick does. This time, we'll make an end of them and cleanse the world of their evil. They're wrong. They're an offence against the natural order of things, don't you see? Abominations!"

The only Miron I'd heard of was an Archmagister of the College of Astrologers five hundred years ago, the man who invented Philosopher's Fire, which burned Nightwalkers but not humans. Miron helped Conqueror Hallow take Eswiland, massacring the Nightwalkers and the humans who lived among them—we Fenlanders were the last remnant of those true Eswyn humans.

"Tell me about the Great Gift this Alberick has," I suggested.

"It's forbidden."

"Tell me anyway."

"I can't!" He started shaking again. "I don't know! It's forbidden for any but the High Circle to know."

"What about the Lesser Gift? Should I guess? You can enter the halfworld."

"I can't, I can't. Only a few are granted even the Lesser Gift. My brothers and sister were blessed, not me. And it isn't the warlocks' halfworld, it isn't. We're pure, we don't use that evil. The Lesser Gift lets us walk the shadow road, blessed by the Powers."

I nodded as if I understood. "Ah. What's this mean?" I dangled his amulet before him.

"It's a symbol. That's all. So that we know one another."

A symbol had to have some encoded meaning behind it, a reason why it was a symbol, but he really was telling all he knew.

"And why did you murder Arvol? I should take you back to Dunmorra, you know, to stand trial for that. He might have been exiled for his crimes, but he was still a subject of my king. I won't," I added hastily. Gerhardt looked like he might weep. "I gave you my word. But you're going to live with the shame of that cowardice the rest of your life, killing a poor old fool that way, and in the end you're going to face Genehar's—Geneh's— judgement with his murder on your soul."

"I didn't want to! The prince ordered it when Labienus told him about the book. It wasn't my fault!"

"I don't think Genehar accepts that kind of excuse. A person's deeds are his own." I hit him with another question. "So Labienus the bookseller is Yehillon too?"

Gerhardt nodded and went on without prompting, trying to buy his own safety by pleasing me and throwing me a different victim. It wasn't nice to see.

"Arvol discovered Labienus was one of us. Labienus has the symbol on his shop sign. Arvol shouldn't have known what it meant, but he did. He kept trying to find out more from Labienus. He hated Nightwalkers. He wanted to join us, he said. As if he could! We were chosen by the Powers in the Years of Darkness. We were sent from Darkness. We're special. You can't just join. You have to be born. You have to be *family*. Labienus kept putting Arvol off. Then he came with this book. He said he'd found secrets, great secrets about the Yehillon that we should know. He showed Labienus."

"What secrets?"

"I don't know!"

"But they were in this book?" I patted the pack where he had seen me stow it. His eyes fixed on it greedily.

"Yes. He let Labienus read it. Labienus told the prince. I was here in Rona watching Arvol—and you. The prince had Labienus arrange for me to meet Arvol."

"And kill him and take the book to Labienus."

"No! I had to take the book to the prince at Labienus's shop. Without opening it."

"What, not even a peek?"

Gerhardt shook his head, and his fear was as much of disobeying his prince's orders as of me.

"Final question. One of our men followed Arvol last summer when he left Hallasbourg. What happened to him?"

"It wasn't me!" Gerhardt protested. "I didn't do it. It was the prince's men. He was watching Labienus's bookshop. There was a meeting there one night and the Dunmorran spy tried to follow Alberick when he left. They threw his body in the river," he added.

We'd feared as much.

I sighed and left off leaning on the boy's emotions. He slumped forward, head on his knees, and burst into tears. I swear I would have done the same if he hadn't been there to see. Or worse, been on my knees throwing up my breakfast. As it was I sat for too long holding my head in my hands, feeling utterly drained and filthy. I think Annot's right.

"Even if you kill me, they'll find you," Gerhardt said faintly, raising his head again. "The High Circle has *gifts*."

"Good for them," I muttered. If he hadn't figured out yet that I did too, I wasn't about to enlighten him. "I told you I'd let you go. First though, we're going to visit Labienus's bookshop. I want to see your prince."

Hope flared in him, and fear again.

"You can't see him. Nobody can, except the High Circle."

"How do you know he exists then?" I asked curiously.

"I've met him," he said. "I'm trusted."

"You're not High Circle."

"I'm trusted. Anyway, he was veiled. We're all safer if nobody knows his face, especially with you dirty warlock-lovers nosing around."

I cuffed his ear, not very hard. He glowered, back to hating me.

"You'll all burn too, once Talverdin falls. And it will. Soon. Prince Alberick has found a way."

"How?" I demanded.

"Don't know," he growled, and I could taste that he was telling the truth. Just what I needed, a new threat to worry about. I drew my dagger, and he whimpered and cringed away. I ignored that and sliced through the cloth binding his ankles. "Let's go."

"Using me as a hostage won't help you. I'd die for him. We all would."

Gerhardt was almost as afraid of his prince as he was of me.

❋ CHAPTER TWO ❋
MAUREY: WITCHES IN THE WESTWOOD

S et a thief to catch a thief, they say. I had set witches to catch witches, and it had still taken them most of the autumn to find the outlaws, the witch-girls from the mountains. The spring before, Robin and Fuallia Shepherd had killed a man and fled down into the Westwood to live as outlaws. If they had not used witchery to raid the king's camp as he traveled to Greyrock Town, if they had not briefly captured Eleanor, crown princess of Eswy and now my brother Dugald's wife, they might never have come to our attention. Or maybe they would have. Maybe the Moss'avver would have dreamed of them anyway.

"They're asleep, and so's their dog." Tam, one of the Moss'avver clansmen left by Korby to serve me, slid from between the trees with a born poacher's stealth. "Mollie's trying to keep 'em under, but that older lass is strong and she's trying to wake. She'd give the chief a fight, I think." The boy grinned. "Like to see that, Y'r'ighness?"

"No. I'd like to get them quietly back to Greyrock Castle without anyone getting hurt."

Tam shook his head at my lack of humor. Fenlanders don't go in for reverence to princes much.

I nodded to Aljess. It was still night, though dawn was thinning the shadows. She and I used that darkness to slip into the halfworld, disappearing as not even Tam—as no full-blooded human—could. The halfworld lies over the ordinary world of nature, another layer, you could call it, a little removed.

Without color, it is a place of shadow and mist and a thousand shades of grey stretched between black and white. Nightwalkers and their white horses and a certain breed of dun Talverdine dog can use darkness as a doorway to enter it and move unseen, unheard, by creatures in the ordinary world. Even witches can't detect a Nightwalker in the halfworld. At least Korby can't, and what he can't do I don't think any other witch could.

We were north of the highway in the central part of the Westwood, and I had left the rest of the troop, Nightwalker and human knights and soldiers, in a camp three miles away. I thought—I hoped—that the spells Aljess and I had cast as we traveled had, this time, kept us secret from the witches, but I wasn't taking any chances. Twenty people on horseback cannot move quietly through the forest.

Even a year before, humans and Nightwalkers forming one military company would have been unheard-of in Dunmorra, but this past summer my aunt Ancrena, the queen of Talverdin, the last refuge of the inhuman Nightwalkers, and my brother, the human king of Dunmorra, had appointed me to be Warden of Greyrock, the castle that watched the Dunmorran end of the only known mountain pass into magically guarded Talverdin. It was an experiment, Dugald said, and so far—so far—the mixed garrison of Nightwalkers and humans had not had any more brawls among the men- and women-at-arms than any small fort could expect. The knights themselves were all carefully polite to one another, leaving brawling to the lower ranks. The humans found being commanded by Captain Aljess, a woman, almost more worrying than being commanded by a Nightwalker and a warlock—or a Maker, as Nightwalkers called those with a talent for sorcery, like Aljess and me.

They'd get used to it.

The outlaws had made their most recent lair in a hollow tree, an oak that might already have been old when Hallow came to massacre my father's people five hundred years before. It was an ugly, twisted boulder of a tree; its heavy, naked branches, thick as trunks themselves, bowed down to rest on the forest floor. Dry leaves rustled underfoot, no matter how quietly Tam moved, but to Aljess and me they were mist-thin.

Mollie, the other Moss'avver witch left in my service, crouched by a crack in the trunk that made a sort of peaked doorway. A blanket woven in the russet, white and blue tartan of her clan (without which no Fenlanders counted themselves properly dressed) camouflaged her as well as a grey jay's feathers.

I stepped out of the halfworld for a moment and touched Mollie's arm. She looked up and grinned.

"I'm still holding 'em, Highness, but th'older lass is starting to fight it. Even in her sleep she knows summat's wrong." Mollie sounded more admiring than annoyed, but there was a sheen of sweat on her lined face. Tam knelt beside her, a hand on her shoulder, probably helping to strengthen her witching. Fenlander witchery doesn't use chanted and object-bound spells like we Nightwalker Makers do, or written symbols and spells like the magic-working that humans call the philosopher's secret arts; it doesn't use made things at all. It's some power in their blood, a matter of instinct and will.

"Better get 'em quick, or they'll be comin' out fightin'."

The rough-cured pelt of a deer was hung over the crack in the tree as a barrier against the wind, which now, at the start of Theyin-month, began to have the bite of coming winter. I used the shadow of the tree to return to Aljess in the halfworld, moving to pass through the curtain, but Al stopped me with a hand on my arm.

"I go first, Maurey'lana," she said. I didn't argue. Even if by some unknown witch-skill they did detect our entering, I didn't believe that a shepherd girl knifing me was going to bring Talverdin and Dunmorra to war, not when my aunt and my brother wanted peace so strongly. However, in a way, I was the symbol of that peace, the half-breed, the person who stood between the two worlds and brought them together. And my safety was Aljess's duty and her honor.

She ducked inside and I followed. So far, so good. The girls still had not woken. But we were as close as we could get in the halfworld.

We both slid back to the natural world. A human would have been blind in the lightless belly of the tree. We were Nightwalkers.

In ordinary darkness, everything has its own color: soft, like pearl and velvet. Night shows the secret shades of stone and wood. They say that from the acorn, an oak grows five hundred years, lives five hundred years and spends a third five hundred dying. This one was somewhere in its last five centuries, a tree ancient enough to be rock solid even in the halfworld, where we Nightwalkers might walk through mere saplings as though they were mist. Although the heart of the tree was eaten away by dry decay, it still had a beauty for Aljess and me to see, a faint amber glow, like sun through honey, marbled with darker streaks. The dry bracken the girls had piled deep for their bed was a paler color, silvery, with a memory of living green. Hair, skin, the threadbare cloaks and blanket sewn of rabbit-skins under which they lay tight together for warmth, with their bluehound— stolen from my brother—on their feet, all gave the faintest light in their own night-colors.

I knelt down by the girls' heads.

"Robin," I said softly. "Fuallia. Wake up now. There's nothing to fear."

Mollie and Tam let go whatever witchery had been holding the girls and their dog in sleep. As Mollie had said, Robin, the elder, knew something was wrong. She came up fighting the moment she was released, a blind punch with the palm of her hand that would have caught my chin if I hadn't leaned back just in time. I seized her wrists. She sank her teeth into the back of my hand. I hissed but didn't let go.

"We're not your enemies," I repeated, but she was a trapped animal, and I don't think she understood.

Fuallia launched herself up with a knife in her hand, but she was slower, and Aljess caught her more securely than I had Robin, holding the silver-haired girl tight against her armored body with one arm, gripping her hand to keep the knife well away from everyone, including the young bluehound, which was barking and leaping around them, not very helpfully. Fuallia hung her head, dropping her blade, as I hauled Robin, still kicking and twisting savagely, to her feet and wrapped her in my arms, crushing her to my chest much as Aljess had Fuallia. My hauberk could turn a sword; let her try her teeth on good Talverdine mail.

Fuallia wept silently, wearily, but Aljess relaxed her grip only enough not to hurt her. "How about some rope?" she asked in Talverdine.

"If we have to," I said. "Robin, Robin Shepherd, listen to me!" I shook her. "We're not here to harm you. Stand quietly and I'll let you go."

"It was me. I killed him!" she shouted. "Let my sister go, she didn't do anything. Look at her; you can't believe she could harm a fly."

"She just had a fairly good go at stabbing my captain," I pointed out. "Robin, lying doesn't serve you. We know it was Fuallia killed that man, and we know the circumstances. It wasn't murder. No one is saying it was murder."

"It was me. Tell the warden to hang me and let Fu go!"

"No one's going to be hanged. Stop kicking and put your feet on the ground, or I swear I'll carry you out over my shoulder like a baby."

"Listen to the Lord Warden!" Aljess shouted over the hound's frantic barking.

"M'lord?" Tam called. "You all right in there?"

"Fine, we're fine," I shouted, afraid of the excitable Fenlanders rushing in half-blind, probably with swords drawn. "We have them. Stay where you are! Fuallia, quiet the dog."

"Taddie, quiet," said Fuallia, and the dog fell silent. It even sat, gaze fixed unwaveringly on Fuallia. I hoped her next word wasn't going to set it at Al's throat.

"Thank you," I said. A feeling like a foul headache was building up behind my eyes, and I'd hunted with Korby enough to know witchery when it struck, however subtle the attack. "Robin, don't do that either. Attack any of us further, in any way, and I'll have *my* witches knock you out again. We can talk to Fuallia alone." The headache fell apart. My threat was empty. Mollie and Tam didn't have a chance of overpowering Robin if she was awake and fighting, and the only witch I knew of who could was far off in Rona. Aljess or I could easily bind her with a spell of our own, but Nightwalker warlocks using magic to arrest humans in Dunmorra...that was a bad, bad idea, even if I was the Warden of Greyrock, arresting them in the human king's name. The old stories about Nightwalkers stepping from the shadows to murder or bespell human victims had not yet been forgotten.

"The Lord Warden?" Robin asked quietly. It was the first thing she had said that wasn't a shout, but she sounded as though the words alone were a mortal blow.

"Yes," I said. "Will you listen now? The king's agents have looked into what happened last spring. We know the truth. Neither you nor Fuallia is in any danger of hanging. We know Fuallia killed that man in defence of her life and her home. Everything you did afterwards...well, back at Greyrock there's a decree signed in the king's own hand, Robin. It says you are

both acquitted of murdering that stranger—that means you're
let off—on the evidence of the king's officers,"—or the witch-
visions of the Moss'avver, but that wasn't the sort of thing to
put on record in the royal chancery—"and that any crimes you
may have committed since, highway robbery or breaking of the
Forest Law, say, are pardoned by the king's mercy, so long as you
give up your banditry. He particularly charges you not to steal
any more of his dogs."

Neither of them smiled. The matter was too serious for
joking. Or maybe they didn't believe me.

"You can go home," I added gently. "Come, let's go outside.
I'll have someone collect your things." They had few enough,
but I knew well how the little things mattered when they were
all you owned.

"Home?" Robin asked. "You're lying. You can't be the Lord
Warden. He wouldn't come out here after us. And that sounds
like a woman." In a different voice—was it astonishment?—she
added, "You're *Nightwalkers*."

When I'm around Nightwalkers every day, it becomes very
easy to forget that not everyone can see in the dark. Robin and
Fuallia had been fighting us without ever seeing our faces. But
Robin had a keen mind. She drew the obvious conclusion from
how easily we had overpowered them, without ever needing to
see our milk-white skin and black eyes and hair. She knew we
must have been able to see what we were doing. I felt her relax
in my arms.

I had rather expected her to start struggling again. Even
if in Dunmorra people knew there was peace, too many still
feared Nightwalkers, and if surprised in the dark, even my own
human knights could be forgiven if the old stories of murderous
warlocks flashed uppermost into their minds.

"We're Nightwalkers," I confirmed. "This knight is Aljess of
House Keldyachi, captain of my guard. I'm Maurey Keldyachi.

And I am the Warden of Greyrock, since this summer past. If I let you go, are you going to bite again?"

"Maurey? The *prince*?" She went tense once more. "Sir, Your Highness, is the warlock queen angry that we went away? There wasn't anybody we could tell we were leaving. I mean, if there had been, we wouldn't have had to leave. Grandda always said the Nightwalkers'd come to us after the king made peace and you started traveling through the Greyrock Pass again, but nobody ever did. And then he got murdered and there was just me and Fu...I knew it was wrong to go, but we had to get away before the old warden's men came looking..."

"Robin, Robin, hush. It's all right. You haven't done anything wrong, anything at all." Aside from robbing folk on the king's highway, including the king himself, and killing game that was the right of the king's huntsmen and the forest village communes, but I knew that wasn't what she meant, even if I didn't have the foggiest idea what she *was* talking about.

"I've been hunting you to bring you the king's pardon, Robin. To tell you that you could go home to your valley. I've had my folk collect what's left of your sheep and put them in with the Greyrock Castle flocks for the winter."

They couldn't really go home to Kanifglin, their barren high valley, with winter coming on and no kale in the garden, no fleeces sold for flour, no cheese in their larder; but there was plenty of room for two young shepherds at Greyrock. My human commander, the Lieutenant-Warden Lord Lowrison, would grumble about two more mouths to feed, but he grumbled about everything that had to do with spending money and using up Greyrock's precious winter supplies. It was his job, and I was glad he knew all the things I didn't about how a great castle and a town should be run. "Why on earth do you think the queen of Talverdin would blame you for not staying in Kanifglin?"

"Because we promised to stay," she said.

"Promised who?"

"The lady."

"What lady?"

"The Lady of Kanifglin."

"Who?" Aljess asked.

I asked, "When?"

Robin shrugged. "When Hallow came."

That was five hundred years ago.

"Who was the Lady of Kanifglin?" Aljess asked.

"A princess," Robin said. "Don't you know, my la—sir— Captain? You must know. Grandda always said you'd come back, you Nightwalkers."

Aljess and I looked at one another. Now Al shrugged.

"But why?" I asked.

"You're supposed to know, aren't you?" For a moment Robin sounded almost on the verge of tears, and she didn't strike me as someone who let herself cry easily. Worn out, frightened, hungry…no wonder.

"Later," I said. "We'll talk about it later. It's not important right now. Nobody wants to arrest you, nobody's angry at you. You're safe."

I let her go and pushed her gently towards the curtain with a hand on her shoulder. All bone. They hadn't been eating any too well. So much for the romantic forest life of Jock Wildwood, roast venison and cider every day. No shoes either. Aljess followed, guiding Fuallia, who now carried the dog in her arms.

Robin didn't try to run, as I half expected. She merely scowled at Tam, frowned and raised her eyebrows at Mollie. The Fenlanders were an unusual sight in the Westwood, true enough, both wearing barbarian trousers rather than hose, both in leather brigandines with their Fen blankets worn as shawls, both with long hair in pigtails: Tam's red, Mollie's yellow fading to white with age. And being Fenlanders, between the two of them they sported a lot more blades than seemed absolutely necessary.

"Make yourself useful," I told Tam. "Pack up everything in the tree as carefully as if it were your own."

"What if it's no' their own to begin with, m'lord?"

"Pack it up anyway."

Robin turned on her heel to direct her glower at me. It was the first time I'd actually seen her by daylight. I could understand how Queen Eleanor had believed her when she claimed to be Fuallia's brother. If you weren't used to seeing women in trousers or hose, Robin, with her tattered hose and short tunic, her curly brown hair, once cropped short, now hanging in snarls below her ears, could pass as a boy—until you looked for her delicate chin and the curve of her hips that not even near-starvation could hide. Fuallia wore her silver-blonde hair in a long braid and a gown whose ragged hem, peasant-style, hung above her ankles, not to be dragging in the dirt; but she was just as gaunt as her sister. Her blue eyes were wide and staring though, while Robin's burned.

"The king wouldn't send the Warden of Greyrock himself out just to deliver a pardon to the likes of us," she said. "He has men-at-arms and couriers and who knows what else for that, if he really cares at all. Tell me the truth, Your Highness."

"I have."

"Not all the truth."

If she was a witch anything like Korby, she could tell when someone lied. He said it was almost a taste. I hadn't lied, but she was quite right, I hadn't told all the truth.

"We need your help," I said. "We need to find out about the man who was killed, and the one who escaped. We want to find out why your grandfather was murdered and who did it."

"Oh, of course, the king himself wants to see justice served on a poor old peasant's killer?" she snapped.

"King Dugald does want justice, Robin. For everyone. When strangers come into the land and murder his folk, Dugald does care—when he hears about it." And there was a new reeve in Kanifglinfoot Village, because the old one hadn't thought the king's warden needed to hear about murder and missing girls, not when there was a fine flock of mountain black-face sheep roaming free for the taking. "You're right though, there's more to it than that, but—"

"M'lord Prince!" Robin flinched as Mollie flung an arm about her shoulders and another about Fuallia. "Look at these poor children!"

Robin bristled. She was probably only a few years younger than me.

"You can sort all that out later, the Powers know you've been waiting long enough already while we chased 'em hither an' yon. Right now the lasses need breakfast and a wash and a change of clothes, don't you, m'dears? And a good long sleep knowin' they're in safe hands with nought to fear when they wake, for the first time in a long while, I'll be bound."

"There's more to it than that, which we can talk about back at Greyrock." I glowered at Mollie myself. She just grinned. Sometimes I could sympathize with Lord Lowrison and his often-expressed desire to thump the Fenlanders round the ears.

"I'll take point in the halfworld, Maurey'lana," Aljess said. She didn't really expect enemies to be skulking between here and the camp; it was a way of being ready to pounce on Robin and Fuallia without warning if they decided to try running after all. My captain ducked back into the hollow tree as the nearest convenient darkness, now that the sluggish autumn sun was finally up. The rest of us, with Tam muttering under his burden of the Shepherd girls' belongings tied up in the deerskin, marched back to the camp through the waking morning forest.

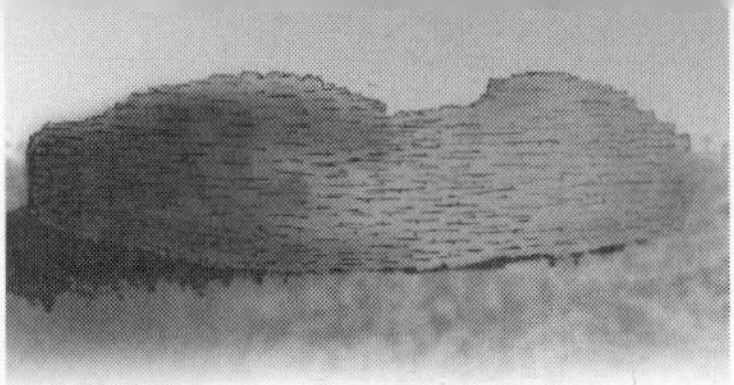

✠ CHAPTER THREE ✠

KORBY: THE VEILED PRINCE

I had to free Gerhardt's bonds to walk through the thronged streets to the bookshop of Master Labienus. I kept my arm linked through his good arm, as if we were two friends out for a stroll. He only tried to break away once. Labienus's shop was built under an arch of the main great aqueduct, a wonder of the world that had carried water to the teeming city from some distant lake in the hills since the days of the first empire. The sign swinging out front was peeling, but I could still make out the Yehillon symbol as well as the words *Magister Labienus, Books.* And for those who couldn't read, there was a picture of a book.

Did it take a barbarian to find that funny?

The front wall, filling in the arch, was old yellow brick, but the door was closed and the shutters were locked over the windows.

"Did you expect him to be closed?" I asked.

Gerhardt shook his head. "No. The prince was going to be waiting in the back, in Master Labienus's private house. I was supposed to go to the back door."

"How many men is he likely to have with him?"

"Probably just one," said Gerhardt. He was lying.

I grinned, and he flinched. I had tanned darker than I thought possible in the Ronish sun, and the contrast showed up the white scars, where the witch-troll had tried to claw off half my face, rather more than usual. "Good effort, but really—four? Half a dozen? Twenty?"

Four was what got a flicker of alertness from him. "Probably a couple of men," he said grudgingly. I didn't call him on the lie that time. Alberick the so-called prince, his usual four guards, Labienus the bookseller, possibly his family and a servant or two...

"Why don't you go ahead and knock?" I towed Gerhardt across the street and shoved him at the door. Someone might be watching through a hole in the shutters, but I didn't feel any minds so close.

I didn't feel the presence of anyone inside at all. Dagger drawn in my right hand, I loosened my sword in its scabbard.

Gerhardt tapped faintly at the door and then looked over his shoulder at me. "He's gone out. Or maybe he's in the house with the prince."

"The house is at the back of the shop?"

"Yes."

"Alone?"

"He has a wife," Gerhardt admitted, "and two copyists and a maidservant."

"And they're all having a friendly drink with the prince who doesn't show his face? Try the latch." I put a hand against the door myself a moment, felt my way into the iron, pushed...I heard the click, if Gerhardt didn't.

"It's locked," he started to say when the latch resisted him, and then, "No, it isn't. It's open."

"Careless of them. In you go, Gerhardt." I propelled him with a knee and followed cautiously into a room like a crypt, its stone ceiling curving overhead, its stone walls lined with shelves. A copyist's desk was set up in front of one of the shuttered windows by the door, and a charcoal brazier burned in the center of the place, probably to keep the cellar-like damp from turning the books to mush.

No indignant servant came bustling from beyond the
curtain at the back to announce they were closed. It was silent.
Not a breath.

"That goes into the living quarters?" I whispered.

Gerhardt was spooked. This wasn't what he had been
expecting, and he was stewing in a mixture of fear and guilt
over his betrayal and relief that he was alive. I hadn't killed him.
I hadn't done anything half so bad as what was going to happen
to him when the prince found out he had failed, found out he
had let himself be captured, learned how much he had talked.
I might be his enemy, but I was safety too, in his mind. He
actually edged closer to me before murmuring, "Yes. Labienus
has the whole arch right through to the lane behind. There's a
storeroom in the middle, then the house beyond. Maybe they're
all in the kitchen?"

A cat, hunched and fluffed up on the shop counter, hissed
as we passed, then leapt down and darted out the door I hadn't
closed.

I drew my greatsword and didn't sheathe my dagger, though
I still felt no living minds in the place other than Gerhardt's.

"Go through," I ordered softly, with a nod at the curtain.

"You go first. You've got a sword."

"What, you don't think your prince is going to be happy to
see you? Go."

Gerhardt set a hand on the heavy curtain. "It'll be dark," he
protested. "We need a lamp."

I held my dagger in my teeth a moment and reached over
his shoulder to rip down the curtain. Light from the open door
behind us poured into the dark room beyond, and Gerhardt
made a protesting moan. The sudden reek of blood was strong.

"Labienus?" I asked. With my sword, I touched the nearest
body, sprawled face-up across the doorway.

Gerhardt gave a jerky nod. "They—you—"

"They're not even cool, lad. I was with you, remember?"

"But…I was just talking to him. This morning. Marcia gave me an almond-bun. She'd been baking." He was too bewildered to be outraged.

"Marcia?" I asked, stepping over bodies. Labienus had been a fit-looking man in the prime of life. He'd been stabbed with a narrow blade of some sort, a knife or a duelling sword, maybe. Taken unawares. One of the young copyists had been killed in a similar fashion. The other looked like he'd been hacked to death. Must have had time to get his hands on a weapon and fight back. The woman, Labienus's wife, was only about my age, barely out of girlhood. They'd cut her throat. And the maid's, over which Gerhardt was bending. The girl was a little slip of a thing, twelve or thirteen. Just the age to get sweet on a doe-eyed boy like Gerhardt.

"She's dead."

"They're all dead." I had my back to the partition wall. There was a door on the other side of the storeroom, beyond the dark stacks of books, the binding press and workbench, and the bodies. It was closed. Heavy old wood, a barrier even in the halfworld.

"You!" Gerhardt spun around and launched himself at me. I kicked him away, and he went sprawling beside the pathetic body of the girl. "You brought Nightwalkers here, you bastard Dunmorran! They did this! It's your fault!"

"Use your head, Gerhardt. Who sent you to murder Master Arvol because he had that book? Because he'd *read* that book? The one you were supposed to take for your prince without ever peeking at it? Who else read that book, eh? Didn't Arvol show it to Master Labienus? Didn't Master Labienus know what was in it? He must have, right, to be able to tell Alberick about it?"

Squatting like a frog on the floor, Gerhardt stared up at me.

"Do you think your prince is going to believe you didn't have a look at it too?"

"I never even saw it!" he howled. "You showed up!"

"So do you think little Marcia was reading over her master's shoulder? Could she even read? Do you think your precious Alberick is going to believe you, or even care? He sent you to murder for him, Gerhardt. He kills his own loyal folk. He kills helpless innocents. What kind of a lord is that? And Powers damn you, stop shouting!"

Well, it's not like I was exactly whispering myself.

The storeroom door burst open and a man, a lone man, charged in. I don't know why, but I left the safety of the wall to get between him and Gerhardt, killing him without even having to beat his light duelling sword aside. Whatever they were expecting, I guess it wasn't me. Maybe they'd thought Gerhardt had disobeyed his orders and come back with Arvol.

"Get lost!" I shouted at Gerhardt, who was scrambling after the fallen sword. The rest of them came out of the halfworld close about us then, three more men in anonymous brigandines with no family emblems or colors to identify their master, and a fourth, handsomely, almost foppishly, dressed in a doublet of plum-colored velvet and hose to match. I figured his jerkin was probably lined with plate though—anyone who went about with four bodyguards wouldn't trust to mere leather and velvet.

And he was veiled, as Gerhardt had said, not a veil like a woman might wear over her hair, but a finely-woven black veil like the priestesses called the Daughters of Geneh wear on the continent—it covered all his face, even his eyes.

I have to say that my first two thoughts about that were, Thank the Yerku *I'm* not so vain as he, and, I wonder what ripped up *his* face?

My blade skittered off somebody's armored chest as he dodged, rather skillfully, and he staggered away, cut badly

on the arm instead, and another man fell backwards over the
maidservant's body trying to get at Gerhardt without coming
within my reach. The veiled man began to sing.

What had Gerhardt said about Great Gifts? Not much. But
I know a warlock's spell when I hear one. The cursed Yehillon
prince clearly knew some very similar style of magic, and I wasn't
keen to hang around to find out what his spell did. Gerhardt had
already decided to take my advice. I just about collided with him
in the doorway to the shop.

"Don't go home!" I shouted after him as he bolted between
the shelves of books and out into the street, though why I should
have cared what became of the murderous twit I don't know.
To give him time to get away, I stood where I was. They could
only get at me one at a time. Alberick kept singing. I couldn't
tell what language, though Maurey would want to know. The
two guards still fit to fight—or were they High Circle, some
priesthood?—hesitated in the doorway. They were between me
and their prince, so at least I knew I wasn't about to be blasted
by a fireball. Presumably he wouldn't kill off his closest servants
quite so uncaringly as he slaughtered others.

I sheathed my right-hand dagger, but this didn't make them
any happier. The greatsword, for those with the strength and size
to wield it, is a weapon for the battlefield, for man and horse in
full plate armor.

Doesn't mean you can't use it in a bookshop.

"Alberick!" I called. "Why on earth d'you want this old
book anyway? I mean, I know old books's worth somethin',
but really! Seven lives!" Eight maybe, if that other bodyguard's
wound festered. I was reaching over my shoulder as I spoke. I'd
put the book carefully on top in my pack and hadn't strapped it
up too tightly, thinking that if we didn't find his prince at the
bookshop I might give Gerhardt a chance to steal it, so I could
follow him. "Bit pricey, don'ya think?"

"Hand it over, and I might allow you to leave," Alberick said. Excellent Ronish, but I was pretty sure his accent was Hallsian, from the kingdom east of Hallaland. The name sounded Hallish of some sort or other anyway.

"Kind of you."

Both his guards facing me looked to be Ronishmen, dark-haired and olive-skinned, like Master Labienus. The Yehillon obviously didn't limit itself to national boundaries.

"So, you two just swords for sale, or are you High Circle?" I asked. Shock of alarm from them both. That answered that. One stepped back into the dark storeroom and disappeared.

"Fescor take you," I muttered. A human had just vanished into the halfworld, something everyone thought impossible. And the Yehillon called that only the Lesser Gift? Alberick was singing again, but even one enemy in the halfworld was one too many. I turned and ran, dropping the ancient book, spread-eagled, onto the burning brazier as I passed. Normally it wouldn't have done more than scorch a little before they could snatch it off the coals, but fire is easy. I called up flames all through the book's dry parchment pages. The brazier was blazing like a bonfire as I plunged towards the street door.

Knowing Nightwalker tactics, I was expecting the blade and the man that suddenly leapt at me from empty space. Last surprise he ever had.

But something punched at my chest as though I'd struck an overhanging branch at full gallop, and I hurtled backwards. I hit the brazier and it went flying, flinging burning charcoal and flaming scraps of parchment everywhere.

My heart was suddenly beating very strangely, out of step, random, staggering. Yerku help me, I thought. Although I'm not a praying type, it was definitely a prayer.

Alberick loomed in the doorway to the storeroom,

shouting at his one remaining man, who was vainly trying to beat out the fire on the book.

"Idiot! Leave it! He's saved me the bother of destroying it."

Damnation. If I wanted to annoy him I should've claimed I was having it set in type at the nearest printers, to be handed out to the public as broadsheets.

"Carlo still lives. Help him onto the shadow road and we'll get out of here. Leave the bandit to burn in his own fire. If Huvehla favors him, his heart will fail first."

It was failing. Alberick and his surviving henchmen were gone, into the halfworld that they called the shadow road and out of the burning shop, invisible in broad daylight. A bell clanged in the distance, summoning the district fire brigade with their bucket chains. Better be gone before they got here.

I was no warlock to fight spells with spells. We witches work with what we have and what we are, and I shut my mind to everything but my own breathing, my own even count, one, two, three, four—grey Harrier's steady hoofbeats, carrying a heavy load uphill, into a gale—slow, faithful and unfaltering. Then I could breathe again, and move, with an ache in my chest that was mostly bruise and coughing from the smoke.

My lord was going to murder me, I thought. Burning books! I still haven't heard the last of that.

I scrambled out to the street, into a gathering crowd, too many to muddle and confuse into forgetting they'd seen me. Not my finest moment. I took to my heels and ran.

That evening I was safe on a sturdy cog heading downriver for the Ronish Sea. The Ronish Empire is too full of soldiers and highway checkpoints and inquisitive provincial governors' agents for a wanted man as noticeable as me to cross it overland. I had no wish to end up sentenced to twenty years in the galleys or the salt mines. No point going to the Dunmorran ambassador and merely ending up trapped in the embassy either. By great good luck though, I had found a Gehtish ship willing to take on a passenger. This was the captain's first venture down to Rona, and she was fed up with Ronishmen asking her where the master was and talking past her to her mate. Now that she had her cargo of Ronish wine loaded, Captain Luvlariana was in a mood to tweak the Ronish nose (what Gehtalander isn't?) and quite happy to talk about the possibility of a few bales of fine Fensheep wool on the leeside of Dugald's export tariffs...

I'm a lord of the Fens. What do you expect? I was born a smuggler.

But just in case we sank or were boarded, or they sold me to the Ronishmen after all, I shut myself in the closet under the aftercastle I was sharing with Erek the mate and unpacked Maurey's speaking-stone.

This was half of a grey, goose-egg of a rock, which like an egg was only a shell. Inside, it was lined with crystals of purple amethyst. My lord had invented it, based on descriptions of such things in old Talverdine writings. I guessed the way it worked was that the two halves of the stone remembered each other and were somehow still connected. Or something like that. Anyway, he had the other half in Greyrock Castle, and I knew the proper Talverdine phrase to recite to make its sleeping magic come to life. I just had to hope someone was nearby in Greyrock to notice when it began to hum and grow warm.

There wasn't enough headroom for me to sit on Erek's narrow bunk, so I sat cross-legged on the floor where I'd be sleeping, holding the stone cradled in my hands.

"Good evening?" I tried softly. "Hello? Anybody home?"

Nothing. My stone was live; I could feel its faint warmth. From experience, I knew this could go on for a while.

We really needed to make a bell chime or something to draw attention to the stone.

I raised my voice a little. Most of the crew were on deck; only the steersmen were in the main chamber beneath the aftercastle, where the massive tiller swung. If they heard, maybe they would think I was praying. "My lord?"

I could hear a dog barking. Well, that was something. "Quiet, Blaze," I ordered on a guess. "Where's Annot? Go find Annot."

Great. A questioning whine and very loud snuffling.

"Don't lick the stone! Go find Annot!"

A sharp bark.

"That's not very helpful, Blaze, my lad."

"Korby! Is that you?"

I recognized Annot's voice—the Baroness of Oakhold, my third cousin, foster-sister and my lord's beloved, to be poetic about it. "It's not the Fuallin queen. Good evening, coz. Is my lord there?"

"He went off to catch your witches."

"Oh, good." And Powers grant he managed it, this time. That pale haunted girl had no business living wild in the forest, and the other one, all smouldering fires and wild stone and water..."How are they?"

"I don't know, Korby. Use your head. He hasn't got them yet so far as I've heard. Where are you?"

"Leaving Rona in a bit of a hurry."

"Who did you upset now?"

"Quite possibly everybody. Listen, I'm on a Gehtish ship, the *Soelvlaks* or something like that, Captain Luvlariana of Hundfiord. We're sailing downriver to the Ronish Sea. With luck and good winds, I'll be back in the Fens in six weeks, a couple of months. I've learned a lot. Have you got a tablet near, something to write on?"

"Not being an ox of a Fenlander, I can remember more than one fact at a time."

"Yes, but I want to spell out some words for you."

"Back in a moment." There was a pause. "Right. Tablet, which hopefully Blaze won't find and chew up before I make a good copy—he loves beeswax—stylus and, lucky for you, someone with legible handwriting to act as clerk. That'd be me. We're still working on decoding your last letter."

"It wasn't in code."

"You take my point, dear coz. Proceed."

I began to lay out all I'd learned recently. Arvol's death. What the Yehillon actually was. The danger posed by the young queen's friend Katerina, a Yehillon herself. The "shadow road" and the Lesser and Greater Gifts. Humans who could enter the halfworld. Alberick, the veiled prince of the Yehillon, and how easily he murdered anyone he found inconvenient. And the manuscript. I spelled out the words *Iarakulanar* and *Iahillalana* and explained my suspicions about what they meant.

"Yaraku princes. The Yerku? The Lesser Powers?"

"Maybe. Didn't Lord Romner say once that he thought the Yerku were Talverdine, not human, in origin, the earliest rulers of the Nightwalkers?"

"Can't you make out any of the rest of it? Even a few words?"

So sometimes I exaggerate how bad I am at scholarship. Annot doesn't let me get away with it. I had actually puzzled my way through what wasn't too hidden by scorching, hiding belowdecks while the captain finished up her business in Rona, and I had been left...puzzled. Even allowing for the fact that I did a lot of guessing at both words I didn't know and ones I couldn't read, it looked to me like the bookseller was right. This was a tale to tell children on a winter's night.

Once upon a time there was an emperor, who ruled a vast empire blessed by the Powers with all the good things of the earth. But a long night came upon his land. Some said the empire had been cursed by the Powers because of the growing wickedness of his people. Some said great enemies had worked evil magic against it. Some said the world was ending and the demons held imprisoned by Geneh were unleashed from the outer darkness to which they had been banished at the beginning of all things. Who can say? But the skies were darkened, and the stars and even the sun grew faint and cold; the clouds rained ash and poison, and winter ate the land.

Now the emperor had two nephews, named Iarakulanar and Iahillalana. And Iarakulanar stood before the emperor and said, "The land is cursed. We die for want of food and our children freeze in the cold. Let us seek a new land where we may live in joy and plenty."

And the emperor told him, "I will not leave the land of my fathers and my fathers' fathers. Only a coward flees what the Powers send him to endure."

But Iarakulanar would not listen. He gathered most of the wise men of the empire, and by his cunning words he persuaded them to follow him. They collected their families and their goods, and they all stole away in the night, abandoning the empire to its sufferings, abandoning their lord the emperor.

When the emperor found that Iarakulanar had done this, his heart broke for sorrow, and he lay on his deathbed. He sent for his other nephew Iahillalana and he told him, "Take the brave knights of your household and find Iarakulanar and bring him to judgement, for like a coward he has fled hardship, and he has stolen the wise men and the cunning men, and left us bereft of hope."

So brave Iahillalana gathered the knights of his household, and they swore an oath before the Powers to find the people of Iarakulanar, no matter how long it should take them, and to bring them to justice for their abandonment of the empire and their defiance of the emperor's decrees.

And they traveled by the shadow road, through the lands of death, and they endured terrors no weaker hearts could have endured...

After that it turned into a story everyone knew: the adventures of the hero Ayill of the Seven Tasks and how he won the hand of the Emperor of Berbarany's daughter. I sketched out the tale quickly for Annot.

"That's it? All that death, for a wonder-tale?"

"Unless there was something in the rest of the book, which," I added gloomily, "I burned."

"Oh, Korby." We were both silent a moment. Then she snickered. "I don't want to be in your boots when Maurey finds out you've been burning bookshops. It must be that story, some meaning hidden in that story. Iaraku'lanar and Iahilla'lana. Yerku'lanar and Yehil'lana. You're right, you must be. And listen, Romner has been studying that book Maurey took from Arvol's room back in Hallasbourg, and he's found something interesting there. What you've found out helps it make a lot more sense. That *Life of Blasted Miron*, as Romner calls it, has a bit about Miron the Burner, the man who invented philosopher's fire, having the gift of Yehillalan, though it doesn't say what that is."

"Yehillon Lesser Gifts and Greater Gifts. Hah. Make sure Dugald knows what we've found out about the Yehillon. If he won't send Katerina away, at least make sure he and Eleanor are always guarded."

"Dugald is always guarded," Annot assured me. "And Eleanor has my Lady Ursula and Lady Joanna and your niece Haidy, and all three of them are good in a fight even if they do have to dress pretty at court. *And* Haidy's a witch almost in your class. She's, er, expecting, by the way."

"What? I'll kill him, whoever he is. She's only twelve!"

"Not *Haidy*, you half-witted lout. The queen."

"Oh. That's all right then."

"Kind of you to allow it."

"That was fast work."

"It apparently doesn't take long." Annot snickered. And sighed.

The one thing that could make me furious with Maurey in those days was that business of grimly refusing to marry until his aunt, as head of House Keldyachi, gave them her blessing. Annot didn't deserve the names she was called behind her back by the snottier types at Dugald's court.

"Korby, take care of yourself. Stay in touch. Keep the stone near. Maurey will want to talk to you when he gets back."

"You mean, Maurey will want me to stare at the manuscript till my eyes cross in the hope that some hidden meaning will magically become clear."

"Something like that. Powers be with you, Korby."

"Hoy, Fen-earl, Mozz-haffer."

I hastily muttered the words to make the stone dormant again and shoved it out of sight into my pack. Captain Luvlariana grinned round the door at me, her fair hair a shaggy mop tied up in a red scarf, gold rings glinting in both ears and a triple string of amber at her throat. "Fens, heh? Half Fens is witches. You is witch?"

There were a few witches among the Gehtalanders. They were mostly respected, not feared. "Maybe," I said guardedly.

"You do winds? You do fogs?"

"Fog is easy. Wind is dangerous."

"Fog then. We have naval galley follow us. Who you kill?"

"I didn't say I'd killed anybody."

"Hah. Sure. Look, we outrun them at sea, not on river. Wind too weak and current carry us both now. When tide come up river they fight it better, you understand? Galley have many oars, but little wind for us. Come make fog behind. Maybe they go aground. Little islands coming up ahead. We try wind later, yes? Get you home to sheeps sooner."

"I'll see what I can do."

She put a whipcord-muscled arm around me, pulled me out on deck. "Good, good. Luvlar smile on me today. Always good, to sailing with a witch. Real pain, my sister, she wind-witch, stay home to have babies this summer. Silly girl."

"Without witches having babies, you won't have any more witches."

"Smart man. Good idea. We think about that later." She tweaked my ear.

"Hey! No! Fog yes, wind maybe, babies no. Anyway, what would your mate say?"

"Not a lot. He be my sister's man, not mine."

"Fog," I said. "You wanted fog."

"Sure, sure. Fog now. Other things later." She patted my shoulder and went back into the aftercastle to give orders to the steersmen at the great tiller. I climbed the ladder to the fighting platform that was the roof of the aftercastle and stood there, watching the surface of the river behind us, dark and silvery, wind-riffled. Finally I shut my eyes, feeling my way into the surface of the water, shaping its memories of cool mornings when the river smoked, of spring thaws, summer nights, winter dawns. White tendrils of mist began to rise between us and the pursuing naval galley.

✣ CHAPTER FOUR ✣
MAUREY: THE LADY OF KANIFGLIN

*Y*ou'll all burn too, once Talverdin falls. And it will. Soon.
Prince Alberick has found a way. Master Arvol's murderer
had screamed those words at Korby, and sometimes
I woke from nightmares with the threat seeming to echo in
my own ears. What secrets Kanifglin hid, I still did not know,
but I was certain the Yehillon did. We had to unearth those
secrets too, if Gerhardt's threat was not to come true. So far
though the rangers Serrey and Arromna had not come back to
report failure; I had had no raven-message from them either.
What that meant, I couldn't decide. In the dark hours of the
morning, I was sure I had sent them to their deaths. Winter
came early among the peaks.

Now that I had the two girls from Kanifglin in my custody,
I hoped I could get answers from another source.

"We don't know anything about a way through the mountains,"
Robin snapped for perhaps the third time, standing before me
with her arms around her sister. In a page's outgrown hose
and tunic and hood, she looked ambiguous, androgynous,
deliberately so, neither girl nor boy, as though she still had
to protect Fuallia by posing as her brother. Her curly brown
hair was cropped short again, as it had been in Korby's visions.
"Grandda never said anything, and he'd have told us if he
knew. I *told* you."

I rubbed my hands over my face. I had been on the verge of shouting. On top of all my other worries, we had heard nothing from Korby since he reported to Annot that he was leaving Rona, and he never answered when I tried to contact him with the speaking-stone. Telling myself he was a good hand with boats and had probably been put to work by the captain did not stop me stewing over what might have gone wrong.

"I'm sorry," I said. "I'm worrying about too many other things and it's making me short-tempered. Robin, Fuallia, I apologize. It's unfair and I shouldn't have kept on at you. Never mind about whether or not there's a way through the mountains. If you don't know of one, you don't, and that's all there is to it. But you do think there's something to do with Nightwalkers, something those men wanted from you or from Kanifglin, don't you? Something to do with this Lady of Kanifglin you mentioned, and promising to stay in the valley? Your grandfather *expected* Nightwalkers to come to you. Can't you tell me why?"

We were in the top room of the great keep of Greyrock Castle, the dim cold tower that was a fort within the fort. It was situated at the highest point of the castle, which bounded down an outcropping of rock in a series of halls and towers and walled baileys on three levels, like giants' steps scattered with the giants' children's building blocks. The keep was mostly used as an armory now, but because it was a stronghold and it was easy to control who went in and out, I had taken this chamber over for my workroom. Many of the papers couriers brought me from Cragroyal held information for which powerful men in Hallaland and even our ally Eswy would have paid in gold. It was also a safe place to talk about whatever great secret it was the witch-girls thought they guarded. Below us, the tower was empty, except for the guardroom on the first floor.

On the other hand, maybe it looked like the lair of some evil warlock out of legend. It wasn't my fault Annot had been using the alchemical workbench in the corner to reassemble the remains of a huge, bone-armored sturgeon that our friend Jessmyn had sent her from Dralla, knowing she was interested in such things. It *was* my fault there was a raven perched on the mantelpiece, but it was too late to chase it out the window now. And the heaps of books were sinister enough on their own to many people, things of power and mystery.

I sighed. "Sit down, both of you." I left my chair and went to sit less threateningly on the hearth, legs outstretched. Taddie, Fuallia's shadow, trotted over to me and I rubbed her ears. Usually Korby is my shadow, and I can forget that maybe to some people I'm fairly threatening on my own. And thinking of Korby again reminded me. These girls were witches, Robin a very powerful one. Korby got sick headaches around what he called the noise of other people's emotions; even Mollie had to get out of the castle for a while every now and then to stop her nerves getting frayed from the press of people in Greyrock. Robin and Fuallia had lived more or less as hermits all their lives, and here was I, urgent and angry and upset, when they were probably already overwhelmed with the clamor of emotions in the castle. No wonder Fuallia was trying to hide behind her sister.

"It's not you I'm angry at," I added.

Robin nodded. "Yes," she said. "I know, Your Highness. But Fu's very…she feels it more. And she's never learnt not to mind it all."

I waved at the comfortable low bench before the fire. They both sat, looking down at me. Robin tucked her feet up.

Fuallia gave me a sudden timid smile. "It's all right, Robin. We're safe with him, really safe, even if he's angry. Mollie and him, they'll look after us. The only secret we have is about the tower, I think, Your Highness."

Robin rubbed her eyes. Headache, I guessed, and probably my fault. "I suppose you ought to know, Your Highness. It's a

Nightwalker secret, really, though it's not much of one. And if Fu says we can trust you, we can. I don't think it's the thing you want to know, but it's the only secret there is, other than us being...I guess you know, sir. Strange."

"You're witches," I said. "Most Dunmorrans don't believe witches exist, or if they do, they think you're just about as wicked as Nightwalker warlocks. I don't think that way. Neither does the king."

"Yes. That. Grandda called it a blessing, because I have these dreams, horrible dreams, and Fuallia sort of knows things about people. Grandda said it wasn't wicked, but we couldn't let anyone find out, ever. He wasn't...like us, but his da was, he said, and our ma was—"

"She could start fires like Tam Moss'avver," Fuallia interrupted, pride in her soft voice. "But she was better. He does a lot of scowling and muttering, doesn't he, Your Highness? She just sort of smiled and held out her hands, like she was inviting the flame out of the wood, and it came..."

"Fu! But that's why no one would help when our da and ma had lung fever. There wasn't anything wrong with Da. He was from Kanifglinfoot, but his family wouldn't speak to him after he married Ma and came up to Kanifglin. Our kin there don't speak to us more than they can help."

"Firstly, there's nothing wrong with you or your mother..."

"I know, sir." Robin actually grinned. "I got that talk from Mollie even before the scrubbing and the clean clothes and the fight about why I wasn't going to dress up like a barbarian, no matter how much I don't want to put on a skirt. But I guess there's knowing in your head and knowing in your stomach, right?"

She had me there. What did it matter what people like venomous old Lord Roshing called my children to come, if they were wanted and loved, right? Such people would despise them for their mixed blood no matter what. But I still wouldn't marry Annot without my aunt's blessing as head of House Keldyachi, because the permission of the head of one's House is what it takes for a Talverdine marriage to be acknowledged, and no one, in either of my countries, was going to name my children bastards. "What kind of horrible dreams?" I asked.

Robin shook her head. "They're never good things. There's nothing—nothing bad now, if that's what you want to know. Couldn't Mollie Moss'avver tell you anyway?"

"Neither she nor Tam has clear visions," I said. "And none of the other Fenlanders here right now is a witch. If you do dream something, tell me or the baroness or Captain Aljess, no matter how small a matter it seems, all right?"

They both nodded.

"The same with the tower. No matter how small a thing."

"You still think there's a forgotten way through the mountains," Robin said, but she smiled, saying so. "The secret's nothing like that at all, Your Highness. We're just supposed to remember, that's all, remember and stay in the valley."

"Remember what?"

"A story," said Fuallia softly. "Tell him, Robin."

"Five years after Conqueror Hallow captured Cragroyal, his army came west..." Robin's story began. But it wasn't a story about the man revered as a Lesser Power throughout most of Eswiland, and how Good King Hallow purified the land of evil warlocks, defeating their wicked enchantments and treachery with human valor and the arts of the philosophers. It was about a princess called the Lady of Kanifglin. She was, of course, beautiful and wise and brave, and she lived in a castle in Kanifglin. Her father had been a human prince of the Westwood, a man who could call birds off the trees with his singing and tame wolves and cougars with his voice, and her mother had been a princess of the Nightwalkers.

It sounded like the beginning of a winter's wonder-tale, all princes and princesses. Soon there would be the wicked stepmother and the evil warlock and the wise little bird. Except that the only warlock in the story was the princess's mother.

The prince of the Westwood sounded like a witch.

Ah, I thought.

"Conqueror Hallow and Magger Miron..." I blinked at that, but then understood. Robin meant Magister Miron, Master Miron, the inventor of philosopher's fire, the cold white alchemical flame which burned those with Nightwalker blood but left humans unharmed. "Conqueror Hallow and Magger Miron fought a great battle in the Greyrock Pass, but the power of the warlocks barred the way to him and his army fought itself in its madness. So instead, Conqueror Hallow built a great castle to guard the pass, so no warlock would ever escape through it again, and philosopher's fire burned either side of the road to the pass, so that no warlock could cross it, even in the halfworld."

The Powers be thanked, the ingredients for philosopher's fire were so rare that those fires had not been maintained for long. Annot and I wouldn't have gotten far if I'd had to run that sort of gauntlet when we escaped into Talverdin.

Robin's voice went on, falling into a storyteller's rhythm. "The Lady of Kanifglin should have fled away into Talverdin with the other Nightwalkers, because her skin was pale as snow and her hair was black as the raven's wing. She should have fled, but she didn't. She stayed, and her people stayed with her. They hunted the knights of King Hallow in the forest and they stalked them in the mountains, until Hallow feared the Westwood and the Lady of Kanifglin, as he had not feared any other warlock or any other human prince. But in the end, there

were too many of Hallow's people and too few of the Lady's.
She knew her fate. She had already sent for her folk, her father's
people, the humans and folk that looked human, like her sister,
and she told them, 'Run away, hide, disappear. Watch and wait
and keep Kanifglin safe, and some day the Nightwalkers will
come again. Always remember.' And her sister—"

"You didn't tell the bit about the sister, Robin. She always
forgets to put the sister in earlier, Your Highness."

"Do you want to tell the story, Fu?" Robin demanded.

"No." Fuallia looked down.

"The Lady of Kanifglin had a sister, who was as fair as she
was dark, and her eyes were blue and her skin was like apple-
blossoms and no one would ever have known her mother was
a Nightwalker. The Lady's sister promised that she would keep
Kanifglin safe forever and would always remember. So the
humans went into the Westwood and into the mountains and
hid. But the Lady of Kanifglin was forced back to her castle in
Kanifglin—"

"We know it was just a tower, really," Fuallia suddenly
injected. "It's not even as big around as Kanifglinfoot's rent-
barn, where they collect what's owing to Greyrock. But the story
always calls it a castle."

"Fu! Don't interrupt."

"Sorry."

"Hallow's army surrounded the Lady of Kanifglin in her
castle. Magger Miron ordered a pyre of philosopher's fire built
before the castle gate, because they knew they would soon take
the castle and drag the Lady out to her burning."

I shivered, and out of the tail of my eye I saw Aljess, on
guard as always, fold her arms close. We had both come too near
such a death ourselves.

"Hallow thought he would capture all the Nightwalkers and
burn them, because the castle could not stand against the great

force he had. But the Lady of Kanifglin was a great warlock, one of the greatest—like they say in the stories about you, Your Highness—and she cast down the castle herself, in fire and lightning, and all the Nightwalkers there died, but so did many of King Hallow's knights, and so did Magger Miron."

The histories I knew said that Miron had died in fighting around Greyrock. Oddly though, there were no shrines to his shade, and his was not one of the tombs in Greyrock's crypt. Just as well. I don't think I'd have slept happily over Miron's bones.

"But after the army had gone," Fuallia said, taking up the story eagerly, "the sister of the Lady of Kanifglin came back, and she lived in Kanifglin, and she married a prince of the Westwood, and they remembered, as she had promised her sister. And their son lived in Kanifglin and his after him. And her name, the sister's name, was Fuallia."

"Fu thinks that's important."

"We're the descendants of the sister," Fuallia said, ignoring Robin. "That's the secret. We promised to stay in Kanifglin and remember the story until the Nightwalkers came back."

"It's nothing," Robin said, in a flare of anger. "Nothing worth Grandda dying for. There's no great secret in it, except that maybe we've got Nightwalker blood, and maybe we were princes once, so far back it couldn't matter even to Magger Miron anymore. It's not something men should come and kill Grandda to find out."

I hardly heard her.

You didn't build a tower in a dead-end valley. Did you? If you were hiding, only hiding, did you build a tower at all?

Had Hallow and Miron thought it was a tower only for defence, a last retreat? Had it in fact been built to guard something else?

I thought I understood. They fought a delaying action to pin Hallow down around Greyrock, while from all over the island, the last Nightwalkers, the last half-blooded, the humans with black eyes or black hair, disappeared into the mountains, through Kanifglin. But the Lady of Kanifglin was forced back, and back...and died at the tower in Kanifglin, a last stand, a last dead end...*because if Hallow didn't believe it was a dead end, he would have followed.*

The Makers, the warlocks, who survived the last battle at Weeping Valley at the western end of the Greyrock Pass, could have sealed a pass at Kanifglin as well, if there was one; the strength of Nightwalker Makers had not yet begun to wane in those days.

Yes. That was it.

Think of the Lady of Kanifglin—half human, half Nightwalker. Her sister looks human; she looks Nightwalker. Her sister can disappear, become human, just another peasant under Hallow's rule. But what of others: black-eyed, black-haired humans, with a Nightwalker parent or grandparent? What of Nightwalkers still in hiding in the east, the south? Not only Greyrock Castle but philosopher's fire barred the Greyrock Pass.

And because the Lady of Kanifglin (the leader of the last resistance of the Nightwalkers and their human allies—the ancestors of the Fenlanders) had died, apparently trapped in Kanifglin, King Hallow went back to Cragroyal, leaving a garrison at Greyrock Castle to watch the Greyrock Pass and catch any Nightwalker refugees trying to escape west. There he began dividing up Eswiland among his barons, thinking he had trapped any Nightwalker survivors east of the mountains, where he could hunt them down at leisure. Kanifglin was so obviously a dead end; the Lady's death there proved it.

Suppose it wasn't? Her death was the best disguise she could give the pass.

Whatever few survivors there were from Hallow's ongoing warlock hunts might find their way there, to the secret pass through the mountains from Kanifglin. They could disappear quietly into Talverdin, while the sister's family, innocent human farmers, still remembered to show them the way.

That was courage. That was a hero worthy of epic. To die for someone else in the heat of battle is one thing, but to coldly calculate what your death can buy, to choose it not in a moment's passion but during a long slow retreat towards your own necessary and terrible end, with escape enticing at your back all the while...

Five centuries is a very long time though, and memory fades. Sacred trusts become romantic stories, and a family of shepherds remembers they promised to stay in Kanifglin. They tell the story. They forget why the story exists. It was a long time since there had been any Nightwalker fugitives to flee to Talverdin.

And how does the Yehillon find out about it?

Five hundred years would mean many marriages with folk of the Westwood and Kanifglin. Pedlars and pilgrims pick up tales. There are histories of Hallow's wars in libraries on the continent that aren't known in Eswiland itself. Who knows? Some rumor came to the Yehillon though. Of that I was certain. And someone, Prince Alberick himself maybe, realized what I had realized. Perhaps he too wondered if the Lady had hidden escape by her refusal to escape. So he had sent his spies to find the root of the story.

"Sir?" Robin asked.

"I think there's more to the Lady of Kanifglin's tale than that, Robin."

She bristled. "That's all there is!"

"That's all that's remembered now anyway."

Robin bit her lip and frowned. "Grandda made us learn some songs. We thought they were maybe warlock magic, but they never did anything. Mollie heard Fu singing to the dog— something Ma used to sing at night, like a lullaby. Fu shouldn't have let her hear, but anyway, Mollie says it's not magic. She says the words are almost Fen-speech, but not quite, and they sound like—just prayers. But even Grandda didn't know that. So who knows what else got lost and forgotten?"

"I'd guess the story of the Lady of Kanifglin was the important thing," I said. "Your family's kept that ancient trust well, to preserve even the story for so many centuries." I took a deep breath. "You're not going to like me asking this, Robin, Fuallia, but understand I don't mean any insult to your grandfather by asking it. What kind of man was he? Would he have told this story to the strangers who came to Kanifglin if they threatened him?"

"No!"

"He wasn't a coward."

"Robin, you were up at the far end of the glen near the ruins of the tower, right? And Fuallia was hunting on the mountainside. Would he have told the story if they were threatening him, if he thought that by telling it the men would go away before either of you came back?"

Fuallia's eyes widened. Robin went still and silent.

"Maybe," she whispered, her eyes on her hands, clenched on her knees.

You'll all burn. Alberick has found a way.

I was no fool. Maybe Arromna and Serrey were still exploring; maybe they were dead in some icefield crevasse or at the foot of some crumbling cliff; maybe they had given up and were even now on their way back to Greyrock. It made no difference. I knew I was right.

Winter would seal the mountains more impassably than any

Maker's spell. Even the Greyrock Pass would be closed by snows within a month. Come spring though, Robin and Fuallia would have to share their pastures with a garrison from Greyrock. Whatever the Lady of Kanifglin had guarded with her death was going to be guarded again, whether I had actually found it by then or not.

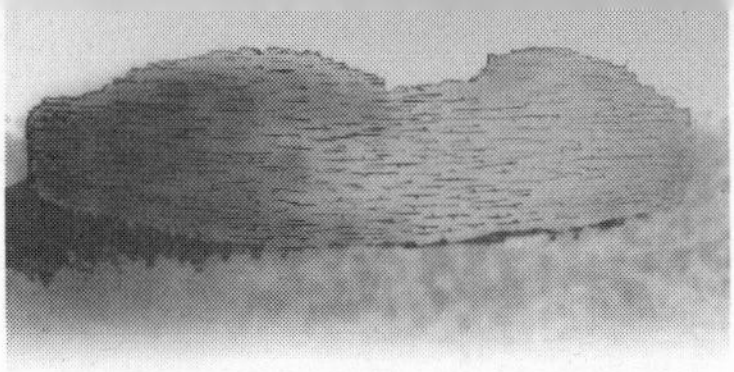

✠ Chapter Five ✠

Maurey: The Spy

The day after my interview with Robin and Fuallia found me hard at work on the dull everyday matters of being lord of a castle and warden of a border fort. A Nightwalker representative of the Embroiderer's Guild and a human merchant were squabbling about formerly agreed prices for silk thread from the east and appealing to the warden's court for a ruling, which was not important in itself but would affect how future legal matters might be decided. Lord Lowrison had sent me reports on all the strangers lodging in Greyrock Town in the last month. He had found nothing suspicious about any of them, but I still had to look through to see if anything odd caught my eye, anything that might hint of the Yehillon. There were reports from Dugald's agents in Rensey and a letter from Korby's niece Haidy, lady-in-waiting to Queen Eleanor, saying that Katerina, the Yehillon spy, had vanished. Lady Ursula, Annot's waiting-woman who had been sent to serve and guard the queen, reported the same thing, and also that a secretary from the Ronish embassy had disappeared at the same time…

Annot gave a little grunt of surprise. I looked up. She was sitting at the opposite end of the big table I used as a desk, half hidden behind a barricade of books. One was spread before her and she had an open tablet by her right hand. All morning she had been scratching down notes on the beeswax surfaces, memoranda for the long summaries and conclusions that she would write up and send with one of my Talverdine couriers to my scholarly friend Lord Romner at his castle in the South Quartering. They were doing some historical research together, and I had been so caught up in my search for the witches and my worries about Kanifglin and what the Yehillon might be that I had only the vaguest idea of what they were up to. Something to do with the ancient stone circles found throughout the island and the north, I thought—something I once would have liked to learn more about myself, except that being master of my brother's spies and more or less the lord of a province did not exactly leave time for such things. Probably, *as* master of my brother's spies, I needed to remind them both that they were supposed to be hunting through Arvol's books and notes, captured by Korby and me last spring, for more information about the Yehillon.

However, Annot was still frowning over the book, chin propped on her fists, so I didn't interrupt her thoughts. Anyway, she made a picture I could lose myself in. Knowing that before long she would be leaving me to return to her manor at Oakhold in the east of Dunmorra for the winter, I treasured the moment even more.

That day she was dressed in Talverdine fashion, which meant a long embroidered tunic over trousers. She was all dark green and chestnut brown, and the embroidery was mostly crimson and yellow flowers and fruit, very autumnal. Her face and slender hands, which went the color of wild roses and cream in winter, never the cold bone-white of my own, were still honey-colored from the summer sun. She had twisted her red-gold hair up into a crown around her head, held in place with gold and copper pins, but it escaped in long, curling tendrils that framed her face. She sometimes grumbled about being too small, not that she was short for a human woman, but she spent so much time around Nightwalker women, who are as tall as their men, that she felt it more. I, however, liked the fact that I could swing her up in my arms so lightly.

She looked up and saw me watching. A smile touched her eyes.

"Are you dreaming of running away again?" she asked.

"Maybe."

Annot pointed sternly at the papers scattered on my half of the table. "You haven't even been back a week. To work, Prince Warden. Earn your keep." Then she laughed. "That was a pun, Maurey. Feel free to snicker. Your *keep*."

"I wasn't going to dignify it with a snicker. What did you find, just now?" I nodded at the book she had been reading.

"Something interesting, I think. When did Nightwalkers come to Eswiland?"

That puzzled me. "You know, I've never thought about it. We've been here for ages. Haven't we?"

"Don't you ever think it's odd, that here, on this one island, there are Nightwalkers, and nowhere else?"

"Well, we don't know that. Who knows, maybe there are Nightwalker kingdoms east of Dravidara or south of Berbarany. Maybe there are whole empires across the western sea, who can say?"

"Perhaps. But I'd think we'd hear *something*, in that case. Anyway, I've been reading *Annals of the First Empire*. Listen. It's talking about Emperor Pios the Fifth deciding that since Hallia was conquered and a peaceful part of his empire, the next place to make a Ronish province was the island of Eswiland, which was inhabited by very primitive and dangerous barbarian tribes. It goes on about their savagery, how they collected the heads of their enemies and allowed witch-born children to live, that sort of thing. The barbarians of Eswiland still made offerings to the shades of their dead in stone temples for the worship of Geneh and the rites of the dead, such as uncivilized men made in the distant past before they knew the arts of the smith and the scribe. And they esteemed most highly those whom they should

most have abhorred.' That means their rulers were often witches,
I'd guess."

"Pios the Fifth was, what, fourteen hundred years ago?"
I've never been good at remembering dates. Probably because
my schooling was interrupted, what with ending up a scullion
in the college kitchens and nearly being executed and so forth.
"What does the Ronish invasion have to do with Nightwalkers?
It sounds like the book's talking about the humans who became
the Fenlanders."

"Patience," said Annot. "Mark of a good scholar, Maurey.
Pay attention. I'm just getting to the interesting part. Still talking
about the barbarians—I wonder how Korby feels about being a
primitive barbarian. At least he doesn't collect heads. Here we
go." Her finger tapped the page. "Pios lands his armies in the
south and they beat the barbarian tribes easily, of course."

"Of course they do. It's a Ronish history written up for the
emperors."

"Be quiet and listen. Then the barbarians make an alliance
with 'the white-skinned foreign magicians,' and 'their new
masters' start holding assemblies in the old stone circles and
building triumphal arches and things—that sounds unlikely.
But listen to this: 'And they brought together all the magicians
in the land and by their arts they raised the sea against the
fleet carrying reinforcements over from the province of
Hallia...' Let's see. So the fleet sinks, Pios and his army are
slaughtered by the barbarians and the foreign magicians, the
survivors retreat home, the next emperor decides to invade
Berbarany instead. You know, Maurey, I think that's the
earliest mention I've ever found of Nightwalkers that isn't
just some wonder-tale full of demons summoned by evil
philosophers, or the children of trolls and human men, or
warlocks being rebellious servants of Geneh, the guardians of
the gates of death."

I made a face. It's bad enough being thought to be evil by your very blood, without being reduced to a wonder-tale monster.

"I suppose I'm not the first one to notice that this is the earliest mention of Nightwalkers in history," Annot went on thoughtfully. "*The Annals* is hardly some rare, lost book, but nobody's ever thought it important before."

"Yes, it's not as if it told you how to get rid of Nightwalkers, after all."

"You should leave comments like that for Romner." She lowered her gaze to the book once more. "He'll want to see this. I'll borrow one of your clerks to copy the whole reign of Pios the whosit, if you have one to spare."

"Of course." I went back to my papers.

Annot sighed. I looked up, but she seemed to be frowning over her research again, chewing on the end of her stylus, so I didn't interrupt.

I realized too late that she had actually been hoping I'd put up more of a fight when she told me to get back to work.

The raven flew in the unglazed window of the tower half an hour later. It was not one of the birds that usually carried messages between Greyrock and the commander of the Weeping Valley fort at the Talverdine end of the pass. This one did not like the tower room at all. It circled, wings hissing like the wind in pines as they parted the air. *Craaaawrk!* it croaked desperately, with the panic of a big bird in a small space. The spell its master had set on it may have urged it to come here, but now that it was here, its bird common sense was telling it to get out, fast.

Blaze knew better than to bark at it, but the big herd-dog lumbered to his feet, watching with interest, making eager little groaning noises deep in his throat, quivering with the effort of not leaping at it. Annot edged towards the door, ducking as the raven hurtled over, making another frantic circle.

I was whistling a soft and piercing note, over and over. The wretched thing was going to hurt itself. There. The sound, half magic and half training, got through to it. The bird dropped to my out-held arm, choosing my naked fist rather than my sleeved wrist. It shuffled from one foot to the other, claws pricking my skin.

"Good boy," I crooned to it in Talverdine. "Good girl?" Only ravens can tell the difference. The raven didn't care. Its glassy black eye studied me. I stroked the feathers at the back of its neck, soothing it. Annot ducked out the door and Blaze padded over, tail wagging gently. He was fairly good friends with one of my own ravens, if friends meant chasing one another in wide circles in the lower bailey, barking and *crarrrwking* and terrifying the horses, which terrified Annot ever since the time Blaze, at full gallop, had smashed his shoulder into a water butt and limped for a week.

This raven shuffled nervously and sidled up my arm.

"Go lie down, Blaze," I ordered, and he obeyed, sighing, with a "nobody ever lets me have any fun" look in his eye.

I spoke the spell for the Weeping Valley garrison ravens, just in case. The raven ignored me and made a snatch for the signet ring on my finger, which was the House Keldyachi unicorn crowned with the Eswyn initial of my name, carved in crimson-flecked green jasper. "None of that," I said. "Sun on the icefields," I tried, "and words on the wind." This was short, as raven-keyed spells went. The raven blinked.

"Wwe'rrre thrrrougha, Maurreyhrnama," it croaked hoarsely, in recognizable Talverdine. "Wwe've come to the hreadwaters of Shennawater. It took a few wrrrong turns and therrre's been a hllanslide thaht blocked the trrail hllong shince, but hwe made it. Not a rrroute frrr narmy, but whone would not need to be a rrrangeerr eitherr. Prrowbly was a rrreal trrack whonce. Hwe'll shenda hyou a mohre detailed hreport whonce hwe'rrre in Sennamorre. Hit's a high hrrroad, schnow hallready. Shouldn't hhaff to hworry abhout Kanifglin till hllate shpring, an' rrrangerrs hwill be patrrolling bhy then."

So…Arromna and Serrey had found a way through the mountains to known Talverdine territory, to the high valley whose springs fed the Sennawater. An army could not cross by that route, but neither was it impassable. The pass had probably been a summer track into Talverdin when it was just a province of the Nightwalker kingdom of the whole island, the sort of thing used by those who wanted to avoid the provincial lord's watch on Greyrock, perhaps. The ancient Nightwalker kingdom had no doubt had its problems with smugglers and bandits and rebel lords, just like any other great land.

Overlooked, forgotten. A route for a band of assassins.

"Good girl," I crooned. "Or boy." The raven made a rattling noise in its throat and dove at my ring again. I moved it to the perch in the corner. "Wait," I told it, as I would a dog. It ruffled its feathers at me. The messenger ravens were highly trained, like good herd dogs or warhorses, and also bound with spells. Training made them loyal and even affectionate animal servants of their masters; spells sent them to particular known places and held a message in their minds until another spell triggered them to repeat it. Message-ravens were clever enough to recognize the symbol I'd painted on the stones above that window. *This window,* it told them. *Come in here.*

That did mean we couldn't leave small objects lying about, because my own birds were in and out several times a day, checking if we were doing or eating anything interesting. Annot complained they had been disturbing her careful stacks of papers, not to mention burying parts of her sturgeon in the ash pail.

Carrying a chunk of cheese, Annot came back from the

guardroom below. She broke a corner off for Blaze and offered the rest to the raven.

"Is it one of Romner's?" she asked.

"No such luck. It's from Arromna and Serrey. They found a way through from Kanifglin to Talverdin." I gave her the details.

"Ah. That's...not good. Not what you wanted to hear."

"At least the pass will be, hah, impassable for the winter, and that region of the border will be patrolled by the rangers come spring. It will have to be watched in the halfworld as well, if this shadow road that some of the Yehillon with that Lesser Gift of theirs can enter is the same thing." Then I realized that this was wishful thinking on my part. "But the Yehillon could already be in Talverdin. It's been months since that one escaped from Kanifglin."

"If they went over in the summer they'd probably have revealed themselves by now. And we don't know if the Yehillon survivor learned the story from Robin's grandfather, or if his High Circle even drew the same conclusions from it as you did," Annot pointed out. "And all you can do about that is warn the queen and Consort Gelskorey, and make sure they take the threat of assassins from the halfworld seriously. Make sure Imurra and Korian are always guarded. Maurey, if your cousins died..."

I nodded. The Yehillon might not need to lay waste to Talverdin with fire and sword. If my aunt and her children died at human hands while I, half human and, bastard or not, the next heir after Imurra and Korian, guarded the border with Dunmorra, the Nightwalkers might lay waste to Talverdin themselves in taking up arms for or against me. A kingdom in the midst of a civil war would be easy prey for whatever fanatical human forces the Yehillon could stir up. Nightwalkers would turn on Dunmorra and no longer hide behind the mountains and the deadly rocks of their spell-protected coastline. They would take what revenge they could, and so would Dugald's folk, and we would be back

in the old days of holy wars with whole villages being massacred
or executed in philosopher's fire.

Surely not. Please, Powers with us, surely not.

"Ahh!" I dragged my hands through my hair. "You're
right, Annot. I've done all I can for now. You wanted to run
away. Let's."

"*Now?*"

"It had better be right now. I'm sure someone will want me
to do something warden-like in another hour or two."

"An hour or two isn't much running away," she protested.

"It's all we can take. Get your cloak." She did so. I found my
own and grabbed her hand. "Blaze can hold the fort."

"He might like to run away too."

"If I'm leaving Aljess behind, you can leave Blaze." There
are times when one wants a devoted dog watching one's every
move—and times when one does not.

Blaze did whine at being left, but now and then, Annot told
him, a dog just has to put up with these things, and we'd be back
before long. I locked the door of my study, and in the lightless
spiral stairway inside the keep's thick wall, I pulled us into the
halfworld.

Sneaking past my bodyguards and the tower guards was
childish. Just then, I didn't care.

"Where are we going?" Annot asked, as hand in hand we
walked past the guardroom, where two Nightwalker knights
of my bodyguard, the brothers Elwinn and Sanno, were trying
to teach the two human men-at-arms on keep-duty, Trefor and
Theo, to play a Talverdine board game. The glass markers glinted
in the firelight, colorless in the halfworld, and the tick of Trefor
cautiously moving a piece on the wooden board sounded sharp
and clean and distant, as though we were on the other side of
some vast still room. The iron-studded oak door stood open,
which made things simple.

"Doesn't matter, does it? So long as it's out and away from all this."

My instinct is always to move softly and quietly in the halfworld, though we could have shouted without drawing the attention of the groom who led a horse almost through us. We walked under the deep arch and down the steep causeway to the busy middle bailey, where the great and lesser halls and the kitchens were. The lower bailey was equally busy, a mixed troop of Nightwalkers and humans riding out, meeting a flock of geese being driven in through the main south gate, from which roads angled away onwards to the ancient stone-paved highway over the Greyrock Pass or down to Greyrock Town. A man following hard on the goose-maid's heels stared our way, frowning right through us to something beyond, or possibly just in a hurry and annoyed at being caught up in the waddling procession. We moved through it all like mist, though one or two tawny, wolf-like, Talverdine dogs following their masters out on patrol looked around and grumbled. No Nightwalker philosopher has yet explained why some dogs can tell there's someone near in the halfworld, when even powerful witches can't. It has nothing to do with the breed; Blaze does it.

Leaving the churned mud of the road behind, we wandered over sheep-cropped pasturage and scrambled over places where earth had eroded away to leave bare the bones of the mountains. Greyrock Castle sits on a steep jagged outcropping, rising like the prow of a galley towards the north, where it drops abruptly away in cliffs and slopes of loose scree. Here we were as good as out of sight of the castle and did not need to hide in the halfworld; to anyone looking down from the towers we would be just two distant figures, shepherds or huntsmen, perhaps. We walked as far as where the dark, incense-smelling, spruce woods spilled away from the north cliff down to a shallow river, before rising again as the mountains piled over us. It was lonely there.

No sound carried from the castle, the sheep had all been driven to more sheltered folds, and only the wind soughing through the spruce boughs kept the silence from being absolute.

We didn't talk. Sometimes you don't need to.

The shadows of the early evening were growing long, and it was dark enough beneath the spruces to step into the halfworld when dutiful guilt drove us back.

And again, there were mounted soldiers going out the gate, human and Nightwalker. This time though, they were in a hurry, and Aljess was at their head.

"Captain!" I shouted, stepping from the halfworld and thrusting Annot behind me as they hurtled by, because a horse chose just then to swerve towards us. In the real world, there were fewer horses. Some of the trailing riders were in the halfworld.

Aljess heard my shout, glanced back and reined in, waving the others on towards the town.

"Maurey! You're not hurt!"

"No. Should I be? What's happened?"

Her eyes narrowed. "What's happened? You weren't even there? What, by all the Powers, do you think you're doing out here then? Yerku damn you, Maurey'lana, you aren't even armed!"

"We just went for a walk, Aljess'den," Annot said, with formal politeness that was meant to be soothing. We were all friends of too long to use the honorifics 'lana, 'kiro, and 'den among ourselves. Aljess saying "Maurey'lana" or "Annot'kiro" was usually for the benefit of onlookers she felt needed to be impressed with our ranks. Or, in my case, a pointed reminder to remember who I was and what that meant. As now.

"I'm sorry, Aljess'den," I said. "We were perfectly safe. We didn't expect to be gone so long, or I'd have left word for you of where we were going."

"But what has happened?" Annot asked.

"Someone was in the upper room of the keep," Aljess said,

with a look at me that promised we weren't through yet. "The guards heard crashing and screaming and barking. They ran upstairs and found nobody but the dog, injured, and blood on the floor. Sanno and Elwinn went into the halfworld and came back to say they had seen out the window someone running across the yard for the gate—one man. He must have passed them on the stairs in the halfworld. Sanno went back to follow him, while Elwinn came for me, since Theo and Trefor couldn't leave the keep unguarded. We've been searching the castle in the halfworld for the past hour, and the human guards on the gate aren't letting anybody out. But we can't find Sanno'den in either world. He and whoever he was following must have gone straight out. Lord Lowrison sent Sir Jehan down to Greyrock Town, but nobody has reported back yet."

"We walked back from the north and we saw no one in the halfworld or out of it," I said.

"You wouldn't. He'll be heading for the Westwood road if he doesn't go to ground in town," Aljess guessed. "Annot?"

Annot had gone pale. I grabbed her elbow and found she was shaking.

"Annot'kiro, the dog isn't badly hurt." Aljess gave her a hasty little bow. "I should have told you, I'm sorry."

Annot gave me a shaky smile and put my hand off. "Right," she said. "I'll look after Blaze. Go on. And be careful, Maurey." She turned and ran through the gateway.

"One of you attend the baroness!" I shouted to the gate guards who were out of sight beyond the deep archway. It was only a guess that the—what, spy? assassin? common thief?— had left the castle. I ducked around to the other side of the horse to mount behind Aljess.

"Ah, no," she said. "No armor, no sword. You go with Annot and find yourself some more guards, Maurey'lana."

"No," I said. Al snorted, but didn't argue further. With me riding pillion, her stallion leapt forward after the others.

"Was anything taken?" I asked.

"I didn't stop to look," Aljess snapped. "I thought they had you and the baroness both."

"I'm sorry."

"Don't go off without telling me again."

"I won't."

"Your word on that."

"My word, Aljess'den. Al, was the door forced?" Even in the halfworld, metal and stone have solidity. So does old wood, though new growth is as intangible as reflection. Other things have varying degrees of presence, often, though not always, related to their age or to how rooted they are in the world. Many objects have no more to them than mist, as though they are mere echoes or mirages of themselves.

I'm the only warlock I've ever heard of who has found a way into a deeper layer of the halfworld, in which it is possible to move through old wood or even stone. It's downright terrifying though, and hard to maintain. Could the Yehillon have discovered the same secret for their shadow road? Hard to believe. But I didn't see how someone could have broken open that door, not without a lot of time with an axe, which is the sort of thing that alert guards tend to notice.

"The door was standing open."

"I locked it. I always do, and anyway, I remember locking it."

"Annot and I are the only other people with a key," Aljess said. "Even Lord Lowrison doesn't have one. But a witch can open a lock. The Moss'avver does."

"Robin and Fuallia would have no reason to break into my workroom. More likely there's another key. I had to come the grand lord over the last warden's seneschal to get any keys at all from him, you remember. When he went back east to join his master, he may have carried off a complete set to all the strong points of the castle, for all we know. If I were trying to get keys for a place, I'd try former servants with a grudge, first of all."

"I can't imagine Fuallia hurting a dog under any circumstance," Aljess admitted. "A person, yes, but not a dog. And Elwinn did say it was a man they saw running in the halfworld."

"Human or Nightwalker?"

"That, he didn't say. If he was wearing a hood or a cap, who could tell, at that distance? I did make sure Lord Lowrison knows that there may be humans about who can enter the halfworld. I let him think it was something new we feared from the philosopher's secret arts. Who knows? It may be. At least the humans know they may be looking for a human."

"Al—there was a stranger coming in the main gate when Annot and I were sneaking out. If we don't find this person in town, we should ask the goose-girl if there was anyone behind her, and the patrol that was heading out if they saw anyone."

"What kind of a stranger?"

I tried to remember. "Human. Not elderly, but beard going white. Wearing a light-colored hood. Snub nose. Shabby but neat in his clothes. I couldn't tell you their colors. He could have been one of the serving-men, though I didn't recognize his face. He wasn't carrying anything. I assumed he was from the town. Probably he's day-labor or something, or a servant sent on some tradesman's business, but…"

"But?"

"But I did get the feeling he was looking right at us. You know how that can happen in the halfworld, when you find yourself in someone's line of sight. It occurs to me, what if he *was* looking at us—what if he was in the halfworld as well? There was nothing to give away that he was, but that doesn't mean much. I always avoid walking through people anyway. Most people do. It's instinct. Probably he's perfectly innocent, but he was a stranger nonetheless and coming to the castle at the right time. If he had honest business we should be able to find it out easily enough."

"A Yehillon on his shadow road spying around the castle, and he happens to see you leaving and thinks the upper room of the old keep will be empty?"

"Annot," I said slowly, trying out a new thought, "has been complaining for some time now about her papers being disturbed. We assumed it was the ravens."

"Better a spy than an assassin," Aljess said. "If he's just a spy, he'll run for it now. If he's an assassin, he'll go into hiding, and you won't be safe until we catch him."

"A spy running for it with what information though? And to whom?"

Aljess didn't answer. "Something's happening at the gate."

I leaned out for a better view.

Greyrock Town has thick walls, but like the castle, the gates stand open during the daylight hours. Though the light was dying, the sun sliding behind the peaks, they had not closed yet. The gateway was guarded by some of the riders who had gone ahead. As we drew nearer, several of them vanished; it was dark enough to enter the halfworld now. Another wheeled her horse and galloped to meet us.

"Maurey'lana, you're safe!" The young knight didn't pause for breath. "Aljess'den, we've finally found Sanno'den. He's very bad, Aljess'den. Sir Jehan has ordered all the gates shut but this. We and the humans are searching the town, and he's sent some to search the forest road too, and a couple of riders in the halfworld to check the highway up to the pass."

Sir Jehan, the lieutenant warden's second-in-command, bowed to me and gave Aljess a nod as we arrived at the town gate.

"Your Highness, Captain. Thank the Powers you found him."

"I was taking a walk with Baroness Oakhold," I said. The more people to whom I had to admit my irresponsibility, the more embarrassing it was going to become. "What's happened to Sir Sanno?"

"We don't know, Your Highness," Jehan said. "I've never seen anything like it. We found him sprawled in an alley, unconscious. Don't know how long he was there. We've taken him into the gatekeeper's house and he's come round, but he's in bad shape. We need to get him back to the castle where a Nightwalker physician can look at him."

"You haven't caught the man he was following?"

"Not yet," Jehan said grimly.

"You carry on, Sir Jehan," Aljess told him. "I'm not leaving the prince's side until we know it's safe."

Jehan saluted her with a nod and went to meet a Nightwalker who appeared suddenly in the lane beyond the gate. "Anything?" I heard him asking the man, as Al and I hurried into the gatekeeper's house.

Sanno was lying on a blanket on the floor in what looked like a kitchen, while the gatekeeper and his wife looked on nervously from the threshold of the other room. A Nightwalker man-at-arms, Dellmurran, was holding a cloth against Sanno's face, and there were soiled rags and a basin of bloody water beside him.

"What happened?" Aljess demanded as I went to Sanno's side.

"We thought he was dead when we found him," the man-at-arms started to say, but Sanno raised a shaking hand and seized my wrist.

"A human in the halfworld, Maurey'lana," he said. His voice was weak and his words stiff and slow. "You warned us.

Didn't quite believe you. He knew I was following—ran for the town."

The man would have to have been in good physical condition to outrun Sanno, even when the knight was weighed down with a hauberk of heavy mail. Pity a horse hadn't crossed his path, but of course he couldn't have gone to get one without losing his quarry.

Dellmurran lifted the wet cloth and I hissed. The surface of Sanno's face was eaten away on one side, livid purple-red, pitted, edged with peeling rags of black-edged skin. A pale curve of bone.

Aljess caught her breath. "Powers! What did that?"

"Did you get it all off him?" I snapped at Dellmurran, whose own gloved hands were blistered, the leather corroded away in patches. Under Sanno's feeble grip, in the waxy, melted scarring which mostly had no feeling at all, I could almost imagine that terrible burning again, eating my arm.

"But what did it? Philosopher's fire?"

"Some alchemical poison the Yehillon use," I told Aljess. "Sanno'den..."

He stopped me. "Listen, Maurey'lana. Followed him to the Three Cockerels. He had to leave the halfworld to open the door. I did too, and followed him in. Told the innkeeper to post his servants at all the doors, let no one out, and I went on up. Expected he'd be grabbing his things and going out a window. Came at me on the landing of the stairs and threw something, a little pot. White stuff, like cream. It..."

"I know," I said. "But you say like cream, not a paste?"

"Yes. Liquid. Don't remember what happened then. Fell. Face on fire."

"It's all right. We'll get you back to the castle."

Sanno made another effort. "Maurey'lana, but listen, the man. Human. Brown hair, beard going grey, short, thickset.

Shouted at me when he threw the thing. Cursing. Dunmorran accent. Think he had a bundle on his back. His left hand was all torn up. The dog got him."

"We'll find him," I promised. "Sir Jehan sent riders out to the road. Lie quiet." Sanno was quiet, his breathing rapid and shallow. He had fainted again. His skin was fever-hot.

"Maurey'lana, the lane where I found him is a couple of streets behind the Three Cockerels," Dellmurran said quietly. "He couldn't have made it that far on his own."

That had Aljess on her feet and out the door, bellowing, "Jehan!" They conferred quietly in the doorway, heads together. "*Dumped him—!*" I heard the human knight snarl, and then he snapped the names of other humans over his shoulder as he swung into the saddle again and spurred down the street, followed by those he had named.

"Better that humans make any arrests, Maurey'lana," Aljess said, coming back to Sanno's side and giving the tenants of the house a hard look that they, at least, had done nothing to deserve. "If the people at the Three Cockerels didn't even try to help…How deep has that stuff eaten into him?"

"Deep."

"Can the witches do anything?"

"I don't know."

Soldiers came with a commandeered cart then, piled with straw to make a soft bed, and Sanno was lifted on his blanket and carried to it.

"Keep cooling his face," I told Dellmurran, who was riding with him. From my own experience, that was the only advice I could offer.

Sir Jehan could carry out the search of the inn and town. Riders had been sent to the highway and the forest road. Nothing more I could do there. I took Dell's horse and rode at speed back to the castle with Aljess, where I found Blaze lying in front of a roaring fire in my bedchamber over the Great Hall, being fed tidbits of roast mutton by Annot and her waiting-woman, Margo. His ruff was partly shaved and his muscular neck sported a line of stitches. The Yehillon spy must have left the halfworld on the stairway and used either a copy of the key or some spell to unlock the door. He had slipped in quietly, knowing Annot and I were gone, not expecting interruptions while he searched for—or read—what? How many times had he done so? But this time Blaze was sleeping there. I suppose the man didn't even notice, if his mind was on rooting through our papers. But Blaze would come to investigate, and he would growl at a stranger. He was very protective of Annot and Annot's places. He wasn't the sort of dog to attack unprovoked though.

The Yehillon must have struck at him, trying to frighten him off, which only had the opposite effect. Threatened, Blaze had defended what was his.

"All that thick fur saved him," Annot said, leaving him with a final pat and coming over to me. She looked pale and her eyes were red. "It's not very deep. Half the blood on him was probably the intruder's. Maurey, what's happened? You look terrible."

I told her about Sanno and our failure to capture the spy. Annot looked as sick as she had when she heard Blaze was hurt. Aljess had already sent for both the Nightwalker and the human physicians resident in the castle, and all the witches, but despite her fear for her old friend Sanno, she was already thinking beyond that. We all had to.

"Did anyone keep a sample of the burning liquid?" Annot asked.

"I told them to keep the rags Dellmurran was washing him with, and his surcoat and anything else that's contaminated," Aljess said. "You think we can find out what it's made of, Annot?"

"If there's enough of it, possibly. We'll want the best alchemist at the university. Or Romner. That won't help now, but if it's going to be used again, the more we know about it, the better."

The rags hadn't shown any sign of being burned, I realized, which was strange. The paste had eaten through my sleeve fast enough last spring and had dissolved Dellmurran's gloves. Korby had said that in the halfworld he saw it—or felt it, sometimes it was hard to tell what Korby meant when he tried to describe witchery—reaching for us in hungry tendrils. Could it be that it sought out flesh, Nightwalker, halfworld-sympathetic flesh, and ate through cloth and leather to reach it, but was inert otherwise? Was it natural alchemy or the magic that the philosophers called their secret arts? I would mention that possibility to any alchemists.

"We should try to find an alchemist with some knowledge of the secret arts," I added to Annot. "Getting Romner here might be best. The compound might be more than mere poisons and caustics. Have you had time to check the workroom? Was anything taken?"

"I couldn't find the tablet I was making notes on earlier, but there are papers all over. It could be still buried, or he could have snatched it. So far as I could tell, all your reports and things are there."

"Which means nothing. Korby and I used to go through Master Arvol's stuff regularly and take our own notes. We weren't such fools as to move things from where we found them though."

"You know, Maurey, you've never had to complain about the ravens shifting *your* papers out of order."

"I'm not so tidy as you," I pointed out. "I might not notice."

"True. It's hard to imagine the Yehillon going to the bother of finding a way into the keep to see what sort of history the warden's pet baroness was reading. But—that tablet of notes is definitely gone and all jokes aside, I don't think Blaze ate it. Why in the world would a spy be bothering with my research?"

"Maybe he thought it was all code for something else. Maybe he wants to be sure you haven't discovered whatever it was in that book he thought was burned, the thing Korby has with the story about Prince Iahilla in it. He might be afraid there's a copy. You're the logical one to have it, after all."

Aljess suggested, "Maybe he likes—what's the Eswyn word for ancient things?"

"Antiquities?"

"That. It's the stone circles you've been reading about, isn't it? Does it matter though? We have to assume he could have read or copied anything."

We did, which meant I had to devise new ciphers for all my agents and warn them all to take extra care, though I kept nothing in writing which could identify any of them.

"Maurey'lana." A young physician's apprentice bowed in the doorway. "The cart with Sanno'den is just coming up to the middle bailey now. We're putting him in the south tower."

"We'll come," I said. Annot took my hand as we followed the girl and Aljess out.

We learned that the Yehillon spy had called himself Todd and had claimed to be an itinerant medicine-seller. He had lodged at the Three Cockerels for a month and was described as a quiet man who kept to himself and sold ointments for skin diseases on market days. He had left behind numerous pots of cheap perfumes and ointments but no documents and no tools of alchemy. We did not find him on the Westwood road, not even in the halfworld, but it is all too easy to elude mounted searchers in the forest, as I know, and by the time scouts and huntsmen were sent out instead of knights and soldiers, he had too long a start.

I sent couriers with a warning to watch for him in Cragroyal and Rensey, but with little hope he would be found.

The innkeeper and the three of his men who had dragged the unconscious Sanno out and abandoned him in the alley were put on trial. We had the witness of various other inn servants and guests, who grew afraid when it became clear that even the king's human officers were regarding this as an attack on one of their own. The three servants were found to be guilty of failing to aid a king's officer in need, which Sanno, sworn to me, was, even though he was Talverdine. They paid heavy fines.

The innkeeper was judged to have the chief responsibility for abandoning Sanno in the alley. He might have paid a larger fine for that, had he not cursed the judges—myself and the two human magistrates of Greyrock Town—with damnation for our warlock-loving ways and shouted that the filthy night-eyes should have died; he meant him to have died, and he'd stick a knife in the next one he found wounded to be sure.

He had intended killing, then, just as much as the man who threw the burning poison, though we could find no evidence he had any connection with Todd, the Yehillon attacker.

The physicians and the witches did their best for Sanno, but medicine could do little, and the witches either did not have Korby's talent for healing or lacked his knowledge. I think even if Korby had been there, he could have done little more than ease the pain.

Sanno died a week after the attack.

The innkeeper was hanged.

A few days later, with the first snowfall of the season sifting lightly down over the dark reaching branches of the naked forest, Annot and the folk of her household set out to return to Oakhold.

PART TWO

✤ CHAPTER SIX ✤
KORBY: RETURN TO THE FENS

Alun was there to meet me when Captain Luvlariana set me ashore in the Fens. My sister Linnet had dreamed I was coming. I made some deals with my allies the Kin'arret, whose clan territory this was, to send the promised bales of wool out to the Gehtalander ship and prised Alun away from the Kin'arret daughters. Then we set out for home. The Moss'avver lands lie far from the coast in the heart of the Fens. In summer we'd have gone by water, but midwinter was weeks behind us. The Fens were deep in the grip of Darthanin-month's cold. Though the salty mouths of the braided rivers were open, farther upstream the waters were frozen, and the boats of reed and bull hide had been wedged into the rafters for the winter. The vast flocks of ducks and geese had flown for Berbarany, or wherever it is they go, and even the reed birds and redwings that made the Fens a riot of song in the spring had gone. The little black cattle and the sheep and ponies were penned up, munching their way through the stacks of hay. People retreated indoors, huddling around the peat fires or working at spinning-wheel and loom. Spinning and weaving are the main winter occupations of most Fenlanders, though a lot of the cloth produced ends up in Gehtaland and Rossmark, and Dugald's excisemen know nothing about it.

We rode up the frozen channels, snow-covered highways much easier passage for the ponies than the broad reedbeds, the silty islands and the bogs, where grass and reed and willows make the ice treacherously unsound and trap the snow. Sedges higher than our heads hedged us in, muttering and rasping like outcast shades, but breaking the wind. In places we had to wade ahead of the ponies, trampling a path through the drifts. We lodged with whomever we found, Kin'arret folk and then Moss'avvers, and passed one night in a den dug into a drift. Alun, thank Linnet, had brought me clothing fit for winter.

We reached my hall around noon on a day of watery yellow light, cloud and more snow promised by a high haze. Not many lords of Dunmorra would have thought the hall fit to be a barn, but it was home. It was built on an artificial island, laboriously built up of timber and brush and clay, and added to every year as it sank a little more. The island was fenced with a palisade, and the walls of the great round hall were built of clay and wattle on a footing of stones dragged down from the north. The steep roof was thatched with sedge, and the eaves reached nearly to the ground. Inside, lofts around the edge made an upper story of sorts, while smoke rose to the peak to lose itself in the thatch and give us all that distinctive Fenlander smell. It isn't the stink of wet sheep, no matter what the Baroness of Oakhold says; it's just that the sheep often smell like peat smoke too. Smaller bothies—huts, those Dunmorran lords would call them—housed things like the forge and the overflow of family and clan hearthsworn to me, which means the warriors who didn't have their own homes and herds elsewhere in the Moss'avver Fens: my retainers, my knightly vassals.

Me being a grand lord and all, we even overwintered most of the ponies and cattle and sheep in their very own barn. Not all of them though. People who sneer need to think about how hard you work to come by fuel—peat and sedge, mostly—in the Fens, and how much warmth is given off by a nice huddle of cows and a pony or four.

Dogs came barking and baying to meet us as we crossed the iced-over causeway to the gate. Cattle and sheep standing about in the mucky yard chewing their cud watched with interest, and a few ponies strolled over to welcome back their herd-mates.

"The Moss'avver's back!" squealed a small child wrapped in a sheepskin with a shawl over her head. She scurried away, still squealing, "The Moss'avver, the Moss'avver! I saw him first! I saw him first!"

Alun took my bridle as I jumped down and headed for the hall. I didn't make it, of course. I was engulfed in a crowd of my folk, all talking at once in the musical, flowing-water tongue of the Fens, the language of home. It might be thought that we witches who find the touch of others' minds so overbearing would go mad, living in such a clamor, so many hearts and minds under one roof, or near as good as, but it doesn't seem to be half so bad when they're all your own blood, one way or another. I don't know why that is. You can crowd plants much more closely and still have them thrive when they're all slips of the same stock, it's said. Which isn't to say I wasn't already thinking it might be good to head off up the river and fish through the ice for pike or eel in a day or two.

"Don't you dare," my sister said, wading through the crowd, a good blond head taller than many of them. Strong men gave way before her; she rarely needed to resort to her elbows. We met in a bone-cracking hug.

Linnet is a good deal older than I am and, really, only my half-sister. She loathed me when I was a child; luckily for me one of us improved with age, because I couldn't ask for a better, more loyal lieutenant, or "voice and hand" as we say in the Fens of a vice-chief. Some hadn't liked it at first, me leaving her in charge whenever I go off with my lord on the king's business; she's not a Moss'avver, my father having brought back a Kin'arret widow, brat in tow, as the bride of his old age. But I was off in Gehtaland playing the fool when the old man died, and it was Linnet who took over and held things together against the ambition of a treacherous cousin, until Annot and my lord the prince could drag me home. She'd well earned everything I gave her, and more.

Linnet and I worked our way through the throng and lost only half of it by entering the hall. Our mother rose from her loom and came to kiss me and tut over the state of my clothes and how cold I must be. She led me to a bench by the central fire, ordering me to get those wet boots off *this instant*. Various small children hung from my arms and crawled over my shoulders. Others peered down from the lofts, wanting to know where I'd been and what I'd done: Lady Linnet said I'd rescued a princess—tell them the story about rescuing the princess! Was I going to marry the princess? Had I killed any monsters and could I tell them a story about monsters...? Linnet's husband, Faa the smith, waded in, plucking children out of his way and sitting them amongst the dogs. Alun squirmed through like a weasel to settle near my feet, and old Nolda shoved a steaming bowl of mutton stew at me, with one for Alun, her grandson, as an afterthought. Ithan brought bread and Iver began warming ale and someone started to tell me about a quarrel with Clan Steaplow to the south about poaching peat-cutting lands, which was among the many excitements I'd missed while wasting my time among strangers...

I was home.

Over the next few weeks I seemed barely to have time to draw breath. Winter might be thought a slow season, but there's always too much to be done, whatever the month. To say that in the Fens we can barely keep our heads above water is more than a figure of speech. I did remember to use the speaking-stone to let my lord know I was back, undrowned and more or less undamaged, and in the evenings when I should have been doing something useful, I pored over the pages I'd torn from the book, trying to find hidden meanings in *Iarakulanar and Iahillalana*. Unfortunately, so far as I could tell, the murdered bookseller had been right. It was just a wonder-tale, with no great secrets hidden in it, though I admit I was still guessing at too many words and had trouble reading the ancient script.

Through the speaking-stone, I learned that Lord Romner had been the last person through the Greyrock Pass to the castle before winter really hit. He claimed he had made the journey because the prince needed a skilled alchemist to analyze the burning compound that had killed Sir Sanno, but probably it was as much to escape his bitter grandfather, Lord Roshing. The fact that this meant he could use the stone to harass me about ancient manuscripts was an extra treat. With him sitting at the other half of it, I went through the manuscript again, spelling out words I couldn't even guess at. We argued meanings and invented new insults for one another that made it a good thing we were three hundred miles apart as the raven flew. By the time Romner gave up on it and me in disgust, I was halfway to sharing his opinion of me and my folk. It says something sad about the Fens when I have to confess that I was the best scholar the Moss'avvers could claim in those days and one of the few who could read at all.

Much as I wanted a second opinion on the story (and my opinion of my own intelligence), I couldn't even send the pages to Annot down at Oakhold until spring. The snows piled high over the eaves, which kept the hall warmer anyway, and the wind howled. Brotin-month was upon us, when we remembered the shades of our ancestors. We made the old, old offerings to Genehar, Power of birth and death, looking beyond the winter to the hope of the new year.

Then everything changed.

Blaze howls as if his heart is breaking. The night flares with torchlight, men shouting, running, horses snorting, hooves loud on cobbles as the big Kordalers are led out. In the distance a woman screams, and torches swirl and run her way.

They have found another body. I know it is another, that this is not the first death. I have seen, will see, an earlier death than this. He is the gatekeeper, his throat cut. Beyond the manor's stone wall, the wind rises, howling, driving snow before it. Torches hiss and sizzle. Even in their light, a hand held out at arm's length is invisible, the snow drives in so thick. The horses pound out the gate regardless, men-at-arms and grooms—the cowherd's son riding my *grey Harrier, old Harl Steward on Annot's Talverdine mare Moonpearl, one of the white breed that can walk the halfworld on their own, a gift from Queen Ancrena herself and an unheard-of honour for a human. No one but Annot should ride that horse. Madness. The horses plunge into the maelstrom of the night and are gone.*

Blaze howls and howls. Other dogs whine and whimper and join out of sympathy. Someone curses them and is slapped for it by a woman in tears.

"Poor dumb beasts," she says. "How dare you curse them for their weeping?" The slapped man rubs his eyes, not his cheek, and walks away.

They lift a woman from the floor. This is earlier. The cowherd's son I have already seen riding is still here, down on his knees, rocking back and forth, straw stuck to his clogs. Annot's chamber, this is Annot's bedchamber. The woman's white nightgown is stained with blood, and a broken sword lies on the floor. Someone stumbles on it and kicks it clattering away.

Blood drips from a trailing hand. Someone lifts her arm, folds it tenderly over her stomach, and for a moment her fingers clench.

They laid her on the bed. Brown hair in a long braid over her shoulder. Not Annot. Margo. Waiting-woman. Cowherd's literate daughter. Swordswoman. Blaze howls, rises from his place by the hearth and goes limping to the bed, lays his head there in silence.

Annot not in the weeping crowd. No voices now, chittering, water-hissing distant noise, and fewer people. Candles burning. Old women sitting by, the vigil one keeps while the body fails, waiting for Fescor to come. Old man. The cowherd, sitting on a brocade chair with a fur robe over his shoulders. Waiting. A grey-robed Sister of Mayn, visiting scholar, murmur of prayers.

Annot not there. Find her. Warn her.

Margo opens her eyes.

"Moss'avver," she says, not surprised to see me.

"No, I'm not here," is my confused answer.

She lifts the hand still stained with her own blood, reaches for mine without effort, and I take it. No watcher stirs. Her eyes are closed, her hands motionless; she has not moved from how they laid her, though a ghost-hand rests in mine. The body barely breathes.

"Are we dead?"

"Not yet. I was once," I add, dream nonsense, irrelevant. Perhaps I was, in the time of the witch-troll. "Where's Annot?" I ask. Why does the damned vision lack Annot?

"A Nightwalker," she says. "Blaze woke us, barking and growling. We had our swords. Men came from the halfworld. They've killed me."

"Yehillon," I say.

"Nightwalker," says Margo, and the voice she does not have is growing faint, a whisper. Fescor's hand is drawing her away. "I saw his eyes by the night-candle as he killed me. Nightwalker."

"No," I say. Her eyes start to close. Her breath is still. Blaze presses his nose to her cheek, whining, and the Sister of Mayn checks in her prayers, gets to her feet, steps to the bedside. The old man bows his head, shoulders shaking.

"No!" I seize her arms, pull her to me as though I dragged her reluctant to some dance floor. "Margo!" Fescor holds her in his arms, but so do I. "Don't leave Annot. I can't find her. Go to her. I send you to her. Guard her, keep her safe till we come, I charge you, by Genehar's blood in me, by Fescor's blood in me, by the love you hold for her and the service you swore to her, go to Annot and guard her till I send you to Fescor again."

I thought the air would shatter, turned to brittle ice. I thought the night devoured all the room till there were only Margo and I, clutched tight as drowning men, though she strained and beat against me and reached for something I could not see. But then she leaned her head on my shoulder and I held her close.

"Go to Annot," I whispered in her ear, and I let her go. She faded like mist in the sun.

Horses in the yard, steaming, snow-caked. Greying light, dawn's footstep. Storm-defeated men. They had ridden in circles, no star, no hill, no light to guide them, storm-tossed as a ship trying to break the spell-wrought blockade of Talverdin's shore. They came to the wall by Huvehla's blessing and followed it round to the gate.

I should wake. I needed to wake. Faint voices. Linnet. Mother. Iver. Alun. Faa.

I was trapped in the storm, circling, blind. I was snow and wind and roaring. I heard Margo call me, felt Fescor's hand on my own shoulder once more and groped for freedom. No storm of nature, this, fixed on Oakhold, tearing like the thongs of a lash whatever it was of me that dreamed.

"Grab," someone ordered, and I grabbed, a small hand that was warm and living, clasped in both my own. "Hold on to me."

I couldn't see her, didn't know her, but then I did. A wind that swam its own way through the winds, a rock that withstood them.

"Tell the prince," I tried to tell her. "Tell him Annot—"

But she flung me through the storm, dropped me free, and I fell through dark water into waking...

I was so sick I hardly remember. So sick that, even when I was conscious again, half the hall still thought I would die. I remember, though I try not to, headaches and vomiting so bad I wished I *could* die. I'd pitched over right under the feet of the pony I was leading out, good thing the little mare was careful where she stepped. Even Linnet at first thought it was apoplexy rather than vision, when I never came out of it—not for three days, they said, cold and hardly breathing all that time, though they piled on sheepskins fit to smother me and nearly burnt the thatch, building the fire so high. And they got no sense out of me for two more, amid the head-pounding illness, no sense beyond fevered muttering and mumbling that Annot needed me, warn Annot, warn the prince, which no one but me had any means to do. That was mixed with nightmares of the witch-troll, which were pretty awful and nothing I really wanted my sister or anyone else to hear, not that I had any choice in the matter. No one thought of the speaking-stone, lost in the hall in some child's game, buried deep in a basket of uncarded wool, its quiet active hum and faint anxious voices calling for me from Greyrock.

Don't play "hunting for treasure" with the chief's magic toys became a new rule of the clan, later.

And also later, when I could think again and knew more than I did then, I worked out I'd gone adrift in the tides of vision. If they could have woken me that first morning when the vision struck, got sense out of me—Margo would still have died that coming midnight, because though we could have told Maurey, neither of us had any means to warn Oakhold in time. I had stolen Margo's shade from Fescor before she had ever died. Even if I had woken and we had both had speaking-stones, could I have warned Oakhold, changed what was to come, when I had already interfered in that future, been part of it?

Thinking of that would give even a philosopher a headache.

Sick and weak, with Linnet practically sitting on me to be sure I stayed in bed, I dreamed, vision or nightmare born of desperate need to know. I saw Annot locked in a cold high room. She paced, slow and halting as an old woman, huddled in blankets, and stared out the greeny glass of the lozenge-paned window, gaunt and pallid, her face battered black as though she had been beaten. What did she see? Flat fields, hedgerows, snow, a dark horizon to the snow that was not sky.

In her nightgown still, barefoot, hair tumbled loose and sword in hand, Margo's shade paced by her side.

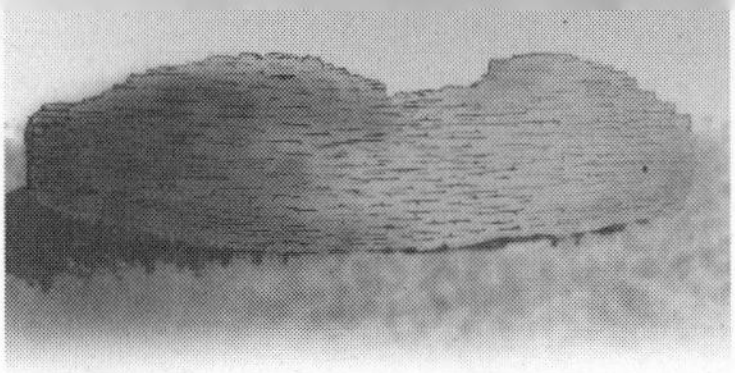

CHAPTER SEVEN

MAUREY: DARK NIGHT

I woke one night early in Brotin-month to the sounds of raised voices in the antechamber, the outer room where a pair of my household knights kept watch. I rolled from my curtained bed, took my sword and went into the halfworld. The room was still empty. Listening at the door, I could recognize the voices. Elwinn and young Palina, Robin and Fuallia.

"I did not say I would *not* wake him, Robin'den." Elwinn sounded aggrieved, his accent grown strong. "I said I wanted to know why."

"She's not hysterical!" That was Fuallia.

"I did not say she was! Tell me what the matter is!"

I slipped back to the natural world and opened the door, yawning. "Too late," I said. "What is it?"

Taddie the bluehound greeted me with a wagging tail, but nobody else looked happy. Both girls were in their nightgowns, wrapped in Moss'avver plaid blankets. To my surprise, Robin was the one twisting trembling hands in her blanket, while Fuallia stood with a supporting arm around her. Both peered into the darkness. I put my hands together on a whispered word, an easy magic, and set a thin blue flame hovering in the air between us.

"Better?" I asked. "Come in and tell me what's wrong."

"Something's happened to the baroness," Fuallia said. "Robin had a dream."

I felt as thought the world stopped around me, if only for a moment. Then everything started up again, but slowly, heavily, the way a dream or fever feels, one's body sluggish and remote. "Get Aljess'den," I ordered Palina, who hesitated. That would leave me with but one guard, if only for the few moments it took her to run to the adjacent chamber.

Footsteps sounded on the stairs, preceded by bobbing light. Everyone armed gripped their weapon, but it was only Mollie Moss'avver, fully dressed and carrying a candle. "I said to wait for me, lass," she said as she came into the antechamber. Palina, with a nod to Elwinn, ducked around her and went for Aljess.

I stirred up the fire, laid on more wood, lit candles, wrapped myself in a fur-lined robe, all without deliberate thought. The three women stood in an awkward row, and Elwinn hovered in the doorway where he could watch both us and the landing.

"Tell me," I said as my captain appeared, shedding Palina in the antechamber. Like me, Aljess was wrapped in a robe over her nightshirt, naked blade in hand, her hair loose. I realized I was shoving around the logs in the fire with my sword and leaned it carefully against the wall instead.

"Something bad happened to the baroness," Robin said. "She's not dead, Your Highness," she added. "But someone else is."

"Are you sure?" Aljess demanded. "Who?"

"I don't know, milady—Captain. I just knew because *he* knew that someone was dead. A woman. He was angry and sad. I don't know, he might have been the one that killed her. He might have been dead and nothing but a lost shade himself."

"Who?" demanded Aljess again.

"The man in my nightmare. The one—I don't know who he is, I know him and I don't know who he is!"

"Shhh," murmured Fuallia, "it's all right. Just tell them."

Mollie slipped out for a moment to the antechamber, which was filling up with Fenlanders.

Robin was shivering violently. I could hear her teeth chattering together.

"Sit down," I said, and the words came out a terse command. Robin almost fell onto the bed, the nearest place to sit, and Fuallia, with great practical sense, if not much thought for how it would look for the girl to be in the warden's bed, dragged the sheepskin blanket over her shoulders.

"Tell me from the beginning."

Robin nodded. "It was a nightmare," she said. "A—a vision, Your Highness. There was a man drowning in clouds, great, blue-black, storm clouds, swirling and swirling. You know when the current in a stream starts whirling when it goes past a rock, round and round, and leaves'll float in and get caught there—?"

"Come to the point," said Aljess. "The baroness."

"Let her be, Aljess. Go on, Robin."

"He was caught there. It was meant to catch people. It was snowing, a blizzard. But I couldn't see the man." Her eyes sought mine. "You have to understand, Your Highness, I didn't see anything, it wasn't like that. It felt like a storm, I knew it was a storm, the worst Tanyati could send, but I didn't really see it. I just...felt it, even the colors of it. The storm was drowning him and he was lost, he couldn't find his way out. I touched him. I think I pulled him out, but I lost him. I felt his hand slip away, but the storm died then, so he was safe, maybe. But that moment when I touched him, I saw things, things he'd seen, things he knew."

"What things?" I asked.

Robin took a deep breath. "They've taken the baroness."

"Who? Where?"

"Enemies," she said simply. "He didn't know where. There was a dead woman..." Robin's eyes widened. "I *do* know her. I saw her here last fall. The baroness's woman. Margo? He thought he'd killed her somehow or done something very terrible to her, and...Your Highness, was he one of the Yehillon?

Did I save a *Yehillon*? He couldn't have been, could he? He wanted me to tell you something about the baroness."

"What?" Aljess asked.

"I don't know!" Robin hunched up within the blanket. "He said, and I heard—it wasn't like the way I saw the storm or knew about the dead woman—it was words in my head, 'Tell the prince, tell him Annot.' That's all."

A Fenlander woman tiptoed in with a cup of herb tea. I could smell the bitter steam of it, and it turned my stomach. She put it into Robin's hands. It was a brew to ease the sickening headache left by visions.

"It's the chief, isn' it?" Mollie asked from the doorway. The Fenlanders were all silent, listening. "This man trapped in the clouds of magic or what'aveyou is m'lord the Moss'avver?"

"Likely," I said.

"Fightin' these Yehillon philosophers and got himself caught. Idiot."

"He wouldn't have killed Margo," Tam protested. "Margo would never have done anything to hurt Annot, so—"

"You know what the chief's like—anyone gets killed an' he thinks he could 'a prevented it an' it's all his fault, right? It won't be more than that. *Idiot*," Mollie added again.

They all seemed terribly far away. All I could think of was Annot; Margo, Geneh bless her and forgive me, was only a distant regret.

"Past or future?" I asked.

Robin shook her head.

"Has it happened yet?" I repeated.

"I don't know, Your Highness."

"Take them back to bed," I told Mollie. "Go away, all of you. There's nothing you can do tonight. Thank you, Robin."

Nobody moved, except Robin, who struggled out of the bedding.

"Everybody out!" I snapped.

"Maurey'lana—" That was Aljess.

"I'm getting *dressed!*"

They went. Aljess closed the door softly behind her.

I dressed, carefully. My fingers seemed clumsy and for a long moment, staring at my boots, I could not think what was wrong with them, but knew I could not put them on. A pair of gloves was stuffed in the mouth of the left boot; that was it. I put on boots and gloves and swung back the interior shutter over the nearest window. Through the panes of rippled glass beyond, the stars swam towards morning. Dawn was only an hour or so away. But that was no guide to anything. The vision might be of something that had happened a week ago or something that would not happen for days yet.

What had Korby said once in fury with his visions? They always showed him deaths he could not prevent.

Aljess leaned by the door, dressed and armed, waiting, as I came out. Lord Lowrison was there, the grey-bearded lieutenant-warden looking grim. I swept them on with me, and Elwinn and Palina fell in behind.

Mollie Moss'avver joined us at the foot of the stairs. "The others'll see to the lasses, get some more tea into them so they sleep," she said. "That Fuallia," she shook her head. "*Now* she's crying, poor thing. Strong enough when she has to be though. The only one as didn't run around tripping over things like a hen with her head off when that Robin woke up shouting. You know it sounds to me like she got dragged into the chief's vision."

"Is that important, Mollie?" Aljess asked when I didn't.

"Could be. Never heard of that happening, except way back in old tales. Two witches that strong though, no wonder they shattered whatever spell was making that storm, whatever kind of magic it was."

"You think it was a real storm, and not"—Lord Lowrison waved a hand—"poetry? A metaphor? What I've read about the philosophers' secret arts, it sounds like they talk about it all as poetry, to hide what they're really up to. Do you people do the same?"

"No." Mollie sniffed. "If she says a storm, it felt to her like a storm, not po'try. Could 'a been both," she admitted.

We left the great hall in silence to head, in darkness, for the old keep. The wind pierced clothing like needles. Romner was waiting with the two drowsy human men-at-arms on duty in the guardroom, though neither party looked happy about it. Romner's sharp face always does look disapproving anyhow.

"Fenlanders babble like starlings," he said. "I imagine all the castle knows by now. Are Fuallia'den and her sister all right?" he added to Aljess.

"They've been sent back to bed."

Romner made a face as though that was not answer enough for him but nodded to me. "Your Sir Jehan has doubled the guards on the gates, for what good that can possibly be. What are we doing?"

"I don't know yet," I answered in Talverdine.

"Hair," Romner said.

I looked back at him blankly as we clattered up the lightless stairs. His black eyes gleamed green, like a cat's, in the darkness. Lord Lowrison stumbled. Aljess caught his elbow. The lieutenant-warden, probably without even realizing it, rubbed her touch from his arm as she pushed ahead, shoving by so that I wouldn't be the first to round the turn. But no enemies lurked in the opalescent night-color of the stones. Elwinn and Palina, reassured of that, went back down to join the keep-guards.

"What?" I asked, my attention back to Romner.

"Hair. Do you have any? Annot's hair, fool. Romantic lovers' knots carried next your heart, a stolen lock wrapped away in silk at the bottom of your clothes chest..."

"No."

"What kind of a courtly lover are you?"

"Not very courtly," I said, but thanks to his needling my mind was beginning to work again. I'd come here with the mindless impulse to call Korby with the speaking-stone, but if Mollie were right and it had been him Robin found trapped in some storm, real or of the spirit, then he already knew and was probably trying to get hold of me. I didn't help Annot by panicking.

"Can you work with something else?"

"Tell me you haven't lovingly saved her toenail trimmings."

"Romner, don't be so foul," Aljess snarled, holding out her hand for the key. I let her open the door and lead the way in past the two twisted tree roots that stood like some strange barbarian carvings to either side of the door now, the anchors for what I hoped was a spell to detect the presence of a person passing in the halfworld. All I could say was that it worked on Aljess and me when we tested it, causing a candle in a lantern down in the guardroom to kindle.

"She left a hood hanging here. Use that. Find her."

Romner's skills had grown since we were boys. I think he'd decided if he couldn't surpass a mere half-human warlock in strength, he'd at least beat him in technique. Spells for hunting and tracking were something at which he now excelled.

Romner took the crimson hood forgotten by Annot last autumn and began examining it closely by the light of a tongue of Maker's flame, looking for lost hairs. Mollie lit the candles, witch-fashion (which worried Lord Lowrison though he tried not to show it), and built a fire on the hearth. The speaking-stone was dormant; Korby was not trying to contact me. I chanted the words to wake it. There was no response. I paced. Korby would hardly be sleeping with his head on it, to notice it was humming and growing warm. Be sensible. He'd have it sitting somewhere there in his dark hall, and amid that swarm of family someone was bound to notice come morning. I just had to keep it by me, keep trying.

A raven's feather, twigs from the pile of tinder, threads ravelled from the hood and a single red-gold hair grew into a triangular frame with a knotted web lacing it together. On his knees by the fire, Romner sang, bent closely over his construction, eyes closed. Lord Lowrison stood as far away as possible. Finally Romner rose and circled the room, the spell-frame stretched on his fingers.

He shrugged. "She's to the east of us," he said. "It's very faint."

"What good is that?" demanded the lieutenant-warden. "I'm sorry, my lord, but we know the baroness is in the east. Nearly everyone in the kingdom is to the east from here."

Romner gave him a sour look. "Don't you humans play games when you're young? You know, hunting for treasure. Hot and cold."

"What?" Lord Lowrison gave me a look that suggested he thought he was being made the butt of a joke.

"Hunt the thimble," said Mollie. "M'lord Romner means it'll tell him if he's getting closer, if he's going the right direction— like that, sir. You must 'av played it. You know, gettin' warmer, gettin' colder?"

"Literally," Romner murmured, wrapping the spell-bound device up in a kerchief.

"Ah." Lowrison did not sound as though "hunt the thimble" gave him any more confidence.

I was only half listening to them as I paced the room. Fear was rising in me, a churning tide, and fury with it. The bodies Korby had found, the Yehillon bookseller's family, murdered because the man had seen the pages titled *Iarakulanar and Iahillalana*. Prince Alberick presumably did not know about Romner. Annot was known as my tame scholar. If Korby had sent the pages to me, Alberick would believe she was the one to whom they were sent.

From what Korby said, Alberick thought the book destroyed though. I slammed the shutters back and leaned on the sill of the unglazed window, letting the bitter wind bite my face. It didn't help to clear my thoughts.

Had the spy Todd been most interested in Annot's papers? Did Alberick not believe the *Iahillalana* destroyed after all? Did it matter?

She wasn't dead. Alberick killed people he even suspected *might* know what he did not want known. Therefore he had some other use for her.

If the abductor was Alberick at all. I was only assuming that, I reminded myself. But who else would want her? Sounded like one of Romner's jokes.

Perhaps the Yehillon feared she might be about to discover something? But killing her dealt with that too. They had taken her alive.

If Todd the medicine-seller had been any good at his work, he would have found out that I was interested, very interested, in Kanifglin. I had tried not to make my interest obvious, but Robin had been right when she said that the Warden of Greyrock, with a castleful of soldiers under his command, wasn't likely to be chasing two shepherds around the forest in person just to deliver a pardon.

Might it be information on Kanifglin that Alberick was after? Had he not learned all he wanted from the old shepherd before he killed the man?

Easier, surely, to abduct Robin or Fuallia. Or perhaps not. By seizing Annot instead of one of the Shepherd girls, Alberick, if it was he, had a good long time to get what he wanted from her before I could react. Even the king in Cragroyal wouldn't find out that Oakhold had been attacked for days, or weeks, depending on the weather in the east.

Behind me, Lord Lowrison was demanding of Romner, "Why can't you warlocks do some magic and find out where the baroness really is and set His Highness's mind at ease? Maybe the girl did just have a nightmare. I assume even witches can have bad dreams from too much pudding, like the rest of us?"

She was alive. That gave us time, didn't it?

Alive, she was…was it my scholar that Alberick wanted, or the woman all Dunmorra called my mistress?

Ah. The simple answer. The one I hadn't thought of at first, because, I suppose, it wasn't something I would do myself.

Hostage. Bait. Trap.

I took another turn around the room. Everyone watched me anxiously. The wind swirled after me, making the fire roar up the chimney, blowing ashes across the hearth, stirring papers.

"Maurey'lana…," Aljess said warningly.

Like a trapped animal, I wanted to strike out at someone, and that was dangerous. When I dragged my hair out of my eyes, sparks sizzled on my fingers. Mollie had a hand to her temple as if stricken with headache.

"You're right, my lord," Romner said to Lowrison suddenly, hard and decisive, not his usual sarcastic drawl. "His Highness and I will do what we can. There's nothing else to be done tonight. Good night, sir." He started walking Lord Lowrison towards the door. The lieutenant-warden shook off his hand and turned back to me.

"In the morning," I said to whatever he wanted.

"Go, my lord," said Aljess. Not even she had authority to give Lowrison orders, but the man, after another look at me, left. "Mollie, go guard those witches in case this is something to do with Kanifglin. We can't assume that Todd was the only Yehillon in Greyrock Town." My captain had been considering the same possibilities as I had. Mollie gave Aljess a salute of sorts and almost ran after Lord Lowrison.

"Sit down, Maurey'lana," Aljess ordered. "You do her no good pacing. Sit down, calm down and make plans."

I shook my head. I couldn't think. I wanted to rush to the stables, get a horse and ride off into the winter night, shouting for Annot as though she were a lost dog and that would bring her back. The fear, the obsessively recurring picture my mind drew, was Annot sprawled on some floor somewhere with her throat cut, as Korby had reported finding the bodies of the women in the bookshop. She was alive now, Robin said. That did not promise she would be in a day, or a week, or a month, or however long it would take me to find her. She ought to be *here*, sitting right *there*, the firelight glinting on her hair, looking up with a hint of a smile in her eyes, some teasing words on her tongue.

"Maurey..." Romner took my arm. The air crackled and smelt of thunder. I jerked away from him, back to the window, where I leaned head and arms on the icy sill, closed my eyes and tried simply to listen to my own breathing, to slow my circling snarling thoughts. I couldn't afford to think about Annot, not that way, not now.

"Aljess, go downstairs," Romner said.

"No," I muttered. "I'm all right."

"You're not."

My failure to control my fury had killed men. Romner and the Moss'avver and I survived because Korby had somehow earthed the storm of power, in that battle at the Westwood stone circle. My old swordmaster was alive because of excellent Maker-skilled healers in Sennamor. The old strong warlocks, the ones like me, must have been men and women of great inner control. Powers knew I tried to build and hold on to an inner stillness, but what were good intentions worth? Little enough, when my friends had to flee me when most I needed them, for fear of the very air turning to fire. And it seemed the more I developed my Maker's skill, the more dangerous loss of calm became. Sometimes I thought I, and those around me, would be safer if I turned my back on magic altogether and let the talent wither away into dormancy again.

"I'm all right," I repeated, pushing away from the window. "Sit down, both of you." I took a deep breath. "We need to make plans."

Fear was dangerous. Anger was dangerous. If I could not set them both aside, I was as guilty as the man who beat his children and claimed lost temper pardoned him. I took another deep breath and sat down at the table, waving them into chairs.

"We need to sort out what we know from what we can only guess. Assuming it is the Yehillon that have her, we need to think of the possible reasons, their possible next moves, and plan for them all. Most important: the Kanifglin Pass has to be watched from our end—I don't trust the ranger captain to take the threat seriously enough. He seems too prone to dismiss all humans as having no mountain skills and no winter skills, just because we don't in Eswiland."

"No, he dismisses everyone that way, Maurey," said Aljess, who knew the captain of the mountain rangers. "The Yerku themselves could show up and he wouldn't admit they were much use till they proved they could dangle down a wall of ice on a rope with skis strapped to their backs."

"And still hit a flying bird with a sling in the middle of a blizzard," Romner added.

"My point is that rangers know how to travel the lower reaches of the mountains even in winter, and in Rossmark and Gehtaland, people don't hide indoors till spring the way we do here either. We can't assume no one will move until spring. We can't afford to wait for spring ourselves."

"You're going after her," Aljess said. It wasn't a question. "I'm not saying 'do not,' Maurey'lana, but remember you are the Warden of Greyrock, the lord of this district. You have a duty here, to your brother, to the folk who live here and to the queen. You can't run off on private adventures without considering the consequences. Even if Greyrock is Dunmorran and as warden you're a Dunmorran royal officer serving the human king whose land this is now, in Sennamor the queen and council have started looking on you as the warden of *their* border, protecting *them* from humans. There's so much trust placed in you..."

"The Yehillon are a threat to the border. I'm meant to be keeping the border safe. Annot as their prisoner is a threat to the border."

"Powers, Maurey, she doesn't have one of the keys to the Greyrock Pass, does she?" The keys, object-bound spells from the earliest days of the hidden kingdom, stilled the guardian enchantments on the Greyrock Pass and let a human travel through them safely.

"No. The Dunmorran ambassador to Talverdin was given one when he took up his position, but he gave it back to the queen once he was at court in Sennamor, of course; Consort Gelskorey has it now. I was given two to keep here, and Annot has had one for years. She left hers with me when she went east this time though, because we didn't think it was safe any longer with Yehillon spies around."

"Have you checked on them lately?" Romner asked. "Since the spy, say?"

"Don't be a bloody fool," I snapped. Papers lifted on the table. I shut my eyes a moment, seeking stillness again. "Sorry. I have, yes. And if you think you can find them or get them out if you do, you're welcome to try."

"Does Annot know where they are?" Aljess persisted.

"No."

So even last summer, when I found myself made my brother's lord of Greyrock and entrusted by my aunt with these precious, dangerous, deadly keys, which could put a human army on the highway to Talverdin, I had in the back of my mind feared this very situation.

"Are you certain?" Romner would be like a terrier with a rat until he was satisfied.

"I'll show you." I pinched out the candle on the table and slid into the halfworld. He followed me. I took his arm, as if I were pulling a human into the halfworld, and before he could react, I dragged him deeper, deeper, to where everything was cold mist and silence, and I plunged my free hand into the massive stone of the hearth. I pulled out the signet ring with the square garnet engraved with the royal oak leaf of Talverdin that my father had given my mother, an old-fashioned ring-brooch in dull bronze that had been unused in generations, and the sapphire pendant that had been in Annot's keeping— as queen, my aunt Ancrena had placed such unheard-of trust and honor in Annot, yet as head of House Keldyachi she still insisted I should marry a Nightwalker and pass on my great power to another generation. If she had only given me her blessing, Annot would have been safe here with me...No. I knew that thought for false as soon as I had it. Even as my wife, Annot would still be Baroness Oakhold, with her own role in the kingdom as one of my brother's great magnates, with her own estates to run. Wed or unwed, Greyrock and Oakhold were still a long way apart.

Romner stared and put a wary hand to the stone himself, flinching as it gave to his fingers like soft snow. I shoved the keys back and pulled us through the more ordinary layer of the halfworld to Aljess.

"Veyros keep us," Romner muttered. He was actually shivering. "That's not possible."

"I'm starting to think we have no idea what's possible."

"What?" said Aljess, who hadn't followed.

"The keys are safe," Romner told her. He shook his head. "Does anyone else know you can walk through stone?"

Aljess raised her eyebrows.

"By anyone, you mean anyone in Talverdin? No. Only Annot and the Moss'avver. And neither of you need to tell. I can't explain how I do it and I don't need—I don't need the queen and consort getting any more interested in how different I am. There's enough fretting over how and why I can do things as it is."

Romner nodded.

I sighed. "So. We need to decide who stays and who goes. We need to figure out how we can travel. We need to talk to the Moss'avver. And consider this: Alberick is supposed to be the prince of the Yehillon because of his gifts, not by some right of inheritance. From the sound of it, these princes come along very rarely. Miron the Burner was supposed to be one, and according to the man Korby questioned, even he didn't have the Great Gifts that Alberick has."

"Ah," interrupted Romner, "something to think about, Maurey, in Cuin's *Life of Miron*, which you and the Fenlander pinched from Master Arvol last spring. I've read it and read it and pulled it apart and thought about what it says and what it doesn't say, and I realized something: Magister Miron invented philosopher's fire. He never actually made it himself."

Aljess frowned. "So?"

"Cuin doesn't say so. He just always says things like 'The Master directed his assistants and his alchemists' and 'Master Miron instructed the astrologers, who assembled the precious powders as he directed.' He's never actually making the damned stuff himself. It would be easier to write 'Miron made philosopher's fire,' but Cuin was there, he was a witness, he was one of Miron's fellow astrologers from the College in Rona, and he never, ever shows Miron doing this, though he's keen enough to show what a master of the arts he is in all other respects."

"So he's too grand to get his hands dirty."

"Maybe," Romner admitted. "Maybe that was what Cuin thought he was seeing, the grand master supervising the lesser lights. But the point remains: if Cuin was accurate, Miron did not make philosopher's fire with his own hands."

"And?" Aljess asked.

I was sitting up straight. *"Ah..."*

"If we assume he was a Yehillon prince, able to enter the halfworld and who knows what else—"

"Philosopher's fire might affect him," I said.

"Which gives us a nasty weapon against Alberick," Romner continued. "One which won't harm Annot, so long as she's in the real world. A weapon against any of them with their Lesser Gift, if that means they can enter the halfworld."

"We couldn't use philosopher's fire," Aljess said. "Powers, Maurey, that would surely be the unforgiveable sin. Even if we knew how to make the stuff, we couldn't. I couldn't."

"I could," I said. "Romner?"

Romner shook his head. "No progress with the alchemical analysis yet. Both natural alchemy and the secret arts are involved, so it's not a question of merely mixing up the right ingredients even once I analyze what they are, but that's all I can tell you so far. I'm sorry. I think I'm sorry."

Aljess did not look sorry at all. Her mother and Romner's father, captive in Eswy, had both killed themselves to avoid execution in philosopher's fire; my father, a year or so later, had died in it; Aljess had nearly been executed by it in Dunmorra, and like me, knew the pain of even coming too close.

I didn't think I could afford to turn my back on any weapon that was offered against the Yehillon, but I won't say I wasn't a little relieved to find that the decision did not need to be made. Yet.

"But what were you saying about Alberick and Miron the Burner, Maurey?" Romner asked, interrupting my frowning thoughts. He seemed glad to change the subject.

"Kill him and we cut off the Yehillon's head for who knows how many generations," Aljess said, which was what I had been about to say.

"And if the Yehillon has Annot either as bait to distract us from watching the Kanifglin Pass or to interrogate her about"— I lost my voice and started again—"about Kanifglin, or about whatever it is they're so scared of in that Yerku and Yehilla story, Alberick is going to be where she is. Isn't he?"

"There, or on his way to Kanifglin."

"With Annot," Romner said. "If he thinks she knows the route of the pass, he'll bring her with him. Either way, you're right. Find Annot and we should find Alberick. And he may be as great a threat to Talverdin and the new peace as Chancellor Holden and Arvol ever were. Or greater. And don't forget that some power trapped the Moss'avver, if he's the man in Robin'den's dream. Anyone that can do that is not someone I want to fight spell to spell, and I'm supposed to be talented. Maurey sitting here watching Kanifglin is a waste of Maker's strength. We're going to need you, Maurey'lana, to defeat this Yehillon prince. Even Consort Gelskorey wouldn't be strong enough."

"I can't fight him as a Maker," I said. "I'm not safe even in an ordinary battle. You know that."

"So learn how to control it."

"Do you think I don't face that, every single day?"

"Gentlemen!" Aljess snapped in Eswyn, which shocked us back to sense. The air had been growing harsh-edged with power again.

Romner sighed. "Maurey, my friend, go back to bed for a few hours, will you? Rest. Shut your eyes, if nothing else. I'm going to go pack up my notes so no invisible Yehillon can get at them, and sort out my warmest clothes, and I imagine Al has quite a lot to look after too."

"Lowrison will be lying in wait for me," she admitted.

"Yes."

"Leave the arguing to me," I told her. "Tell him we'll all meet to make our plans mid-morning. Up here, not in my council hall where there's a danger of being overheard. I want Lord Lowrison, Sir Jehan, the quartermaster, Mollie Moss'avver... Aljess, you know which of your people should be here. We'll be ready to leave tomorrow morning."

I was no fool, to insist we ride this very day. Haste in a winter journey would leave us crippled or dead and no use to Annot or the safety of Talverdin. But I felt like a chained dog. I needed to be on the forest road, moving fast as horseflesh could take me.

"Soon," I promised, as Aljess and Romner headed for the door with repeated orders that I was to get some rest. "I'll rest soon. There are things I want to see about here first."

But all I did when they had gone was pace, and look at maps, and pace again, until the dawn.

✳ CHAPTER EIGHT ✳
ANNOT: THE CAPTIVE

The abduction and imprisonment of the Baroness of Oakhold,
as set down in later years:

There was nothing to do but think, and most of the thoughts the baroness had were bleak ones, or nightmarish torments that made even cold, hunger and grief a distraction. The nightmares were memories from which she could not wake. Blaze's fierce barking. *The first man stepping from the darkness, caught as a shadow against the glow of the fire.*

How did Korby cope, when his life and his memories were full of the clamor and stink and fear of battle? She had killed a man. She knew she had. That first man, who had reached for her as she ran for the door, sword in hand. *She whirls and chooses her moment and stabs blind in the dark at the bulk of him. She feels her blade drive in, and he groans...*But she had an effort to tug her weapon free again, and by then it was too late. Margo had turned back to her aid, and there was a man between them and the door.

Aljess had made her promise not to let her guard down, not to think her own familiar hall safe. If they had not slept with swords by their bed, would they have simply run, swift and sure in the familiar room, and made it out the door?

Probably not, she decided.

She and Margo, shouting to raise the household, surrounded, unable to reach the door, trapped back to back. Margo's opponent jeering about little girls playing with men's toys. Ronish accent. He dies, fatally surprised. Someone kicks Blaze hard in the ribs, knocks him flying, and she screams at his pitiful yelp, shrieks, a sound to carry through heavy doors and sleep-heavy heads. She has men-at-arms. Where are they?

Blaze lying motionless, his head on the hearth. Stunned, please Vepris, who loves all beasts, only stunned.

The room had been all darkness, the men moving shadows. One had to strike at edges caught in the dim glow of the embers, at dark masses, at a gleam of eyes.

A man swings a heavy blade two-handed, smashes her sword from her grip and turns on Margo. Her blade cracks. Then she gives the strangest gasp and crumples up, a heavy weight against Annot's knees, and a man stands there where no man was, out of the halfworld, and his eyes, his familiar face…His sword dripping with Margo's blood.

He drags a dark veil over his face, hastily, as if he had forgotten it, and knocks Annot to the floor as she lunges at him bare-handed. All the others draw back.

The newcomer had caught her wrists and dragged her up. She had kicked at him, but he twisted aside, let go one hand and clouted her hard over the ear. She had fallen again, ears ringing, eyes running, face burning. She tried, staggering, to get her feet under her, but he twisted her arms behind her. She shrieked in agony and rage. Noise was her ally, noise to wake all Oakhold.

Colorless, grey-lit halfworld about her. Now they take their time, lashing her hands together. They drag two bodies back into the halfworld. Half the men hold fast to the other half. Yehillon of the Lesser Gift? They can call it the shadow road all they like; she knows the halfworld when she sees it. Their leader, veil in place, heaves her over his shoulder. She flings her weight sideways, and they both fall heavily to the floor, but he does not lose his grip on her. As the door opens finally, too late, and her chamber fills with milling, shouting servants and men-at-arms in various degrees of dress, undress and armor, the Yehillon sweep out unseen. Blaze staggers to his feet and stumbles after them, snarling. Someone catches his collar, thinking he growls at poor Nebbie Halffoot, the butler, who comes limping in behind the rest.

Blaze howling, howling, howling.

The baroness had flung herself sideways again. That time, her head struck the tiled floor of the corridor, cruel stone, hard even in the halfworld. Darkness took her, shot with red pain.

There were other nightmare memories after that, vague glimpses: howling gale, cutting snow, pellets of ice like stinging darts. Smell of horses. Movement. Flaring light.

And then she had woken in this place, ill, weak, with a headache that would not go away and made her stomach lurch if she so much as turned her head. Her wrists were black with bruises, her face was swollen, her forehead was swollen and too painful to touch, while one ear was deaf to all but its own ringing.

Weeping—for Margo, for Blaze, for herself, for rage and misery—did nothing but make the headache worse and congest her already clogged nose, which bled down the back of her throat. She lay on a straw pallet, covered in a pile of moth-chewed blankets. She had vague memories of waking there before, of being ill, of a girl moving around her, muttering and changing bedding. That embarrassed her, but at least they hadn't left her lying in her own mess. The clothes she wore were not her own: a white shift too loose and too short, a heavy quilted gown over it, plain brown and possibly a man's because it was too long. No belt, no shoes, no stockings or drawers.

What would Maurey do?

Maurey had learned to walk through walls, something no other Nightwalker could do, something he kept very, very secret. Maurey would already be out of such a place.

What would Korby do?

Knock someone's head against the wall. The baroness choked on a giggle that was one breath away from sobbing again. Perhaps they'd send her a smallish guard, and she could try it. But probably not. She made a careful exploration of the room, moving slowly. A pool of vomit on the floor was not going to improve the atmosphere. A jug of water and a chamber pot stood against one wall, which might be useful in more ways than one. She rinsed her mouth and drank straight from the jug. Ice had begun to form around the rim, and the freezing water threatened to rebel in her stomach. She sat down on her knees quickly, eyes closed, swallowing hard.

After a few moments it seemed safe to continue her exploration. The door was locked, no surprise. There was no fireplace. The room was square and seemed to be under a narrow gable. She looked up into the dark beams and the underside of a steeply pitched roof; the walls, quite low to either side, were plastered and painted, though the red paint was mottled with damp. The floorboards were scuffed and scratched. Not the best guest bedchamber. Was she in the attic of a house? The window was glazed, and when she worked the latch loose and pushed it open, dislodging an avalanche of snow from the sill, she could lean out to see that two stories below, the stone wall plunged into a moat—black water with ice along the edges. Away to her left, another wing of the house ran along the moat, showing rather grand windows and decorative stonework. Open water meant the moat must be flowing, fed by springs, but that did not make it much warmer than ice. If she hung from a blanket and dropped, she would survive the fall but not crawling ashore soaked to the skin. She would freeze to death, even if she did manage to claw herself up the low stone wall fencing the moat. More likely she would drown, numbed by cold. Well, it might be better than the alternatives.

If she did make it out of the water, there was no shelter in sight, only flat, snow-covered fields broken by the dark lines of hedges. If she was to be a hostage against Maurey, better to choose the moat...

Where was she? The view from the window told the baroness little. Or did it? Snowy fields, blue with what looked like the shadows of late afternoon. She faced east, to judge by the angle of those shadows. There were no buildings in sight, though there must be a village close to support this manor house and work these fields. Probably it lay nearby in the other direction. Anyhow, it would be something to avoid, not a refuge. Where the snow seemed to reach the horizon, the sky was strangely dark.

No, it was not the sky. She was looking at the sea. The horizon was farther yet and streaked with wisps of cloud. There was no sign of the blizzard she remembered, which ought to have turned the hedges to white drifts and hadn't. The snow did not look very deep.

No hills were in sight. How far could they have brought her? The valley of the River Kor rose into sweeping hills that ran north past Oakhold as far as the southern edge of the Fens, except along the coast, north of the mouth of the Kor and southeast of Oakhold, where the land sank down into a small plain, the Ytimmaed. There should be fishing villages along the coast, which must be her destination when she escaped. She could find a boatman there, someone to take her north to some other village from which it would be a short ride to Oakhold. Or down to Korharbour, where she could demand the aid of the king's authorities and *sack* this place... The baroness imagined herself presenting Maurey and Korby with Alberick, abjectly bound and gagged, her foot on his neck. It was a pleasing picture. She sighed and sat down on her pallet, wrapping all the blankets around her shoulders. A child's daydream.

Alberick. His eyes... Her own eyes opened on nightmare again: that face, that moment in firelight before he pulled his veil across. She had to tell them; she had to warn them somehow.

The baroness rested her head on her knees and tried not to think of Margo, but the tears came back regardless.

The baroness had been injured more gravely than she realized, probably those several blows to the head. She missed time and did not think she had been sleeping. The broth and sops they fed her, invalid's food, turned her stomach. The headaches and attacks of weakness, during which she could hardly stand, came and went. The hearing never returned to her ear, though the ringing died away to a faint whine. On the edge between sleep and waking, especially in the twilight of dusk or dawn, she thought she saw someone near, a pale figure, like a shade, but it was never there when she looked directly at it. Sometimes— too often—she thought Margo was imprisoned there with her, sobbing quietly to herself, cursing angrily in words a lady should not know but a cowherd's daughter might, trying to cheer her and offer encouragement, promising to keep her safe. Sometimes the dreams seemed more real than the waking.

One day her jailers—always two, and never decently undersized—came in to find a blanket knotted to the window latch. While they went shouting and clattering through the attics beyond and down the stairs to pull her body from the moat, the baroness crept out from behind the door and followed.

She was caught in the kitchens. They were fools to imagine that the window latch could have held her weight, even for a moment.

A cook's boy and an armed man marched her before Alberick. He sat, veiled, at a wide table scattered with papers and books. An open chest held scrolls in leather cases and books that had not yet been unpacked. Most of the volumes open on the table looked old, the work of scribes rather than presses, and many had an unevenness of script and lack of ornament that suggested they were original texts, not fine copies. There were equally old parchment pages unbound and tied together with string. She usually traveled with a similar chest herself, these days. This was a portable library, an ancient library, from the look of it—the Yehillon library? The Yehillon archive, all its records and history? A second table by the wall held alchemist's equipment—flasks and stone mortars and stoppered jars, an alembic for distilling. For a dizzy moment the baronness was not certain where she was. It ought to be Maurey sitting there, but her own chair was missing.

The men stood flanking her as if she were a criminal brought to judgement, facing the magistrate's throne.

A couple of wood-backed wax tablets, folded closed, lay on the table. She recognized the nearest. The toothmark in the corner had been left by Blaze, trying, in a particularly bored and wicked moment, to treat it as a honey-scented bone. Her eye wandered to the nearest writing, an open book on ancient yellowed vellum. She read, upside down and in Old Ronish: *...to bring the Iarakul'lanar and all who followed them to judgement, for they had no leave to depart...They and all who come after them are outcast and condemned until they shall return to the seat of judgement...*

Alberick leaned forward and shut the book.

"If you make more trouble, Oakhold, you will die," he said. He spoke Ronish, with a faint Hallsian accent. "I have no good reason to keep you alive. You're a filthy *wallachim*, a disgrace to your noble name and a traitor to your own kind. You deserve to be killed like a base animal. I don't need to prove to the half-breed that you are alive. Once my messenger reaches him to tell him you are hostage and he must come here to speak with me, privately and secretly, hope would bring him even if I order you killed here and now. Or if not hope, revenge. Either way, he will come."

"What about Kanifglin?" the baroness asked, just to see what Alberick would say. Powers, what possessed her tongue? She was witless as a baby. She wanted to know what he knew about it, but asking only revealed that they knew about it themselves.

Alberick snorted, distracting her thoughts. "There's nothing you could possibly tell me about Kanifglin that the old peasant already did not."

"I probably could." She bit her tongue and frowned. Was he doing something to her mind?

No. It was her injury, her madness. More and more often she woke into consciousness in the night to find she was talking to Margo. Sometimes she even thought she saw her, a woman spun of moonlight and rainbow-glimmer, standing guard beside her.

"I very much doubt it," Alberick told her. "The Yehillon have Gehtish-bred mountaineers now, woman, and they mapped me a route through the mountains while you and your warlock half-breed were busy turning the Eswyn king into a puppet of that *wallachim*, Dugald, who stole his daughter. The Yehillon don't fear the winter like you soft islanders. Before long, we will be ready to cut down the lords of the warlocks in one night and begin the purification of this miserable island."

And there were those in Talverdin, even in the queen's council, who would be all too quick to think themselves betrayed by Maurey, the half human who guarded the Greyrock Pass. Romner's grandfather, Lord Roshing, would be among the first to cry that Maurey and Dugald had planned such a massacre all along. And if Maurey had deserted Greyrock to come to Annot's rescue, that would only give Roshing the proof he wanted of Maurey's treachery. *The lords of the warlocks*...if the queen and her children died, Maurey was the only heir of the royal family remaining, and it would look more than ever like treachery, an attempt to seize the crown as a puppet of Dumorra. It was nonsense. Surely even Lord Roshing wouldn't believe that of him. What point would there be to usurping the kingship of a wasteland, its folk all slaughtered or burnt? But Roshing's hatred of humans left no room in his thoughts for logic, no more than Alberick's did.

"It won't work," Annot said. "Talverdin is too well defended. Every man and woman has some training in arms. Even if you attack the queen and her lords, the whole country will rise against you. And Dugald wouldn't stand by idly either. Dunmorra and Talverdin are allies now."

"But the eyes of the fool Dugald will be opened to the evil he has set free, when his abomination of a brother rides armed into the heart of his land to attack a peaceful human manor. No matter how deluded your king is, his barons won't let him ignore that. No, your corrupted king will not be able to ride to Talverdin, even if they would welcome him, which they will not, believing it his folk who have attacked them. Dugald's power is ended, though he does not even know it yet. This summer I will lead an army of the virtuous knights of Eswy and Dunmorra into Talverdin, to carry on the work of the Yehillon. Our time for hiding in the shadows is nearly over."

"Miron the Burner and Conqueror Hallow in one?" her reckless thoughts asked aloud. "But you're skulking back here out of danger. Do your men really admire you for that?"

"There are other evils that must be purged before Talverdin is cleansed. The greatest evil of Talverdin is in Greyrock, and I alone have been given the blessing of the Powers, the Great Gift, to destroy him."

"You mean you're scared of Prince Maurey. I don't blame you—I suppose you heard all about what happened in the Westwood from your little spy. You don't want to find him attacking you from behind while the Yehillon are slaughtering innocents in Talverdin. Or is that just your excuse? Are you afraid to go to Talverdin while your followers are using philosopher's fire and your other poisons? Are you afraid you couldn't avoid the fire? Magister Miron managed somehow; can't you use his excuses, whatever they were?" Powers help her, strike her dumb.

Alberick sprang to his feet, like a cat leaping, and came around the table in three long strides.

"You know," she told the stolid Hallalander guard holding her arm, "have you seen your prince without his veil? He isn't even—"

Alberick knocked her down. Hazily, as the world closed in red and deafening about her, the baroness saw him stumble back, clutching his chest as if he'd suffered some moment of pain. Then he turned on his heel and stalked from the room. Margo crouched beside her and Annot tried to catch her hand, wanting to join the shade, to be nothing but a light and a shadow in the air, free of pain, no hostage, no weapon against Maurey any longer. But Margo was not free of pain. Tears shone on her face when their cold hands could not clasp.

The baroness wasn't alone when she woke. Beside her was not the imagined shade of Margo, singing old lullabies of their childhood with an incongruous sword laid across her knees, as she was sure it had been a moment before, but another young woman, singing, dolefully, the Rose Maiden's "Song of the Starling." Speak of a warlock, as the saying went, and he will appear. She could wish that were true. Speak of a little Yehillon spy...

"Lady Katerina!"

The Hallalander girl broke off her song. Katerina was the dear friend of Eleanor, Crown Princess of Eswy, Queen Consort of Dunmorra. She also stood revealed by her own words and actions as a traitor, one of the Yehillon. And yet Eleanor had forgiven her and taken her to Cragroyal, to Dugald's court. The pert round face was tear-streaked now, and a bruise was fading to yellow on her cheek. Her fair hair was well-dressed though, coiled up neatly under a velvet cap trimmed with fine lace, and her dress was a fetching buttercup yellow, in good heavy wool, with a dark brown over-robe trimmed in rabbit fur. She wore jewelled rings, and the pins that held her cap in place were gold and topaz. The dowdy Penitent waiting-woman was long gone.

"What are you doing here?"

Katerina turned a brown-eyed gaze on her and frowned. "You asked me that not an hour ago."

Annot would have shaken her head, but she knew that to be a bad idea. "I haven't seen you since I was last at court."

"You woke an hour since and asked me why I was here. I told you, I'm here to watch you."

"For Alberick."

"For the prince, yes."

"So you've betrayed Eleanor again."

"I didn't! He is my prince. My..." Katerina flushed. "My husband."

"Your *husband!* Mayn help you, why? He's a brute. And I thought you hated—" The baroness choked off the words she was about to let slip. Too dangerous. They might kill her. It was insane to think Katerina did not know what Alberick was, but...was it mad to think the girl could not know?

"I didn't ask to be. He's..." Katerina shivered and said no more for a moment. Then she went on, looking down as if confessing something shameful, "When I was born, it was all decided, between my mother and the High Circle—they're like his council. My father never knew anything about it, of course. He doesn't know my mother is Yehillon. Father doesn't know his own father was Yehillon, because grandfather died when he was an infant and there was nobody to teach him the mysteries. But the High Circle knew and made sure he married my mother. I was chosen because of my ancestors. I have no gifts, but my grandmother was Alberick's grandmother's sister, so they think..." She glanced at the door as she said this, and then back down at her hands, clasped tightly together against her stomach. "Alberick was only a child too, when I was promised to him. I thought he might have…thought of me more. *I* always knew that some day—my great secret—my prince would send for me." She looked up. "They came to me in Cragroyal and told me that he and the High Circle had come ashore secretly someplace up the coast and it was time for me to join him. They brought me here and we were married, just like that. Do you think I could tell them no?"

"Ah," the baroness said, "they want to be sure they have a spare prince started, since Maurey's going to kill Alberick."

Now the baroness remembered, as if it were another dream. She had woken, and Katerina had been warming her hands at a charcoal brazier. There was the brazier, so it was no dream, though she had certainly slid into uneasy darkness again and did not remember hearing about husbands. She did now vaguely remember asking where they were and being told Katerina did not know either.

Katerina told her that again, when she asked, but did say that the baroness had been there two weeks already. Two weeks. She did not remember nearly so much time passing. And longer than that since she was taken, perhaps three weeks? If her people sent a message to Cragroyal, allowing for snow, and Dugald borrowed a message-raven from the Talverdine ambassador… Maurey might know soon.

Blaze lying motionless, his head on the hearth. Alberick's sword black with Margo's blood.

Such visions came and went, overwhelming what was real and present. She had no interest in Katerina's problems.

"I think you're very ill," Katerina said, and her worry seemed real. "Did you truly kill three men when they captured you?"

"Margo and I did."

Katerina looked…respectful.

"Is Margo dead?" Katerina asked. "Huvehla bless her. She was kind to me when we traveled back from Rensey, you remember, and so many weren't."

"Alberick killed Margo."

"You…you talk to her, you know."

The baroness clenched her lips together as if to stop madness spilling free.

"It's…I won't tell, my lady. I think, perhaps the blow to the head? Perhaps it will pass as you heal."

"What do I say?" the baroness whispered, afraid to know.

"Sometimes it's difficult to know. I don't hear her half of the conversation." Was that a faint attempt at humor? "You ask, 'Where is he now?' You say, 'Tell him Alberick is here.' 'Warn Maurey.' You tell her all about the Gehtalanders Alberick has sent to wherever it is, the place with the funny name. You say, 'I know it hurts, I'm sorry, I don't know how to let you go, and I need you, please stay.' Things like that. It frightens me," Katerina admitted. "And there's something…nobody likes to come close to you, have you noticed? Nobody likes to touch you. They made me…when you had to be washed. It was not only because I was the only woman here except the manor servants, and they don't want them to have anything to do with you, in case they get away and betray us. It was because they don't like to touch you."

"Because I'm mad?" the baroness asked.

"I don't think they know that. They just…they're afraid, when they come too close to you."

"So are you."

Katerina shrugged.

Men brought food, stew and meat pie, dried fruit compote and watered wine, a table and chairs. Heaps of fur blankets and a whole bedstead with a better mattress appeared at some point while she was unaware.

"What kind of prince keeps his wife locked up in the attic?" the baroness asked. "What did you do?"

"Nothing!" Katerina shouted. "It's you, your fault, that stupid trick to escape. Someone has to stay with you."

"So despite what he says, Alberick actually thinks I'm more valuable alive? That's nice to know. But it's still no way to treat your bride."

Katerina burst into tears. The baroness scowled, unrepentant.

"Did you try to escape yourself?" she asked, when Katerina was done blowing her nose on a dainty linen handkerchief.

That was a mistake. The only answer she got was another bout of tears.

Answer enough, probably. Poor child.

The baroness slept fitfully through that day. She leaned at the window, open a crack because of the poison fumes of the charcoal brazier, and found she could not remember all the Dravidaran names of the stars, once so familiar. That made her furious, made her head ache and tears prickle. Margo leaned beside her. They whispered together, while Katerina slept.

She woke with the dawn to find a girl being noisily sick in the chamber pot, and asked, "Katerina! What are you doing here?"

The baroness did not want to admit herself mad beyond cure. Strange to take hope from Katerina, who assured her she had been injured in the head and that she would surely recover. Perhaps the mind was like any other injured limb and needed to regain its strength through use. That she was so often surprised to find Katerina locked in the room with her, knitting stockings or doing Alberick's mending like a dutiful wife, terrified her almost as much as her recurring belief that Margo was beside her.

The days passed slowly though, and there was little change. Once or twice Katerina was escorted away to dine with her husband, though she went scared and came back silent with misery, saying he only wanted to question her about Maurey.

"He wants to know all the old stories, all the things the ballad-singers tell about how it was discovered who he was, and how you rescued him and ran away together to Talverdin, and came back to save the king from his wicked chancellor. This time he wanted to know why Maurey took Eleanor to the stone circle when she was hunted in the Westwood, what he was trying to do there. The prince wants me to find out what you know about it. And he wants to know if you've ever said where Maurey's mother's ring is, the key to the Greyrock Pass."

"Maurey has it. Hidden. Alberick will never find it, no one ever will."

For her own safety, the baroness wasn't supposed to know, but she had a very good idea how the keys were hidden, if not precisely where. Think of something else, quickly, she ordered herself, before her stupid babbling mind told Katerina how very clever and very powerful a warlock Maurey actually was. What had she been scratching notes about on that tablet the spy had stolen, that day back in Greyrock? Stone circles. What did she know about the wretched stone circles? Nothing. Pure chance led Maurey and Korby to one; Romner was interested in anything old.

She started to recite aloud the names of the stars of the Brotin-month sky. Too many still escaped her memory. Katerina stared, a little afraid. Perhaps it sounded like an incantation. The baroness broke off to ask, "Why doesn't he ask me himself?"

"He says you make him sick," Katerina said spitefully. "He cannot bear to look at a perverted *wallachim* like you."

"Why do you keep calling me that?"

Katerina went suddenly prim. "It means a nasty person who does wicked things with warlocks."

The baroness laughed out loud. "Katerina, dear fellow prisoner. It's a Talverdine word. *Wallacarim*. It means something like, oh, someone who works with someone else, who helps them. A collaborator, a member of the same guild, something like that. An ally."

And how could she forget the stars, the names her father had taught her up on the tower roof with his precious telescope? What else was missing? She set herself to assemble, in her thoughts, the dull quiet histories she had been reading before she left Greyrock, the descriptions of stone circles, ancient shrines reused by the Nightwalkers as meeting halls and places to pray. Something about that research interested, or even worried, Alberick. What had she found? Paragraph by paragraph, she reformed the summaries and conclusions she had written for Lord Romner, proving to herself that her mind was still her own. At least when she forgot details of her recent studies, they were not some precious piece of her past. It did not hurt as much to discover them gone.

She is on the roof of Greyrock keep, looking at the stars through her telescope. Of course they make a pattern, if you look at them the right way, she says, though who is listening, she cannot see. But you can't look at them sideways, she adds, and that seems perfectly reasonable. She floats up beneath a ring of stones, as though she is rising through deep water, stars all about her. She knows the pattern the rings of stones and the scattered three-stone gateways make, but in the manner of dreams she cannot think why she knows it, or why it should matter. She must tell Maurey, tell Romner...

She can feel the circle around her. She shuts her eyes, and she can feel the ring of free-standing stones enclosing her, feel the breath of the gaps, the gateways. The road turns there.

The road?

The road turns to cold lightning. She is at the center of a web of cold blue lightning, fibers of fire, branching and branching, a globe flattened into a disc, a spider's web of impossible complexity. The pattern of the path between the stones lies over it, so vast she cannot imagine the reach of miles and years it encompasses. She does not move. She pulls a thread towards herself and the whole thing swirls and flies around her. She ignores the forks, the branches. The stone rings, their gateways, guide her. Her way lies ahead, and the forks lead only to…dangers, unknowns. She will be lost, lost forever, wandering, if she does not remember her way. The road is a line of cold fire in the darkness between the stars. The gates are signposts, nothing more. It seems suddenly obvious, something she has always known. "Here," they say,"this branch is the path we walked. Turn here." She has only to turn onto the marked way, still pulling the road towards her. Another gateway opens up. Turn, turn, turn.

"Have you…have you ever seen his face?" Katerina asked in a whisper out of the darkness one night. No guards stood at the door, but Katerina still whispered, always afraid of being overheard from the halfworld. There were still a half dozen High Circle in the house who could "walk the shadow road," as Katerina called it, though three had been lost in capturing Annot. Both the men killed, and the other, who died of an infected wound afterwards, had been blessed with the rare Lesser Gift. One of the dead was Todd, the spy from Greyrock, the killer of Sanno. Annot had not recognized him in the dark.

The baroness felt less useless, less a helpless wonder-tale princess awaiting rescue. She and Margo had done something worthwhile after all. They had cut down the number of the most dangerous enemies to Maurey and to the peace.

Though Alberick may have sent most of his halfworld-gifted followers to Kanifglin.

"Have you?"

The baroness hovered between sleep and waking. Margo had been telling her something vital, something she needed to know.

"Have I what?"

"Seen his face?"

"Whose?"

"The prince's."

"My prince's, or yours?" the baroness asked nastily, and Katerina, to Annot's shame, turned away and began to cry. She cried embarrassingly easily, small wonder. She was alone and expecting a baby, ignored or rejected by her husband and locked up as nursemaid to an enemy madwoman.

The baroness rolled over in the bed, carefully, and tried to rub Katerina's shoulder. "I'm sorry. I'm sorry. I don't mean to be cruel. The thoughts just keep coming out, you know, the horrible things one thinks but doesn't mean. I'm not like this really, Powers help me. Nothing that's happened to you here is your fault, you know that?"

Katerina snuffled.

"You've seen his face?" the baroness asked.

Katerina shook under her hand. "No one is allowed to except the most senior of the High Circle. Not even me. It was...it was always dark."

"But did you?"

"I wasn't supposed to. I didn't mean to."

Wasn't that some old wonder-tale, the disobedient bride forbidden to look on her husband's face, who pulls the bed-curtain back in the moonlight only to see him turn into a white fox?

"Oh, Katerina…"

"You know, don't you?"

"He's a Nightwalker," Annot said.

Katerina's sobs grew until she shuddered with them.

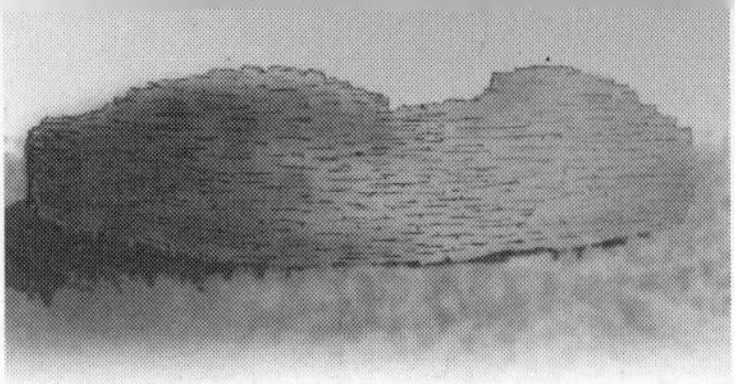

✠ Chapter Nine ✠

Maurey: Winter Journey

"…So that's the situation," I said, my lips close to the raven's sleek head. It tilted a clever black eye towards me, growing impatient with the length of the message. But it was my best bird. I knew it was able to carry all I needed it to. "Romner can find her. I've made plans with Lowrison for the defence of Greyrock and for keeping a watch on Kanifglin even in the halfworld. We should look on this as a chance to scuttle the Yehillon attack on the pass, to strike them when and where they're not expecting us, before they can get their plan, whatever it is, under way. We'll rescue Annot before they can make good any threat against her or Talverdin."

I was being more than optimistic; I was telling my brother the lie I wanted someone to tell me, and I didn't believe it.

"Sending out your own men after Annot might do more harm than good at this point. We don't want the Yehillon to be expecting us. An uproar in Cragroyal would warn them. But Dugald, if you could alert our agents in all the ports and issue warrants granting me leave to bring a force in from Greyrock and allowing the Moss'avver to lead a warband out of the Fens, that would help. Korby must already know what's happened, if Robin's vision is true, and you know he won't wait for your leave to set out, not when that could take until spring. Thank you. Make an offering to the Yerku for us," I added. My brother and his wife were more devout than I, and prayers, I often thought, were more comfort to the people offering them than to those for whom they prayed. "That's all."

I spoke the concluding words of the spell and tossed the message-raven out the window of the keep. The sky was still pink with dawn. The bird soared low over the middle bailey, where the milling confusion of the stableyard had already sorted itself into order, the big mules all laden, the horses stamping and snorting clouds of frosty breath. We were too large a band to be entirely secret outside of the halfworld, too small to be any threat to a well-defended stronghold. Sheer force was not going to help me though, and now, more than ever, I could not leave Greyrock ungarrisoned.

In the end I had chosen two dozen Nightwalkers: the five surviving knights of my bodyguard and Aljess; the rest, men- or women-at-arms. Of the humans, I chose five human knights led by Sir Jehan, with their squires, and a score of my brother's Dunmorran men-at-arms mounted on good horses, with the tall mules they bred in Eswy to carry the baggage. Romner and the half dozen Moss'avver hearthsworn Korby had left with me were coming too, as a matter of course, and so were Robin and Fuallia Shepherd, at their insistence, because Robin had some notion they would be needed. I had wanted to leave them behind for their own safety—the Yehillon might be waiting a chance to seize them—but when even Romner took their side, I had given in, though I thought he merely wanted them along so he could continue to pester them about what little they knew of their ancestry and the history of Hallow and Miron the Burner.

Over the past weeks, when he had not been scorching his hair and poisoning himself with fumes from alchemical experiments in the cellars, or quarrelling with Korby by means of the speaking-stones, Romner had been with the mountain-witches. He was fascinated by the story of the Lady of Kanifglin and for a day or two even started chasing the idea that it was human blood that made my sheer power as a Maker so exceptional—like the Lady of Kanifglin in the Shepherds' tale, he noted. But Aljess had pointed out that her grandmother was half human and not a Maker at all, so he had abandoned that notion and for some reason started harassing the elderly herald-librarian of Greyrock for information on my mother's family. This had not distracted his attention from Robin and Fuallia though. Several times I had told him to leave them be. Each time he had given me a narrow-eyed look and said nothing. At least his was not the sort of male pushiness that I worried about bringing harm to fragile beautiful Fuallia, and riding through the Westwood would not give him much opportunity for historical interrogations. Mollie would sit on him if he became too great a nuisance to the girls anyway.

I took the second bird from its perch on the back of a chair, spoke the priming words over it and started again in Talverdine, a briefer message for the queen, a renewed warning of the possible threat through the Kanifglin, as well as information on the steps I had taken against that threat.

"Leaving it a bit late, aren't you?" Aljess asked, coming in the door as I launched the second raven. "Neither will be able to send a reply." The birds couldn't usually track a person; they flew to a place.

"I suspect that's the idea," Romner murmured at her shoulder. "One can't defy orders one hasn't received."

"Something like that." I fastened the shutter firmly in place. "Are we ready?"

"We're just waiting on you, Maurey'lana."

I nodded. "Then let's go."

That desperate expedition through the clutching grip of winter was the worst, and seemed the longest, I had undertaken. I should

order Rossian skis made, I thought, for winter patrols. Next
year. If there was a next year. Snow slowed us to a walking pace
much of the time. In deep snow and the chest-high drifts in the
west of the forest, we went afoot, leading the horses, trampling a
path for them. When the snow was crusted, it cut up the horses'
legs, and again we had to trample ahead, clearing their way. In
the halfworld, where we often traveled, every human and every
Dunmorran horse and mule had to be led by a Nightwalker.
Even in the halfworld the snow was still a problem, though thick
crusts were not so dangerous. There the snow seemed more like
water, deceptively easy going at first, but heavy as we continued
to wade through it, wearing us and the horses down, a dragging
weariness from which no night's sleep was ever long enough to
restore us.

In the halfworld, cold and wind still bit through fur and
wool and leather, cutting to the bone. At night we dug pits and
pitched our small tents buried in the snow, which, like a good fur
blanket wrapped around the tent walls, kept in the warmth of
our bodies, packed tightly, Nightwalkers and humans, knights
and soldiers and serving folk, all together. When we were by
a village, we lodged with relief in their barns and claimed my
right as the king's officer and lord of the western Westwood to a
night's food and fodder; but I told them nothing of why we rode
east with such urgency, save that it was on the king's business.
I rode under the banners of the king and Greyrock, as well as the
unicorn of House Keldyachi and the royal oak leaf of Talverdin.
That so many of the company were humans wearing the king's
blue and black reassured them. And it was a lie. I was not on the
king's business.

We lost one mule and two horses to serious injuries along
the way and left behind a man ill with lung fever in a village,
another with a broken leg at an isolated charcoal-burner's hut.
One of my Nightwalker grooms fell ill as well, and when she

could no longer keep in the saddle despite medicine and witchery, we had to leave her, though one of the Fenlanders stayed with her to make sure she was safe—he had a more than comradely interest in her well-being, I think. The elderly widow we left the couple with seemed more happy to have a strapping young man in residence to look after her goats than worried by a feverish Nightwalker installed in her one and only bed. At least I was able to see that those who took in my strays were well paid for their care, with promises of further reward in the spring when my people were returned to me, which made me more confident they would be well looked after in the meantime.

I took better care of my folk than I did of myself, I suppose. Most nights I couldn't sleep. If I sent one of the sentries to bed and took his or her place, or sat up with notebook and pencil devising spells by a flame of thin blue warlock's fire, Aljess and Romner got angry with me; so I mostly lay through the nights, staring at the low roof of the tent overhead, trying not to toss and turn and disturb those sleeping by me. I knew I had to sleep, had to eat. People, not only Annot, depended on me to have strength and wits about me. I should not be a shambling dull-minded sleepwalker when we came to the crisis. But knowing I needed sleep did not bring it, and knowing I needed to eat did not give me appetite. And I dared not give way to the grief and fear and fury I felt; wrestling those feelings down—every breath of that weeks-long, centuries-long ride—ate up everything I had in me, until I was more than half a shade myself.

One good thing came of all my fretting over spells. I found a means to push at the weather, though Mollie Moss'avver warned me that what she called "messing with" the wind and rain could bring down disaster on "other folks you haven't even thought of." There may have been wild gales off the south coast of Eswiland—well, I knew there were, because I could see them in the sheet of ice I built into the heart of one weather spell—but no blizzards rolled down off the mountains over us in Dunmorra, and, for Brotin-month, the weather was mild. Nonetheless frostbite took its toll, but the witches had better success fighting that than pleurisy, if it was caught early enough, and no one lost any fingers or toes to the black rot.

The only comfort I had was Korby. By the time I finally did make contact with the Moss'avver through our coupled speaking-stones, he was on his way to Oakhold, and somehow (at that time he refused to give me details, saying I would not like them—and I didn't, when I found out what he had done to Margo's soul) he had a vague, dream-carried contact with Annot. He was able to tell me she was alive.

"And well, is she well?"

"She's not getting any worse."

"What does that mean?"

"She's not well, m'lord. She's hurt. I think it was in the attack. But she's not getting any worse."

"Tell her—"

"I can't tell her anything, m'lord. I can't speak to her. She's—I can't explain. I can try to let her know we're on our way, give her hope, but even that's—I don't know what she understands. I have no way of knowing." I heard his sigh, even through the thin voice of the stone. "I only saw her once from outside, if you follow, right after she was taken. I guess she's somewhere in the Ytimmaed; it has to be either there or the marshes of Hallaland, and I doubt they've gone overseas. She's in a room of the upper floor of a house with a distant view of the sea and no other buildings in sight. I can feel my way towards her though, like a goose heading north in the spring. Probably no more accurate than Romner's toys. But between us, we should close in on her."

"If they're not burning beacons from the Fens to the River Kor already, to warn the kingdom the Fens have gone to war," I said, because it was the kind of thing I knew I would say, and I was trying to hide, even from him, the howling emptiness that was eating me up from within.

"Um," said Korby.

"They're not, are they?"

"Not yet. Bit of a scuffle skirting by the old Lord of Platt's place, but nobody killed on either side, and we pushed on. Once we're to Oakhold, I'll…I'll do something. I don't know what yet. Ride under the Oakhold colors, maybe."

"Just how many men did you bring?"

"All the hearthsworn. Annot's our kin, my lord."

"That's enough to hang you." For a Fen lord to bring more than a dozen armed retainers with him out of the Fens was, by law, treason and armed rebellion.

"Yeah, do speak to your brother about that, if it's not too much bother. 'Course, riding out with all the hearthsworn doesn't leave much behind if the Steaplows get pushy. I may not have anything to go home to but ashes anyway."

"Your neighbors are too scared of Linnet to start a fight, aren't they?" I asked.

"Mm."

"What does that mean?"

"Linnet's riding with me. I wish I had my niece too. The only chance we have of sneaking up on the Yehillon, once we figure out where they are, is with every witch I can muster doing everything we're capable of to hide us."

"I sent a raven to Dugald before I left," I admitted. "I warned him this is what you'd do. You may already have your leave to ride out, witnessed and signed and sealed and in the chancery. But I can't say that for certain."

"Only helps me after the fact anyway. Anyone who sees us

coming is still going to be turning out the village levies and digging out the crossbows." He laughed, and Powers, hearing Korby laugh gave me hope as no reassuring words from anyone else could have done. "The trick is not to let them see us coming. Do you have a map, my lord?"

"Of Dunmorra? Yes."

"I don't, but I can root one out of the Oakhold library, I'm certain."

I saw what he meant. "Between Romner's spell and your…"

"Feeling," he said. "That's all it is, my lord. Don't put too much faith in it. Not even so good a guide as wind on the cheek."

"We can get an angle on where she is, not just know the direction." We would be two corners of a triangle, and where our line and Korby's intersected, there would be the third: Annot. A doubtful, desperate plan, but to me it blazed with hope. I asked him, again, for everything he knew or could guess about her, told him again to tell her we were coming, everything would be all right…I think I was more than a little incoherent.

Nearly six weeks of struggling winter travel left us all weary, aching and stretched too thin within ourselves, but by the time our converging directions led us to one small manor on the flat fields of the Ytimmaed, a new year had dawned. Pepsmahin-month and an early spring were upon us. Annot was still suffering some illness, some troubling scar—Korby would never lie to me, but he was good at simply refusing to tell me things and at leaving things unsaid—and I was fevered myself. Whether it was a fever of the body or the mind I don't know. It didn't seem safe to think, to speak. I rode shut away in silence, no longer making plans, no longer thinking. I had long ago exhausted all the possibilities, all the marshalling of resources I had—if Alberick did this, I would do that…When it came down to the blood of my heart and the marrow of my bones, I was not the Warden of Greyrock, nor a prince of Talverdin. I had no duty, no loyalty, no honor to hold me to the course of the greater good of either kingdom. Whatever came, I would have Annot away from the Yehillon. That was all.

✤ Chapter Ten ✤
Annot: Travelers on the Shadow Road

"What did you do when you saw Alberick's face?" the baroness asked.

"I must have made some noise. He woke up. I dropped the candle and tried to get away. He hit me. He shook me. He said I was a fool. He said he was as human as me. He said it was the sign the Powers sent: the more of the Gifts you had to fight the warlocks, the more you looked like one. It was a curse and a sign of your blessing. He said the High Circle would kill me, or he would kill me himself, if I told anyone. That's why I tried to get away, why he keeps me locked up with you now. That's why he cannot stand seeing either of us. He knows we know. He sees that we despise him."

"He's certainly despicable."

"He knows he's hideous. He hates everyone because of it. He has this great blessing from the Powers, and it's made him so terrible no one can ever love him. All he can do is serve the Powers; he can never tell himself that when it's over and the world is cleansed of warlocks, he will settle down with his wife and his baby…I think he even loathes himself. Every time he looks in a mirror, he must have to remember. I should feel sorry for him and I cannot, I cannot. He makes me sick. Even when I can't see his face, I know he's looking at me with those black eyes. I know it's not his fault. But I can't help it. And what if my baby…?"

"At least you're having a baby," the baroness snarled, to her own surprise. "And Powers curse you if you treat it as a tool in this stupid evil war against Nightwalkers, whatever color its eyes. You are wrong; everything you Yehillon do is wrong. The Powers must weep to see it, and Mayn damn you if you don't love that child, if you don't keep Alberick and his High Circle from poisoning its heart the way his was poisoned."

Annot turned her back and dragged the blankets over her head. Katerina lay the rest of the night in chilly silence. Neither of them slept.

The baroness is back on the road of cold fire. She floats slowly this time, as though she moves in thick water, swims in honey. At the knots where the threads of still lightning tangle together, she sees strange lands. She has lost her memory of where the stone-linteled gates stand; she no longer remembers the map for this maze. An ocean lashed in storm. A desert from which cold bites. A forest of unimaginably tall trees, where strange glittering creatures fly. Barren rock, red. Barren rock, black. Dust and cold and ice. A lake of fire from which harsh vapors reach for her like licking tongues. She cannot remember the turns. She is lost. She cannot retrace her steps. She will wander, a shade, trapped, not even in her own world but in this empty unreality, this void between worlds.

There are other shades on the road, an endless snake of them— men, women, children. Horses, dogs, cattle, oxen pulling sleighs. Leading them are a man and a woman. The woman carries a spear, the man a sword, naked in his hand, as though attack might come on them even in this place, even hazy and unreal as they are. All are bundled up against great cold, but the man glances towards the baroness, seeming for a moment to meet her eyes. His eyes are black as ink, black as Maurey's, in a gaunt, pale, rag-bearded face. They are all haggard with hard times, even the little children. Some wear long coats with the fur turned inwards, others are wrapped in cured pelts, not even trimmed and sewn into cloaks. The horses and cattle and dogs are all shaggy with winter; she has never seen horses so heavily furred. Warriors ring them. Are they prisoners? No. The warriors are most numerous at the rear. They fear whatever they are leaving behind more than what lies ahead. The travelers grow fainter, dissolving into the tracery of cold light. Gone. Other shades follow, men and women—a mere handful by comparison, a couple of hundred—snow-skinned, black-eyed. They have no children, no cattle, no dogs, few horses, but they are all armed, their fur-lined coats painted between the shoulders with bright symbols.

Hurry, hurry, hurry, she thinks at the vanished army of refugees. They're close behind. But for all she knows they are miles, stars, decades behind. There is no way to know. The second company fades away, leaving her alone, lost. She is lost, and nobody will remember.

"Oakhold!" The cry comes faintly down the blue trail of lightning. "Annot, my lady!"

She reaches a hand for Margo's voice. Shade touches shade. Her head explodes in a thunderstorm of pain. She thinks she curls, groaning, weeping, moaning, with her head in Margo's lap, but it is Katerina who holds her and cools her temples with wet towels and whispers desperate prayers to Geneh and Huvehla that the baroness not die here, where Katerina will be blamed for failing to save her. The girl calls, loudly, until someone hears and comes, but they will not fetch a physician or an herb-wife. They want no outsiders. The half-breed must be killed; he is the only one who could threaten their prince, their revered master of the Great Gifts, but he will come if he even hopes his mistress lives, they say. Meanwhile she must be punished for her corruption. If she dies in such agony, it is the judgement of the Powers. If she does not, the prince will see to her fitting end. Eventually. Eventually the pain ebbs.

"I saw the shadow road," the baroness says to Katerina, who is in the dream too. Powers grant it is a dream, because she should not be telling Katerina these truths that have come to her out of

the darkness of mind, the dreaming of witches, the wild, inspired guesses of inspiration piled on the scraps of history. "But it's a road of light, through the shadows, a road through the great darkness. You have the name tied to the wrong place. It's not the halfworld at all. I saw the Yerku, the prince and the princess of House Iarakulla, and Prince Yehilla hunting them, and you're lost, you've lost your way long ago. You are nothing but children who didn't understand what your elders taught you, just like the Kanifglin shepherds. You don't even remember who you are."

She starts to giggle, absurdly, and then to cry for Margo to come to her, to take her away, out of this pain and madness; for Maurey's strong arms about her, her face against his chest; for Korby the brother of her heart; for her long-dead father; for the warm absolute love of Blaze. She will be a filthy scraggle-haired witch, rocking and wailing alone in the marketplace, telling fortunes the fishwives do not want to hear. Maurey will have to lock her up, like the tale of that queen of Eswy a century before, who went mad after losing her child and sang and danced naked in the king's council hall, poor thing.

The baroness circled the room, her lips moving silently, eyes almost shut, changing direction with every circle so as not to grow dizzy, which happened all too easily these days. It was useful to be mad. Katerina hardly listened any longer. Annot whispered things she wanted to remember, needed to remember, things that Maurey must be told. She fixed the words in her mind, the careful paragraphs leading to conclusions, theories to be tested, though how she could test a theory spun out of cobweb and vision she had no idea.

However, walking, even if only winding about the room, kept her warm and strengthened her weakened body, without making it obvious what she was doing.

"There's a man hiding in the hedge at the edge of the first field," Katerina said.

The baroness joined her at the open window, hope flooding her. Fear came with it. Something unusual had been going on in the house below all day. Busy footsteps up and down stairs, thumping, creaking...Their dinner at noon had been cold meats left over from the day before, slapped all anyhow onto a plate. They usually treated Katerina with at least a veneer of respect and presented her food as if she were a lady at table, though thank the Powers they never stood by to serve. It would have made squirreling away the nuts and raisins and long-keeping gingerbread she had persuaded Katerina to crave more difficult. Not to mention stealing the knife that lived in her stocking, now that Katerina had knit her stockings.

The stranger had left the shelter of the hedge. The snow was melting in an early thaw as the month of Pepsmahin turned winter into spring and a new year began. The man picked a way around what remained, walking only over patchy sodden grass, leaving no footprints. He was dressed in dull browns, a hood pulled low, shadowing his face. Katerina clutched Annot's arm.

"It's..." She said nothing more. The man disappeared behind a row of what were probably gooseberry bushes in the garden, and then his upper body appeared again above the waist-high wall bordering the moat. He stared anxiously upwards.

He was not anyone the baroness knew after all. Not a scout for rescue, but some boy come to meet his sweetheart from the kitchens, perhaps. But Katerina leaned out, looking frantically around, and then waved.

The man pointed at Katerina, at himself, and beckoned. Katerina shook her head, hesitated, and then mimed someone turning a key in a lock, pointing to herself.

"Don't shout," the baroness warned, seeing Katerina was on the verge of doing so. The man below was frowning, apparently puzzling over what her gestures meant. "Who is he, your brother?"

"My uncle! The prince said—the prince said he was a traitor, he said they were hunting him and when they caught him he would be executed and I would have to watch, he said…He has to get away, they will catch him. Gerhardt!"

The baroness grabbed Katerina away from the window. "Fool! He knows he's in danger, that's why he's creeping around in hedges. Are you utterly stupid?" She caught back the words. It was so shaming and infuriating, the way thoughts just spilled out. "Forgive me, Katerina. But don't call to him."

"He has gone now," Katerina said. "But he will come back. He will save us."

"I don't need to be saved. They're already—" The baroness clenched her teeth on the words, before anything else escaped her. Things she must not say, things she must not say, Margo had told her…*Margo gasped and crumpled up, a heavy weight against Annot's knees, and a man stood there where no man had been, out of the halfworld…*Margo was dead and did not tell her anything; what she thought she knew was only a wish. Maurey would come, but he could not possibly be here yet, even if Korby had dreamed of her, and she didn't know that he had, she only hoped. "No, you're right. We need his help. It's not as if we're that well guarded; I could have gotten away almost anytime since I got my strength back. It's the problem of staying free, once we're away."

Katerina looked doubtful. The baroness did not know or care whether her doubt was for the state of Annot's health, or for the claim that they could have escaped. Hadn't she noticed the fools had locked their captives in a room where the door had only strap hinges and opened inwards? Their captors had never noticed when she had hidden that knife from their supper. It was almost insulting, as if resourcefulness could not be expected of mere females. Or they trusted Katerina, despite her attempt to run away, to be still loyal enough to report such things.

It would take the baroness half an hour at most to dismantle the hinges and twist the door open on its latch. The problem lay in what to do afterwards; that was why she had waited. But if they had an ally on the outside, even a former Yehillon murderer...

"What's stopping us is the difficulty of getting away from the house and surviving once we do, despite all the food we've stashed. But if Gerhardt has eluded them for this long, he can't be as much a fool as—" And she swallowed the thought. "But you do have to choose, Katerina. Right now. Are you Yehillon, or are you not? Your brother—"

"Uncle!"

"—is a traitor to the man who's married you, a traitor to the Yehillon. Which one are you going to betray? What path will you set your son's feet on?"

A straw-blond young man, sword drawn. The blue fire of the shadow road crackles beneath his feet. His eyes are black as the raven's feather, and he turns away from her, towards a cluster of figures like shades, half dissolved in flame. But he fades into the stuff of the shadow road himself and is gone, all are gone...

Katerina's brown eyes swam and she sat down on the bed. The baroness blinked herself back to reason.

"I don't know what I think anymore!" the girl wailed. "I don't know who I can believe. I don't know what to do."

The baroness sat beside her. "Your first thought was for your kinsman's safety."

Katerina sniffled.

"So you care about him. You're afraid of Alberick. Which do you betray? Which do you trust with your life and your baby's future? Which do you want?"

And Mayn grant you choose well, the baroness added, hoping the thought stayed silent. If she could get herself out and safely away, the game changed. If she could put a hostage in Maurey's hands, bait that Alberick would come for, his child...she would. Talverdin would not burn.

"Can we make a rope from the bedding?" Katerina finally asked. "We'd have to swim the moat."

And die of cold. The baroness had already thought of all those things.

"What if we can take the door apart?" she asked. "Pry off the hinges? You know your way around the house, don't you? Can you get us outside without being seen?"

The village, assuming there was one out of sight on the other side of the house, would be no help. There might be other villages along the coast, but between here and the horizon there were empty fields in which they would be as exposed as a mouse to a hunting owl. Alberick could probably see in the dark.

Was he really a traitor Nightwalker, kidnapped, perhaps, and raised on lies by the High Circle to be a weapon against Talverdin? She had dreamed the answer, she knew, but in her waking and rational mind she distrusted that insight. It didn't really matter. He was Nightwalker, one way or another. Assume he could see in the dark. Night would not hide them.

"I...I don't think I can get us out," Katerina admitted. "There's only one bridge over the moat. Porters keep watch at the door."

"Are they Yehillon, or are they local?"

"Yehillon. Everyone here is either High Circle or someone who's been serving the prince personally a long time. Or, well, there's Sir Ervin."

"Who?"

"The man who was Warden of Greyrock before the king took it from him and gave it to your—to Prince Maurey. This is his house, I think."

"He's Yehillon? Powers, and he was warden for so many years..."

"No, he is not. I know he helped with the arrangements to get Alberick and the High Circle ashore without the portmasters knowing and warning the king, but he is not Yehillon. He wanted to help defend the kingdom against the warlocks…" Katerina abandoned that line of explanation. "I think he's confined to his bedchamber now. He may be ill. He told his servants he was, and sent them away. One of the High Circle is a physician, and Sir Ervin is under that man's care."

"Powers, Katerina, the poor man's a prisoner too, then. Ill? Terrified, more like. If not murdered already, now they've got his house. How many other people are here you haven't told me about?"

"None! Those are all. All Yehillon. Only the kitchen servants belong to the house, and did you notice, it was not the usual boy who carried the food today?"

"And it was yesterday's leftovers. Do you suppose they've sent the rest of the servants away too? We have to get out of here now, Katerina. They're packing up to leave: that's what all the noise below is."

Why, why, why? Were they afraid and fleeing? Had Maurey found them? Why wasn't he here, then?

The baroness knew she was too weak to have any chance of overpowering anyone. Katerina was unreliable; she would not trust the girl not to lose her nerve.

"It will have to be the window then," the baroness admitted. "We can't do anything for Sir Ervin, not till we're free ourselves. As soon as they've brought us supper and cleared away, we can start cutting the blankets. Pity they never let you have scissors for your workbasket; my knife is pretty dull. And pray to all the Powers we can find shelter quickly, and a fire."

They never had a chance. There was no supper. The baroness began pacing again, while Katerina sat chewing her nails, rocking back and forth as if she already soothed a baby. The shadows thickened into dusk. The baroness had decided they would be left alone for the rest of the night, when, just as she was about to begin tearing the blankets, feet came thumping up the attic stairs. She hastily shoved the dull knife out of sight again.

Two men, booted and cloaked for riding, strode in.

"Time to go, my lady," the Hallalander said. His Ronish partner merely stood scowling at the baroness, a hand on the hilt of his dagger as if he expected trouble.

"Go where?" she demanded.

"Not you, *wallachim*. You remain here." The Hallalander bowed mockingly to Katerina. "My lady, Katerina." He took her arm.

The baroness put herself between them and the door. "Where are you taking her?"

The man didn't bother to answer. His partner swung the baroness out of the way. She stumbled and fell by the bed. The Ronishman raised his fist as she struggled to get up, her traitor head spinning and lurching sickeningly, and Katerina shrieked, "Do not dare!"

The man shrugged and stepped away, when the baroness did no more than crawl up to sit on the bed, a hand to her head. She wasn't pretending illness, unfortunately. She couldn't find her balance to stand.

"Where am I going?" Katerina demanded of the men. "Is my husband coming too?"

"He will be joining us later," the Hallalander said, smirking. "Do not you worry your head about where. Someplace safer."

"The baroness must come too. I need a companion, a lady to wait on me. It's not fitting for me to be surrounded by only men and vulgar servants, in my condition. I insist she come with me. I will not move a step outside this room if she is not allowed to attend me." Brave of her, but Katerina's voice quavered.

The Ronishman rolled his eyes, grabbed her by her elbows and marched her out the door.

Katerina shrieked. "How dare you lay hands on me! My husband will hear of this! Annot!"

The Hallalander went out and locked the door without ever looking at the baroness again. Katerina's voice, cursing the men in Hallian, died away in a final shriek.

The noise in the house, the slamming of doors, continued for a little longer and then ceased.

At least they had left her Katerina's night-candle to see by.

"My lady, we have to get out of here," Margo said. "There's something very wrong here." The shade was there beside her, shadowy but with a dim light of her own within. Or lit by the light of some other place. No dream, no madness, and it seemed perfectly natural for her waiting-woman to be with her, to be speaking, a voice known and familiar, though it sounded…not faint, but somehow remote, as if Margo stood in some other space of other echoes. But Margo had been there all along, the baroness remembered now. Margo spoke to Korby, told him things, told Annot things. Memory was a fish that slid free of her hands and was gone, lost in dark waters, the moment she turned her attention to something else. Or else she was mad. Katerina had never seen or heard Margo; no doubt the Hallalander would have screamed in proper womanly fashion if she had. Did that make the baroness mad? Or blessed with a vision meant for herself alone? Or was choosing to whom they would appear some gift given to shades, when they had grave tasks laid on them? She had never seen the bound dead of the Greyrock Pass except in her nightmares, though Maurey had spoken to them in the waking world.

Mad or blessed, did it matter? No one else was offering even the little advice the shade had to give.

"My lady—"

"I know, I know. Can't you go and see what's happened downstairs?"

"I can't leave you unless he calls me, my lady. I told you that."

"You did, yes. I'm sorry. I can't seem to remember things very well." The baroness leaned out the window. The moon hung low over the sea, silvering the snow. Still more snow than naked grass. Other than that, the fields were cloaked in darkness; no shadows moved, no torches. Well, she had long ago concluded that whatever road passed by here, and whatever village served the manor, must lie to the west, out of sight.

"My lady, do you hear...?"

"Not very well," she said glumly, turning from the window. "What is it?"

"I'm not sure." Margo, shade or not, had her ear pressed to the crack of the door. The baroness joined her. It did no good. Whatever noise Margo heard was drowned by the whine in Annot's left ear, which was dead to the world, otherwise. But she could smell...

"Margo, something's burning." Now she could hear it, with an idea what to listen for. Roaring. "The house is on fire."

Powers help her, Mayn, Asta, the Yerku, please...Was Maurey down there?

"Margo, where's Korby? You know where *he* is, don't you?"

Margo seemed to be listening to something far away. "Near," she said at last. She pointed to the south. "That way. I don't know how far." Such coldness in her voice when she spoke of Korby, whom she had always, the baroness thought, rather fancied, though he had never singled out her or any other girl for particular attention. Now Margo seemed to fear him, hate him even. She would not say why; she carried the messages he gave her and refused to speak of him otherwise.

"So there's just me." The baroness's voice was alarmingly calm and steady, as if she were the girl who rescued princely scullions from dungeons without hardly batting an eye, rather than this mad ill creature who believed she conversed with a shade. "Locked up here to burn while the Yehillon vanish again. Punishment for my corruption, I suppose. They lure Maurey here; then they burn the house…Do they expect him to destroy the village in revenge? Or is it enough to have a burnt house and a woman's body and an enraged warlock here for the world to see? Everyone will decide it's a massacre, and they'll attack the Greyrock Nightwalkers. Korby's such a fool; he's brought an army out of the Fens to get himself beheaded if Dugald can't twist the law somehow, and meanwhile, Alberick slips off after the assassins he's sent to Kanifglin…Powers, why couldn't we have killed him when we had the chance?"

"Because he's a better swordsman than either of us," Margo said tartly.

"Why didn't Korby kill him in Rona then? Idiot." She pushed herself away from the door. Fingers of smoke were feeling their way under it. She took a blanket from the bed and blocked the crack. "I'm going to die from that stupid moat after all. I might as well have jumped out weeks ago. I hope they took Sir Ervin away with them. I certainly can't do anything for him now."

From under the mattress, she dragged the knotted scarf that held her hoarded nuts, raisins and slabs of tough gingerbread. She rolled it up in a blanket with Katerina's change of gown, along with the girl's abandoned clean linen and another pair of her stockings. She tied it up in a tight bundle, including for weight, so that it would go further, Katerina's alabaster darning egg.

"What are you doing?" Margo asked. "My lady, there's no time."

The baroness flung open the window fully. The draft sucked a storm of smoke in around the door. Coughing, she took careful aim and threw the bundle out. No splash but a reassuring thud, as it landed safely in the garden beyond the moat.

"Dry clothes," she said. "Food. We're going to want both. Or I am, anyhow. Freezing is just as deadly as burning. Powers, I wish you could help."

"I'm sorry."

"Don't be silly."

The wool blankets turned out to be too thick to cut with a table knife, but Katerina, or her honor as the Yehillon broodmare, had warranted linen sheets. They were still tough. The baroness managed to rip one into two strips and knot it securely, but by then the smoke was rolling around the door in clouds. Her eyes poured tears, and she coughed and coughed. No time for more. By feel, she tied the other sheet on whole and shoved the knife back into the top of her stocking.

"Just jump, my lady. Annot, jump!" Margo paced the room, a thing of shadows and misty color, shedding a faint light of her own, frantic, waving away smoke that was no more solid than she.

The baroness, the neck of her gown pulled up to cover her mouth and nose, tied her rope around the leg of the bed. The moat was probably only deep enough to drown her, not deep enough to cushion a high fall, and she was still going to drop at least a story.

"Annot! Go!"

"Powers be with me," she muttered, choking, and had one knee on the sill when something hurtled by her head. Something rough and hairy dragged over her hand and she flinched away, but then she saw the grappling iron scrape over the floor, to lodge under the overhang of the windowsill. She didn't bother to look down, simply seized the new rope, so much better than her own, and slid, clumsy and frantic, afraid her weak body was going to betray her and let her plummet.

Her foot hit the water and kicked frantically for something, anything, to stand on.

A man shouted incomprehensibly. The words were Hallian. Foot? Ladder? She found a toehold on the protruding stone edge of the foundation. Above her, air roared. To her right and above, a first-story window shattered, flames bursting through. Her other foot kicked something solid. She finally dared to look down and found that a ladder had been laid across the moat to this place where the foundation stuck out a little farther than the wall. It made a bridge, of sorts, and she lost no time in crossing it, though the rungs were a slippery and uncertain footing, and more than once she nearly went in. She did fall, at the end, but the man was there to grab her and drag her over the waist-high wall.

"You are—where is Lady Katerina?" he demanded in Eswyn. He thrust her aside and started onto the ladder himself. Fire glowed in the attic room now. The house roared and creaked in its dying.

Her teeth were chattering so that she could hardly shape the words. "Taken away. I don't know where."

He cursed in Hallian and spun on his heel, about to rush off.

"Wait!" The baroness groped around. Her hand found the bundle she had thrown and she grabbed it, running stiffly after him through the kitchen garden towards the hedge. "Gerhardt! What are you going to do?"

"Find my niece," he said. "She is not safe with him."

"Help me get someplace safe," she pleaded. "I'm not saying take me with you. Just find me some place to wait for my friends, to get help."

"I have no time. I cannot help you. Who are you?"

"Baroness Oakhold. I was a hostage," she added helpfully. "They decided they didn't need me any more, which means my friends must be close."

Gerhardt ignored her as though she were a little dog yapping at his heels.

"Look, you can't leave me to die in the cold."

He had broken a hole through the hedge, angled so that even by daylight it would not show when viewed from the house. She squirmed through after him. Stubble stabbed her shoeless feet through stockings already cold and slimy with mud. The air was warmer than she had expected, and tongues of mist rose from the patches of snow. To the east, the moon lit up a high bank of fog, like a wall of cloud, hanging over the sea.

Gerhardt followed the hedge to a low stand of thorns in the corner of the field, where two cobs were tied.

"Hiding in the shadows won't do any good," she told him, untying the reins of one horse as if he'd already agreed to help her. "Alberick is more or less a Nightwalker. At least, he's a human who looks like a Nightwalker. That's what having the Great Gifts means. Or did you already know that? Katerina said she'd been told you were a traitor and they wanted to kill you. Is it because you discovered what he looks like? She did. She's terrified, poor little fool."

She finally had his attention.

"But...I heared"—Gerhardt's Eswyn was fracturing— "someone tell me, someone who do not know I am condemned, he tell—*told* me Katerina is married to Alberick!"

"She is."

"But that is horrible! He corrupt—corrupts everything, he corrupts us and he kills humans without caring. I have to take her away from him. She is so...so innocent. I cannot let her become a part of that, but..."

Innocent was not the word the baroness would have picked for Katerina. "Perhaps you mean naive?" she suggested.

"But a Nightwalker! That explains why he is so callous of human life. How did a warlock take over the High Circle? Like

a worm in heart. That veil! What happen to the real Prince
Alberick?"

"He is the real Alberick," the baroness said. "And your High
Circle must know all about him. They brought him up, Katerina
says. He is human, Gerhardt, no matter what he looks like; he
says so and in that, at least, I do believe him. And you know, I'm
sure they exist, but I've never met a *Nightwalker* murderer."

That was something she probably should not have said.
Gerhardt turned towards her. Murderer, yes, and she was armed
only with a dull table knife that she would have to hoist her
skirts to reach. Night hid his expression though.

"Master Arvol, the man you stabbed in the back, was my
cousin," she added, which was probably even higher on the list
of things she should not say. "I didn't like him very much, mind
you. Another murderer."

Gerhardt merely grunted. "Oakhold. I know you now.
You are another of the damned *wallachim*. The half-breed's
mistress."

Not a good time to argue with either his words or his tone
of voice. "That's me, yes. Can you give me a hand up? I'm not in
very good shape at the moment."

To her surprise, Gerhardt took her bundle, shoved it into a
saddlebag and cupped hands for her foot. "I take you with me,"
he said. "I leave you at the first safe place."

"Thank you," she said. "You haven't seen any Fenlanders
around?" she asked him, once she was in the saddle and gathering
up the reins. With her skirt hitched up to her knees the wind,
warmer than Brotin's breath or not, bit deep. They had better
come to some shelter quickly.

"Fenlanders?"

"Barbarians," she suggested. "Korby, the man who made
you take him to the bookshop in Rona. People like him. Long
braids. Plaid cloaks."

"Phaydos be thank-ed, no."

"Any Nightwalkers?"

"*Powers*, no."

"King's men?"

"Madam, no! I come in secret, I am hided in a ruined windmill. I am unseen. I see no one. I wish to see no one. I am taking you away from Alberick only because he is an evil Nightwalker. I leave you to shelter. You must save yourself, after."

"I'm very good at saving myself," she muttered, sounding childish to her own ear. "And I like evil Nightwalkers. It's the evil humans I'm trying to avoid."

Behind them, the house lit the sky scarlet and orange. Gerhardt swung into the saddle of his own horse and took the reins to lead hers. She did not protest. He kept to the thickest darkness, following the tall hedgerows that marched along the field boundaries to gates or barred gaps and causeways over ditches. The flat fields of the Ytimmaed weren't the naked, exposed place she had thought. They traveled in squares and right angles, as though they slunk through some giant's game board. Always, the manor house lit the sky behind them. Always the dense hedges screened them from the village she guessed must lie nearby.

Margo strode alongside the horse, a pearl-mist glimmer.

"Do you think I should trust him at all?" the baroness asked her. She knew she shouldn't speak. Gerhardt might hear. Yes, he looked her way, but her head ached and she could not seem to care what he thought. She could feel the madness taking her again. The horse, even at a walk, jarred her head without mercy. Mind and vision lurched and swam. The bank of sea fog rolled over the land from the east, fast as a horse could gallop, faster, eating up the fields, the stars, reaching for them. The roaring in her dead ear grew louder. Gerhardt and even the horse the baroness rode seemed as intangible as Margo when the fog took them, transforming them all to shades.

Once upon a time there was an emperor, who ruled a vast empire blessed by the Powers with all the good things of the earth...
The words of the story *Iarakulanar and Iahillalana* rambled through her mind, almost in Korby's very tones, though he had not read the full tale to her, only given her the outline of it. But her dreaming mind made it a tale such as it must once have been, put the storyteller's voice back into it, the lilt of the Fens—Korby perhaps, aged to some old white-haired patriarch, a dozen grandchildren at his knee, though why he should be speaking Eswyn rather than the Fen-tongue...She struggled to wake herself. This was no place for dreaming. It was said those dying of cold wandered lost in pleasant dreams of warmth and sleep. She could smell peat smoke, feel the warmth of the fire...
But a long night came upon his land...the skies were darkened, and the stars and even the sun grew faint and cold; the clouds rained ash and poison, and winter ate the land...he has stolen the wise men and the cunning men, and left us bereft of hope...they swore an oath before the Powers to find the people of Iarakulanar, no matter how long it should take them...and they traveled by the shadow road, through the lands of death...

"Here, here, you go down here." The man's whispering voice was urgent. The baroness surfaced to the headache and nausea that were all too familiar. She was cold too, shudders traveling her body in waves. Her clothes felt damp.
"What?"
"Shelter. I promised. They are holy sisters, a shrine. A safe place, just a little farther up this lane."

She blinked. It was still dark, and fog was thick and blinding around them. The faint pale smear that should be the moon was high overhead now. She could not see anything of where they were, but it felt like a black tunnel, smothered in fog. When she slid obediently down, steadied by Gerhardt's courteous grasp, her stockinged feet sank up over the ankles in thick-churned icy muck.

"A shrine, where?" she asked.

"There ahead. You go that way, not much farther. You come to the gatehouse. You can walk so far, my lady?" he asked. He did not wait for an answer. "Well, I leave you." And he did, mounting his cob again and riding away at a trot, leading the second horse. He kept tight against the hedge where the dead grass cushioned the sound of hooves.

When the baroness moved, the mud sucked noisily at her feet. "Wait!" Too late; he was riding away with her blanket, her dry stockings and her food. Without them, if this shrine turned out to be no refuge after all, she would die. But he was gone.

She trudged in the direction where Gerhardt had claimed a gatehouse, wishing for him to run slap into Korby. That would teach him.

Better yet, she should be wishing that *she* run slap into Korby. Every step she took felt like she dragged some great weight behind her. She got turned sideways in the fog and walked into snaring thorns that tore exposed skin and clutched hair and clothing. She struggled free. Even the moon was lost now.

"Margo! Margo! Where are you? Which way?" The world had shrunk to a tomb of empty darkness. Even an outstretched hand was lost. She wanted to sink to her knees and shut her eyes and simply stop.

"No, don't!" Margo, a dim glow that was the only feature in the fog, knelt face to face with her. "It's not much farther. He told you truth. Come on, my lady. Just a few more yards.

Come." The shade walked backwards, hands reaching out as if she tried to coax a toddler.

The baroness struggled up, wet now to the knees, and plodded after the retreating shimmer.

Gerhardt hadn't lied. A squat stone building rose from a stone wall. The low archway was blocked by dark doors, and the chamber above had peaked windows alternating with stone shields displaying the royal rayed tower and the simple old-and-new moon disc of Mayn the Mother. This wasn't a mere shrine but a full House of Mayn under the king's patronage, and there were only two of those in the whole kingdom, one in Cragroyal and one, yes, somewhere in the Ytimmaed. If she'd known this place was so close…Just as well she hadn't, her wiser mind said. To have fled to this house of peaceful scholars pursued by Alberick and his murderous followers…But it would be a sanctuary now that they thought her burned. More than a sanctuary: active aid. She knew many of these women. Senior Sister Rowena had helped the baroness to find female scholars to be masters at Asta College.

The heavy iron ring of the knocker on the gate bit her fingers. She had to lift it with her hand wrapped in her sleeve. The baroness had barely raised it for a second thud when one leaf of the gate opened and she was dragged within. Lantern light gleamed on the edge of a sword. Then, above in the porter's room, a dog, hysterically, frenziedly, furiously, began to bark.

PART THREE

✴ CHAPTER ELEVEN ✴
KORBY: TO LOWATER MANOR

I had a more difficult time getting my folk to Oakhold than I let on to my lord, but at least nobody got killed, and we didn't have to do too much damage along the way either. We traveled at night, some on ponies but most of us afoot, and hid up during the day. Linnet and I, with the help of the other witches of the clan, raised a bank of fog around our camps. Fog, as I'd told Captain Luvlariana, was easy, especially with all that snow around. A mysterious pool of fog in some copse or little valley tended to keep folk collecting wood out of it, but they didn't go dashing off to their lord yelping that the Fens were rising again either. It was bad luck, or Sypat reminding us not to get cocky, that we ran afoul of old Lord Platt out deer hunting. And since I'd warned the lads and lasses what'd happen to them if I caught them cooking up any supposedly straying sheep or hens, and since we aren't really known for traveling with much of a baggage train, the scent of roasting venison had him roaring about poachers as he came through the fog. Spurring through a beechwood in thick fog is a stupid thing to do anyway. We kept him prisoner through the day, even told him we were riding to the aid of Oakhold, which had been attacked by Hallalander agents—for some reason he didn't believe me about that—and dumped him and his huntsmen in his own hunting lodge on our way past that night, tied with knots it shouldn't have taken them more than an hour or two to get out of. Since I sent his horses off straying into the forest, I figured he wouldn't catch up before we were out of his lands, and he wouldn't want his neighbors knowing he'd been so shamingly overcome, so he'd stop pursuit at his own borders. If he lost a cask or two of ale and a few hams and cheeses through it, well, he had only himself to blame. Any truly chivalrous knight would have joined us, not used such language that Linnet sent all the young lasses to picket duty to get them out of earshot.

Oakhold itself was cut off from the rest of the world by more than natural winter. The closer we drew to it, the harder we found the going, until people and ponies and dogs alike were floundering, almost swimming, through drifts such as I have not seen outside of the mountains of northern Gehtaland. Oakhold's villages were huddled hummocks with smoke rising unexpected from the white mounds, and the old yellow-stone towers of Oakhold itself seemed to float above the white waves like the last glimpse of a foundering ship. Was this not the hardest winter I'd ever seen? old Harl Steward wanted to know, when we were finally stamping and steaming in the yard.

Only, Linnet retorted, for a dozen miles around Oakhold. The rest of us had had no more snow than one might expect for the time of year, and had they sent a messenger to Cragroyal yet?

Of course they had not. I couldn't blame them. I wouldn't have sent one of my own folk out to travel through what lay beyond Oakhold's gates, not knowing how little of it there actually was.

Of course, I would have sent someone to find out.

When we went on, it was under the Oakhold colors, as I had told my lord, and we carried a number of Oakhold men-at-arms with us. There was not time to summon Annot's knights from their scattered manors. I collected my big Kordaler chargers, Harrier and Boots, and borrowed a few more for some of my hearthsworn. My plate armor was at Oakhold already, so we rode led by heavy knights, not Fenlander skirmishers.

Blaze came with us. It was a long hard journey for a dog getting on in years to be making, especially one who had twice been badly injured in the past months and had moreover been pining for weeks. But he knew me and saw me as someone connected to Annot. When we'd arrived he had roamed among my band searching, sniffing every hand, in case I had brought her back to him. Annot had vanished and not come back and now I was leaving; his logic said that one disappearing human was going to join the other. The morning we left, he stuck so close to me, shoulder to knee, that I fell over him every time I turned. Hanna Stewardswife, the one who'd been feeding him by hand all these weeks, said that she'd better shut the poor old boy in the kitchen or he'd be off after us, closed gate or no, and I agreed. Blaze, sitting on my foot, stared up at me in naked honest faith. There's no love so simple and true as that of a dog. He'd been Annot's only friend in the black days after her mother's murder, when her cousins had kept her prisoner and bait for the king in Cragroyal. If he didn't have a right to come seeking her, I don't know which of us did.

"Let him be," I told Hanna Stewardswife. "Can you find him an old fleece or something to sit on, so his toes don't get too cold? Alun!"

Alun was leading a team of Oakhold cart horses to one of the provision-laden sleds. The Oakhold folk had no idea of traveling light, but then, we'd all be eating better for it.

"M'lord?"

"Shift a couple of those meal sacks and make a place for a passenger, eh?"

"M'lord. He'll want a blanket too, if he's not going to keep himself warm by running."

So we broke out the banners of Oakhold and the Moss'avvers, just as if the king had given me leave to ride out, and Blaze came with us. Sometimes he rode on a sleigh amid the baggage, wearing a plaid cloak and looking down on the lesser dogs like some dignified old senator being carried through Rona in his palanquin, aloof of the mob, and sometimes he trotted amid the rest of the hounds we hadn't managed to leave behind at home in the Fens where they belonged.

Between Romner and me and the speaking-stone and a map from the old baron's collection, we soon had Annot located in the Ytimmaed, and then in the area around Lowater Manor and the Holy Dragica Sanctuary of Mayn, the biggest house of the scholarly Sisters of Mayn the Mother in all the island.

I couldn't suspect the Sanctuary of harboring Yehillon kidnappers; Senior Sister Rowena not only sat on the king's council but was a friend of Annot's. Even better than mere friendship though, the Sanctuary of Holy Dragica had high walls encircling a large compound. Plenty of room for a gang of Fenlander raiders. Of course, as they indignantly pointed out when we arrived, they only had a small guesthouse inside the gate and men weren't allowed beyond that, but Senior Sister Rowena and I came to an agreement: We'd camp in the various outbuildings, and the lads would be turned over to Linnet with my compliments if I caught them where they oughtn't to be.

My lord and his troop from Greyrock rode in near dusk two days later. They'd been able to travel faster than us, being all mounted on good horses and having a bit easier going when in the halfworld, but they'd also had twice as far to come. It was amazing we'd all managed to get ourselves to the same place at almost the same time and, Powers loving us, without the entire kingdom knowing about it.

The question that mattered though was, had we managed it without *Alberick* knowing all about it?

We knew precisely where Annot was by then, of course. However, we didn't dare go scouting out around the manor of Lowater, not knowing who might be sitting watching us from the halfworld or what Alberick might do to Annot if he thought she was in danger of rescue. But the Sisters of Mayn knew the place pretty well and helped Linnet make a map showing hedges and village buildings and other cover. And then there was Margo.

To this day, in my nightmares—when they are honest nightmares born of my own mind and not vision-sent—I am Margo, lingering in all the pain of death, cold and inutterably alone, cut off from the warmth of life that enfolds us all unknowing like a mother's arms, cut off from whatever rest and cessation of pain we escape to on dying. Whether Fescor truly carries us to Genehar's realm or whether that's only a false comfort we give ourselves, facing the end of all that we are, I don't pretend to know. Perhaps Fescor's embrace is nothing but a metaphor and what I dragged Margo from was only the shade's own slow severing from the body, the last light of the mind fading. Heresy, yes, but there you are. Either way, I had trapped her, enslaved her, and she was suffering because of it.

Living, Margo would have done anything for Annot. She had. She had given her life, and what more does anyone have to give? Dead, her loyalty to Annot did not change, but I had betrayed her. She feared me and hated me and fled me. In my dreams, I had to hunt her. Like the bound shades in the old tales, she would only answer what I directly asked and pleaded with me to be set free. It was enough to break a heart, if you had one—she said that I did not—but leaving Annot alone with only treacherous Katerina for company, friendless and unguarded, was something I would not do. Margo's presence did protect her, even the shade admitted as much. Without ever letting them see her, Margo had cast a fear of touching Annot into them, even into Alberick. Margo also told me how badly injured my cousin was, how she wandered in her mind and fell into visions like a witch. I wouldn't have kept her bound a prisoner to the world even for that knowledge, not even for the descriptions of the visions Annot muttered to her, fever-mad, believe me. But to keep Alberick from Annot...for that, yes. Anything.

I suppose it's fear of that sort of power over others even in death, that sort of evil, that drove most of the peoples of the continent to purge their tribes of witch-blooded children, back in the grim old days before history began. One of the old secrets that we only speak at the Brotin-month prayers tells that the first witch was a child of Genehar. The Great Power of Life and Death loved a mortal man. Her love destroyed him, and he became Fescor. But their human daughter was the first witch. And those of us who come after her, those of us strong enough, we have a toe in Fescor's gate. I don't know if I believe that or not. Maybe it only hides some greater truth in its poetry.

Be that as it may, even while hunting and trapping Margo in the wonder-tale wilderness that her dread and anger threw up against me, a dream-wilderness through which she fled as a white hart, a silver falcon, a snow-pale hound, I thought about those shades the Nightwalkers had trapped to guard the Greyrock Pass. They were the ghosts of old invaders, men who had followed Hallow and others who had come after, but they all patrolled the Greyrock to haunt humans who tried to break Talverdin's borders. They had begged my lord to free them, when he was a boy. They had known him to be of Talverdin's royal blood. A word from him might have done it, though every surviving Maker in Talverdin was supposed to have worked on the defences of the Greyrock, of which they were a minor part. Feeling Margo's misery, her pain cut off from the peace and rest we say is the final gift of Genehar...to do what I had done to her, what the old Makers had done to their enemies even in death, was one of the great sins. Slavery, even of the dead, did no honor to the kingdom. I would tell the queen so, I resolved, next time I went with my lord to Sennamor. And if Ancrena still refused to allow the shades their rest...I do not think the old Makers, no matter how powerful, could have bound the dead without witchery involved. I would see them freed, one way or another.

I owe my lord my life and blood and death, but in some things I owe older duties before the Powers, or whatever shapes this world. I don't think I thought of it as in some way atoning for what I was doing to Margo; you can't keep accounts that way, tallying good and evil acts. I just understood for the first time, deep in my bones, what it meant to keep those souls bound there, how great a sin it was. To have the power to free them and to do nothing made the sin mine.

Anyhow, thanks to Margo, Annot should have known to expect us that night. I was not so sure she would though. Although I had confessed Margo's binding to my lord, I hadn't told him that the shade thought Annot had trouble holding on to some thoughts from one day to the next. He had enough to worry him. Maurey distracted, going into a fight, was a very bad idea for everyone.

Our plan was simple. Around midnight, we humans would travel to Lowater Village, keeping as much to the shelter of hedges as possible, in case they were watching for us. The Nightwalkers would ride with us in the halfworld, dealing with any sentries there that we humans couldn't see. Still in the halfworld, they would enter the house, overwhelming any Yehillon they found and heading straight for the attic room in which we knew Annot was kept. We would give them time to get in and find her; then we'd assault the main gate of the moated house, and the Yerku with us, most of the Yehillon would rush to defend against the obvious attack. The Nightwalkers would get Annot out. She and silly Katerina, if the Hallalander girl wasn't screeching and running in the other direction or trying to stab people, would be rushed away to safety. The Sanctuary of Holy Dragica was to be guarded by nearly half our forces, under Linnet's command, both to keep Annot and Katerina from being retaken by the Yehillon and to protect the holy women from any vengeance-seeking Yehillon who escaped us. Also, we really had no idea how many men Alberick commanded here. All Lowater Village might be filled with an army. We might find ourselves needing a stronghold to retreat to. Meanwhile, my lord and the others would find Alberick. My own opinion was that the Yehillon prince would keep his guards close about him once things started to go wrong, more concerned for his own safety than for any larger plan. He'd been told too long he was special; in his own mind he *was* the cause, not the servant of the cause, or so I suspected.

And if what Margo told me was true and Alberick was, or seemed to be, a Nightwalker, I figured that simply ripping his veil off before his men was going to cause even more confusion than a gang of Fenlanders rushing the gate. I hoped I got the chance to do it myself.

The sun had finally set. Most of us were already armed, though the horses were not yet ready. We were doing all the things people do in the final hours before a fight—checking the shoes of the horses and ponies, checking armor buckles, praying if we were so inclined—when one of the men stationed in the Sanctuary's gatehouse came rushing to the library, which Maurey had taken over as his headquarters without a murmur of protest from the sisters. Somehow the rules about males not entering the main sanctuary buildings had quietly vanished once the prince showed up. He has that effect on women. He doesn't notice.

"Highness," the Oakhold man-at-arms said, "come quick. The house is burning."

Senior Sister Rowena and the librarian started up from the table where they were going over maps with Linnet and Sir Jehan one more time.

"No," the man gasped, as the librarian rushed to her shelves to begin grabbing books. "Not here. The other house. Lowater."

My lord didn't even curse. I did, under my breath, despite where I was. "They know we're here," Maurey said, and his own knights dodged out of his way as he strode for the stairs. Aljess and I went after him, and the rest came thumping and clattering behind. Word had spread swiftly as fire itself, and unbidden, people were assembling, grooms running out the horses as they got them harnessed.

"Lady Linnet." Maurey nodded to her. "Make sure everyone I put under your command does stay. The Yehillon could mean it to be a diversion, to draw us out and leave the Sanctuary undefended."

Linnet's eye was already roving over the milling men and women. She started snapping orders, sending folk to their posts, never exactly shouting, but she didn't have to. As for the rest of us...if my lord meant to wait until everyone was here and every horse and pony saddled...

"Ride when you're ready," he called over the hushed and urgent beehive noise of the yard.

"Highness!" Sir Jehan protested. "Even if...You have to wait until...It's a trap, an obvious trap." He gave up and shouted for his squire to find his horse.

My lord almost rode him down. Someone had found *his* charger fast enough. Romner's Sennana flashed after him. I plunged into what was rapidly becoming chaos, planning to grab the first saddled heavy horse I came to, but there was Harrier, not only saddled but full barded—how had anyone had time to get his armor on him? He thrust his way through the crowd with Aljess's white stallion jostling beside him, both led by a scrawny crop-haired girl in a Fen blanket she had no claim to wear.

"Don't let the prince go alone!" The witch-girl glared at me. It was the first time I'd seen her outside of vision, and I hadn't expected the color of her eyes. Like a rain-washed sky in Ferrin-month. Silly thing to think at the time, but there you are. That's how it was. Like falling off a cliff, no way back.

"I wasn't planning on it," I snarled at her. "Get out of the way. Al! Here!" The captain heard and was in the saddle before I.

Overtaking my lord was not going to be possible. Kordalers like Harrier aren't built for speed. Aljess left me behind before we were out of the gate.

We rode into fog more blinding than a moonless midnight. The Nightwalkers and their horses could probably see where they were going, but Harrier and I might as well have been eyeless. Still, the thorn hedges kept us on the road to Lowater. Good thing we were both armored.

The fog around the manor house was lit lurid orange by the flames. A black-pointed Talverdine stallion stood stamping and snorting, tied to a small garden tree he was near to uprooting—Maurey's charger, Lightning. His eyes rolled with panic and ash settled over him like snow, turning his white face black as his ears and mane. Romner's mare had tugged herself free and stood farther off. Aljess flickered in and out of sight. I don't think it was the fog. She seemed to be riding a circuit around the burning house, weaving in and out of the halfworld.

The heat of the blaze drove me back. I barely kept Harrier under control.

Something was wrong, very wrong, here. A massive fire like this and the village we had charged through, not a quarter mile back, hadn't poured out to watch the fun? No one slept that heavily.

"Captain!" I shouted, and Aljess was beside me. "Ambush," I said. "Why aren't the villagers out here?" I could feel their fear, even from this distance, but what had them frightened I couldn't tell.

"I know. But I don't see anyone." She disappeared.

"Where's my lord?" I howled at the fog. Stupid question.

Al reappeared. "Inside. Him and Romner." She grabbed me as I started to dismount. The drawbridge leading to the fancy gatehouse was lowered. "Don't be a bloody idiot, Moss'avver. At least the fire can't touch them in the halfworld."

"They can still fall through a floor."

"And a fool of a Fenlander won't? The smoke may be bad though."

"Don't you know?"

"I've never been stupid enough to run into a burning building, in the halfworld or out of it. You can smell smoke in the halfworld. And I don't know, such a great fire—they may not be immune to it, even in the halfworld. It's not like a candle or a cookfire. Greater presence. Like an old tree, you know."

"There's no one alive in there," I said. I could feel no one. Not Annot, not silly Katerina, not any panicking Yehillon. Not Romner or my lord, which might only mean they were in the halfworld, and Annot with them. "No one at all."

We were both grimly silent after that, waiting, the horses head to tail so that we watched both directions. Nothing stirred in the fog until, almost at the same time, the drumming of hooves from Lowater Village and a crash from the manor sent us spurring opposite ways.

I'd been wondering if everyone else had gotten lost in the fog. Sir Jehan, sensibly I suppose, had held up the soldiers until the whole company was ready to ride. No point straggling up and getting picked off in twos and threes, after all.

Jehan and I swerved to avoid one another. I wheeled Harrier back towards the house. Part of the roof to the far right had given way and flames roared up into the fog through the void. Only the gatehouse was not burning, which seemed a bit odd, when the rest had been so thoroughly fired.

My lord and Romner, reduced to ghastly black puppets by a coating of soot, came staggering across the bridge, holding one another up. No, they were struggling with one another.

Men shouting. When I looked to its source behind me I saw the fog lit oddly, weirdly white, smoking and swirling.

"Yerku keep us," Aljess whispered. She and her horse vanished into the halfworld, though that was no protection against philosopher's fire. She reappeared a moment later. "A couple dozen men with torches of philosopher's fire. Running up from the village. And more men behind them, armed mostly with bows and billhooks. Villagers." Of course, in night and fog, she would see better in the halfworld. "The Yehillon are all yours, Moss'avver, till you get those torches out." She raised her voice. "Keldyachi to me!"

"Yours, sir," I shouted to Jehan. I wasn't leaving the prince now.

"My lord, Moss'avver." Jehan saluted me with drawn sword, lowered his visor and circled, leading the royal soldiers back through the Nightwalkers. "Yehillon coming—go for their torches first!" he ordered. Aljess, at the same time, had been shouting orders to her folk in Talverdine. The Nightwalkers, man and woman and horse, all vanished into the halfworld. "Don't kill the Dunmorrans! Disarm them!" Aljess finished as she too winked out of sight.

A new roaring joined the din, the ragged, sea-wave noise of a crowd singing the warsong of a clan, each in his own key and to his own time. I guess Jehan must have left my lot behind on the way, slower on ponies and afoot. They were here now, and from the screeching and wailing, they were the last thing the unlucky villagers of Lowater had expected to find emerging from fog and night behind them.

"Th'chief'll want the peasants left alive!" I heard Mollie screaming. Good head on her. "They're no enemies of the king. Get the damned Yehillon afore they burn someone!"

The torches of oily, white, philosopher's fire wavered, and their close formation scattered apart.

As ambushes went, I've never seen one go more wrong, more swiftly. I suppose the Yehillon had worked some sort of spell of their Great Gifts or the philosopher's secret arts to learn when my lord arrived so as to prepare their trap—and Powers help us all if he thought his arrival had caused Annot's death in that burning house. By not springing their trap till the main body, as they thought, arrived, the Yehillon had missed their chance to take the prince. But they hadn't been expecting Fenlanders, or such numbers: With our witchery we'd sneaked past them two days before, like their own fog.

Now, even with the village men forced or tricked into fighting for them, they were badly outnumbered. Not my concern. My lord was.

"It was not she!" Romner was bawling in Talverdine, as though Maurey were half a mile away. They still struggled on the bridge. Maurey was trying to go back. "Too broad! Had to be a man!"

Wildfire flared up around them as Maurey wrenched himself away. Romner—I had one ghastly glimpse of his face wreathed in sudden flame—dove off into the moat. The chains of the bridge twisted and flailed around like live things, and the bridge flew apart as if ripped by a whirlwind, timbers flying over our heads. A wind tore the surface of the water, driving the flames every which way, and my lord in the middle of it all stood on the threshold of the door, his back to us. He had lost his helmet and his hair whipped around like the flames that had engulfed Romner. Neither flame nor wind-lashed water seemed to touch him.

I screamed his name. Then he vanished.

Aljess swore and flung herself from her horse. I leapt down after her, grabbing her shoulder as she entered the halfworld.

She raised a hand to strike me off and then seized me instead. In the grey light of the colorless halfworld, the fog was the faintest hint of mist. The smoke might have been light fog. The flames of the burning house were pale and cool. But the doorway to the gatehouse where Maurey had vanished was empty.

"Switch sides," I said. I'm left-handed, and the captain, who was not, was clutching my left with her right. We switched, never breaking our contact, and ran, swords drawn, to the edge of the moat.

Romner clawed himself up out of the frigid water. His surcoat was charred away and his mail hauberk was blackened with soot, but he was cursing Maurey steadily. I hadn't realized Talverdine had so much foul language in it. He stared towards Harrier, looked around for me and then came into the halfworld himself.

"Bastard," he said and fell across my feet. "Help me up. Idiot." I wasn't letting go of Aljess or my greatsword, though how we expected to fight like that or what there was to fight I don't know. Romner grabbed my elbow and heaved himself to his feet.

"Body in there," he gasped, his voice grating in his throat. "Locked room round the back. Broke down the door and found it. Room was on fire by then. Big man. Partly burned. Not Annot. The idiot's not hearing me though."

"Annot was upstairs," I said. "There's no one alive in there."

"Where'd he go?"

"How deep's the moat?"

The three of us went in one after the other. Yes, and me in full plate. It is possible to swim, though I wouldn't recommend it for your morning exercise, and the Talverdine mailshirts were just as heavy, if not heavier. The shock of the water was like ice in the veins. We made it across, barely, and heaved and dragged one another out, over the threshold and into the passage of the gatehouse. I was already beginning to shiver as I forced myself up onto one knee, pulling my helmet off to shake the water out of my eyes and ears. Romner, his voice still breaking and weak, grabbed my head and started muttering, casting that spell of his that'll hold humans in the halfworld on their own.

"I'm not going to be the one to hold your hand once you start swinging that great scythe about," he said.

"Maurey!" Aljess shouted. "Maurey'lana!"

There was no sign of him. The fire hadn't reached the gatehouse yet. She went through into the central courtyard, which was built like a hollow square. Romner and I checked the doors to either side of the arched passageway.

"*That's* what he was saying," Romner said. "We already checked here as we went in the first time. And we left these doors open. I didn't understand him. The doors were closed, he said, and—and someone was calling him?"

But there was nobody beyond to the right. To the left, two newly dead humans, armed with light duelling swords. One lay by the wall with a broken neck. Maurey's doing. The other had several bad sword cuts. He'd only worn a brigandine for armor, and leather leggings aren't much protection against a sword of war. Maurey's not such a fool as to bother about fighting prettily when it matters. It was probably the thigh wound that had killed the man. A narrow stair spiralled up to a larger chamber over the archway. I followed Romner up. The room was empty and no other doors opened out from it, a dead end.

"Nobody," Romner said, frowning, and led the way back down to rejoin Aljess. "Tell me, Moss'avver. There was nobody in the gatehouse when Maurey and I went in, dead or alive, in the halfworld or out of it. So where did those two come from?"

"My lord's been moving too quickly for the Yehillon all along. I'll bet Maurey wasn't supposed to show up here for another month. When Alberick discovers he's at Holy Dragica and sets out to spring a trap on him before Maurey pulls the house down round his ears, my lord goes tearing through the village before the ambush expects him, and then we do the same, and Jehan, and the poor fools get themselves sorted out just in time to get clobbered by my lot. And then before that, the two of you come in here in the halfworld. Maybe some of his High Circle types are lurking around to watch the fun, and they see you go into the house in the halfworld, so they go after you. But either they get cold feet about jumping two warlocks at once and decide to hide instead, or you take them by surprise by leaving before they're ready. Whatever they were here for."

My lord had certainly taken them by surprise; that was plain.

Romner grunted. "So where is he now?"

I was very much afraid he was still looking for Annot.

I followed Romner into the courtyard. What Aljess had feared was true. Even in the halfworld we felt the heat, though out of the halfworld I don't expect we'd have lasted long at all, standing there. We steamed, while flakes of ash fell around us, blackening the paving-stones.

Fire barred all the other doors to us. The windows had all shattered. Maurey could not have gone into that. Surely not. Even in the halfworld, he couldn't have lived inside.

"Send me out!" I screamed at Romner. I could barely hear myself over the roaring of the flames.

"You'll roast!"

"I can't work in the halfworld. Send me out!"

He spoke a word and gave me a push. Yerku, but the heat was bad. My lungs caught on the smoke and I choked. I went to my knees. Less smoke down there. I shut my stinging eyes and reached for the fire.

There was poison in the flames. They were fed not only on old timber and polished panelling, on wallhangings and furnishings. They had been born from alchemy; they still devoured pools and splashes of oils and powders meant to keep them burning against any warlock's Making to extinguish them. Only the gatehouse had no alchemical fuel encouraging it to burn; quite the opposite. I could feel something of the philosopher's arts protecting it, and something that felt to me like a warlock's spell. Someone had wanted it *not* to burn. No time to worry about why.

I fed the fire memory of cold and rain and snow. I dreamed the moat into it. Bit by bit, I pushed it down. The mass of the fire fought back, a wild, exultant hunger that would grow and grow until there was nothing left to burn. I did not think I could master it, but then it got suddenly easier, as though someone were standing behind me, back against mine, bracing me as I shoved. Two of them. Three. They didn't know what they were doing, but that didn't matter; they weren't trying to shape anything, just feeding their strength into mine, as a spinner feeds more fibres into the strand of yarn. Like rolling something downhill, it got easier as we got going. And the fire was out, the courtyard lightless now that the house no longer lit the fog. I started coughing so I could hardly breathe and flailed my hand around. Someone caught it and I was in the halfworld, Romner kneeling beside me.

"Nice," he said, dragging me up and pounding me on the back. I nearly fell again.

"Where's Al?"

He nodded towards the door in the eastern wing. "She went that way as soon as the fires died. Annot could see the sea, you said. He'll have gone that way."

Both of us wheezing, we went after the captain.

We caught up to Aljess picking her way over charred and smouldering timbers and heaps of unrecognizable rubbish. Fog coiled over our heads, thin in the halfworld, or maybe it was thinning anyway. I could even see stars. Much of the roof and all the floors between had come down. "Maurey'lana!" Aljess called, fear in her voice. "Moss'avver, find him!"

I pushed Romner's hand off my arm and left the halfworld again. It was filthy hot, hard to breathe, and embers still gleamed red. I could feel no living person.

"He's not here," I told the empty air. Unless he lay dead under the mess with that other body they'd found, and I'd have known. I know I would have known.

"He's gone deeper," Romner said, appearing beside me. "Gone where we can't follow him."

"Why?" Aljess demanded, more of the smouldering ruins than of either of us. "He can't imagine Annot could still be alive in this."

"Cellars?" I suggested. I didn't think anyone could have survived the heat and smoke even in a cellar, but a man desperate with hope seized any chance.

Under all the ruin, we could not find any way down to the cellars, other than a place the floor beams had collapsed. Good thing we were all back in the halfworld then, or I at least wouldn't have seen the gaping pit. Water stirred murkily below. Some wall had cracked, and the moat was flooding in.

One person would know where Annot was, though I had no great hope I could catch her, being awake and in the halfworld. Still, I started to cast my mind loose, just enough to reach beyond the edges of waking. I called her name, without hope, expecting to have to pursue her, if I could touch her at all without being in a dream, but there was no need.

"You should leave now."

I blinked and was back in awareness of the smoke-reek and the ruins again, Romner's hiss of indrawn breath at my side, the sudden rasp and jink of metal rings as Aljess turned.

Margo stood before me, pale and cold in her nightdress, hair blowing loose in a wind that we didn't feel, sword raised. Stood before *us*, there in the halfworld. Aljess lifted her sword.

"Margo?" she asked in disbelief. They both knew about Margo, but seeing a shade is a different matter from knowing one exists. I was already cold, armor wicking away the heat of my body, but Margo brought her own chill air with her.

The shade's composure shattered. "Get out of here!" she screamed at me. "If you die I'll be trapped forever, out here, alone and cold! Oh, Powers, Powers help me, get out of here before it's too late!"

A section of roof beam, stretched skeletally against the sky, cracked and fell under its own weight and took a good chunk of nearby floor with it, but it was Margo's frenzy that convinced me. I saw nothing, no vision, but I felt the edge of something coming. Summer thunderstorm. Romner was still clutching my arm, too weary now, I think, to repeat his spell, or too annoyed at me for breaking it in the first place. I sheathed my sword and grabbed Aljess.

"Run."

The level of water in the moat was lower now. We waded, shoulder-deep, and with difficulty climbed out covered in muck and oily soot and Powers knew what else. The fog had lifted. The horses were where we had left them, and from the look of it, the battle, such as it was, had ended. Horses snorted and whinnied, harness jingled, but there was no clash of weapons, no shouting, except for one voice raised in a torrent of abuse of those who, it said, fouled their blood by lying with filthy night-eyes. It went abruptly silent. All the other voices were low, no shouting, no fury any longer. "I see no one else in the halfworld," some Nightwalker woman reported. A last torch of white philosopher's fire, still burning on the ground, went out as someone dumped a shield full of snow on it and beat it.

Sir Jehan spotted us as we came out of the halfworld and cantered to meet us.

"The prince?" he asked.

Aljess shook her head.

✠ Chapter Twelve ✠

Annot: The Sanctuary of Holy Dragica

"What do you mean they've gone?" The baroness did not wail like a weary child, but her heart felt it. She sat on the floor where she had collapsed when Blaze hit her, her arms and lap full of quivering, whining mastiff, trying to keep his joyously slobbering face out of her mouth and eyes, winding her hands in his silky long fur. "Silly dog," she crooned. "Blessed dog, darling of Vepris, *good* dog. It's all right now, *everything's* all right now."

But it was not. The grey-haired Nightwalker soldier who stood before her was someone she did not know well, an old House Keldyachi retainer in Maurey's service. Even after half a year in Greyrock he spoke no Eswyn, and her mind would not work. She fumbled the Talverdine language in which she had been fluent for years. The man's human partner had gone running off to fetch the sisters, not staying to talk to her. Everyone knew she spoke Talverdine.

"Tell me again, slowly," she said.

The prince had arrived late that afternoon; the Moss'avver and his followers several days before. They had been scouting the area, laying careful plans. The manor neighboring the sisterhood's own estate was held by Sir Ervin, the former Warden of Greyrock, who usually wintered at court in Cragroyal…she knew all that. Powers forgive her, the poor man must have burned. She could not have gone back through the house to find him. He had lent the house to a Ronish scholar, they believed, though the scholar had so far declined the invitation of the senior sister and librarian to dine with them in their guesthouse.

Then Sir Ervin's house had blazed up like a bonfire on the horizon, and the prince and the Moss'avver had gone.

And there had been that fog come like an army of shades in from the sea, which explained how Gerhardt, no matter how good he might have been at sneaking cross-country, had avoided discovery by Fenlander scouts or Nightwalkers in the halfworld.

"But it's a trap," the baroness said, struggling to her feet. "It must be a trap. They have to be warned."

"Annot'kiro, please, wait for the holy women to come." The man caught her arm and was still holding her up when the swarm of grey-robed Sisters of Mayn swept in around her, carrying lanterns and blankets.

She had not realized how dreadful she looked till she saw the shock in their eyes.

What followed was a confusion. She was rushed away, bathed, her hair washed and combed and braided, and finally was dressed in a clean nightgown, smelling of lavender, and fed soup. A young female physician, one of the sisters, examined her *all over*, asking terribly intimate questions about what had happened to her. The woman sent for another sister, and they both felt their way over her skull, pressing gently, muttering to one another.

"Well, it's healed now, thank the Mother," the elder one said at last, "but what damage has been done only time will reveal."

"What's wrong with me?" the baroness asked.

"Nothing, my lady, nothing at all," said the younger one soothingly.

The elder, more blunt, said, "You've had a fractured skull. Do you have headaches, Baroness? Seizures? Loss of memory?"

Visions? "Bad headaches," she admitted. "Dizziness. And sometimes I don't remember things. But I'm getting better. It will all come back. It will, won't it?"

She got the feeling they were eyeing one another over the top of her head.

"It's very hard to say, my lady," the younger said, being soothing again. "With time and rest, perhaps, the Mother willing. We'll pray for you. The best thing you can do for yourself is rest and grow strong. Don't fret about things."

Don't fret. They made her drink a cup of stewed herbs and honey. No doubt it was meant to make her sleepy, but instead her thoughts raced, and she felt herself slipping away again. She had to find Maurey, warn Maurey. Lowater House was a trap. It had to be. Maurey's arrival must be what had set Alberick to flight, and she knew the Yehillon prince had not gone with Katerina. *"He'll be joining us."* If she must fall into this drifting dreaming madness, could it not be some use? If she could not warn Maurey, then perhaps she could dream herself into Korby's visions. *Find Maurey,* she told herself, as if she spoke to a dog. *Find Korby. Find where Alberick's gone. Warn Maurey of the danger.*

Margo was there, of course, sitting on the foot of the bed, arms wrapped around her knees. The sisters had chased Blaze off the foot of the bed repeatedly. Now he lay by the head, getting up every few minutes to snuffle loudly in her ear, making sure she was still there.

"Someone should stay with her," one of the sisters said. "She may take seizures. Head injuries sometimes do. Shall I send for one of the novices?"

"We'll stay," a familiar soft voice said. "We can't sleep anyway; we'd just sit up waiting. And she knows us. She'd feel better, if she woke, to see a familiar face."

"That's very kind. Mother bless you. I'm just down the passage to the right. Come at once if you need me."

The baroness forced her eyes open, but could see no one. All the lights but a single night-candle were extinguished. The flame blurred in her vision. The light of the candle grew and grew. She wished they would put it out. It sparkled and glinted off snow.

A dark moving line cuts it, a broken snake gliding across the whiteness. She knows the shape of those rising shoulders of stone, though she has never seen them under snow, never seen them so near, so vast in their weight, towering over her. This is the view looking west from the spearhead of Kanifglin, snow glittering as dawn light floods it. The snake is a long file of men on skis. They travel roped together in sections of five or six. She counts. There are easily two hundred of them. A few, unroped, force their solitary paths to the sides, scouting the way. So many. From what Gerhardt told Korby, they had thought the Lesser Gift rare. How large is the plague of Yehillon across the world? Or has Alberick summoned all those he commands, to hazard all on this mission of assassination, the destruction of Talverdin from within? No. She thinks of herself led by Maurey, leading Blaze, a children's chain-dance into the halfworld. The leader of each roped file will be the Lesser-Gifted one, able to take the others with him. Or her. There are a few women among them, but only among the leaders, which strengthens her theory that these are nearly all the Yehillon of the Lesser Gift. Alberick is hazarding all, even some of his breeding stock.

They wear cloaks of Dunmorran blue and black over their winter furs. Some even have the royal rayed tower between their shoulders. But Dunmorrans do not speak to one another in Ronish, or the thick-tongued language of Gehtaland.

Maurey would not have left Kanifglin unguarded. The baroness flies back over the track of the skis as she flew through the star-labyrinth of the shadow road. She pulls the mountains past herself. Kanifglin lies in curves of wind-sculpted snow, but there is something new, a tower near where once she saw ruins. This tower is built of logs; it was so hastily thrown up that the bark has not even been stripped from them. Green wood too, which is why the tower smokes so much as it burns. The flames lick up gold and scarlet, and she wants to escape the fire, fights her own impulse to flee. She must take note. It is important to see, to know. Maurey must know.

Much trampling disturbs the snow about it, and some patches are scattered red. There is no sign of any defender left. It could never have held more than a handful: a lookout post watching for furtive Yehillon scouts, not this. She can imagine it. The shiver of snow that would alert only the most wary watcher that something drew near in the halfworld. An attack on the pathfinders by the tower's Nightwalkers in the halfworld? The Yehillon gliding on their skis from the halfworld, the dark hiss of arrows from the tower, the rush on its narrow doorway...Did anyone escape? Ravens circling. Perhaps they had got a warning away?

But the rangers who ought to be guarding the other end of the pass are not likely to be expecting any move by the Yehillon until spring. She cannot believe they will be ready, or there in enough force. The Yehillon will be hunted. Talverdin is warned. But it is hard to hunt a fugitive with the halfworld as his cloak, if he is able to forage and live off the land and willing to kill rather than be discovered. Some will find their victims, perhaps young Imurra and Korian first of all, the royal heirs, to sow the most distrust and anger, to shatter Talverdin's heart. The prince should have been here to guard Kanifglin. Even the baroness thinks that. Her fault he was not. Her fault, this terror and death coming to Talverdin. And she has not found him, to warn him not to go to Lowater, to tell him she is safe and he must not seek her in burning Lowater.

The light is growing brighter. The candle comes nearer.

"It's all right," a voice says, soft and implacable. "We'll help."

The headache was fading beneath a cool hand on her forehead. The baroness opened her eyes. The night-candle still burned. She could not think where she was, till she saw the faces peering down at her, felt the cold wet nose pressed against her ear yet again.

"Blaze," she said and blinked at Fuallia, smiling shyly around her sister. Robin took her hand from the baroness's head.

"Did that help?" she asked. "You were making a lot of noise. We didn't want the Sisters to come back."

"Yes. Thank you."

"I, um…" Robin rubbed her face. "I saw what you were seeing, I think. Sorry. Nobody told me you were like that too, like him. So loud and big. Getting into my head and I don't know how to stop it."

"I'm not. What him?"

Robin shrugged.

"Mollie says it's her lord, the Moss'avver," Fuallia volunteered.

Despite herself, Annot snickered. "Loud and big. That's Korby. I'll tell him."

"Don't!" Robin flushed. "My lady, please."

Fuallia, shy, gossamer Fuallia, smirked, looking sidelong at her sister.

"Lady Linnet said you'd be wanting these, my lady." Robin turned away and came back with a bundle, which she laid on the bed. "She says she'll do as her lord and fool of a brother said—that's what she said to say, m'lady—and hold this place fast against all comers, but it's not here nor there the prince needs his reinforcements, and so she sends us to him, and our menfolk and the Holy Sisters can yell at her later if they dare. That's what she said. Not that *we* have any menfolk."

This time Fuallia blushed.

The baroness explored the bundle. It contained some Fenlander woman's gear, from clean undergarments to a horn-lined brigandine and a cloak. Possibly they were Linnet's. Annot had to turn the legs of the trousers up, not to trip on them. The boots fit, over two pair of stockings. A dagger but no sword. She couldn't have managed one anyway. Linnet would have sent a sword if she thought it would be needed.

"How long have I been sleeping?" the baroness asked. She felt steadier on her feet, stronger than she had been in weeks. It couldn't have been the soup. Robin's doing?

"Hardly any time at all," Fuallia said.

"Do we take the dogs?" the baroness asked. She couldn't imagine how she could leave Blaze behind and not have him howl the roof off.

"They'll slow us down," said Robin.

"They'll howl if we leave them," Fuallia countered. "You know what Taddie's like."

"We're going into a battle," Robin said. "I'm not having any more dogs get—"

"They'll be safe," said Fuallia, with calm certainty.

Robin snorted and took up a bow and quiver from the floor, but she did not protest when the young bluehound sitting alert on the hearth padded, nails clicking, at Fuallia's heels to the door.

They escaped the infirmary without being seen. Light glowed from scattered windows and lit the thick mist, but though the Sanctuary was not sleeping, no one seemed to be looking out into the yard. It was impossible to see from one side of it to the other anyway, because of the fog. The whole place had been turned into a stableyard. The baroness thought she recognized the freckled carthorses sleeping in the lee of the wellhouse as some of her own.

"This way." Robin led her into the small stable where the sisters' few riding mules were kept. A pale face, ash-grey about the nose and ears, thrust at her, and Moonpearl whickered a greeting. The baroness found her harness neatly hung nearby and began saddling the mare. Robin and Fuallia were busy farther down the line, beyond the mules. They led out a mountain of shadow.

"Is that a good idea?" the baroness asked, as Korby's black Kordaler charger, Boots, lowered his white-masked face and lipped at her hair.

"He seems friendly enough," Robin said. "Lady Linnet said that Baron Moss'avver—the Moss'avver, I mean—left him for her, but that we should take him."

"He's a long ways to fall."

"We've ridden all the way from Greyrock, my lady. We don't fall anymore."

"Much," Fuallia added, but the baroness gave Robin a little bow by way of apology.

The same Talverdine and Dunmorran were on guard at the gatehouse as when the baroness had arrived. They told her she looked much better and opened the gate without the protest or argument she had expected.

"The Yerku ride with you," the Dunmorran wished them.

Outside, the fog was even thicker, closing them in. The baroness gave Moonpearl her cue to step into the halfworld and found the fog thinner there, swirling currents rather than a dense wall. A few moments with ropes—such oddments were always to be found among Korby's gear—and they were loosely leashed together, dogs and all. She led the parade down the thorn-hedged lane at a rapid trot in the halfworld and then, when Blaze had no trouble keeping up, a gentle canter towards the pallid glow that was burning Lowater.

"He's drowning himself again," Robin said suddenly and reined Boots in so sharply that the rope-end tucked through his cheek-strap pulled free, and Annot lost them all. She turned back out of the halfworld to find Robin pale and sweating, eyes clenched shut as if against some throbbing light, and Fuallia behind her reaching around for the dropped reins. Boots turned his head, wondering. The baroness caught up the reins and passed them to Fuallia, taking Robin's arm.

"Wake up," she said. "You'll fall."

"I's going to eat him," Robin said though clenched teeth. "I's huge fire."

"Yes, I can see it." She glanced over her shoulder. Even in the dense fog of the real night, the fire lit the world crimson. "Powers, are they in that? They went in looking for me, the fools!" Moonpearl danced and wheeled under her touch.

"No!" Fuallia shouted. "Baroness, don't! Help Robin."

"Help her what? Maurey will die in that!"

Fuallia had dropped the reins again, her arms wrapped tight around her sister, her head pressed between Robin's shoulders. She freed one hand to grope in the direction of the baroness. "Here."

She returned reluctantly. The dogs sat panting, observing with interest. Boots ducked his head to catch a rein and chew it thoughtfully. This wasn't a picnic. They couldn't just stop. Maurey was in that burning house.

Fuallia caught her hand.

"Now what?"

"Help Robin."

"Help her what? How?"

"I don't know!" Fuallia shouted. "Just hold on."

The baroness shut her eyes, since she thought both the others had too. It made it darker. Did that mean the fog was thinning, or the night was dying? Both? Fuallia's hand was cold. Where was Margo? Fog amidst the fog? She felt the rushing world move about her, the feeling with which she had drawn mountains and stone circle maps past herself, but it was Fuallia who engulfed her, a tumble of spring breeze and rain-scent, and then snow and rocks and the tang of pines and the shriek of eagles that was somehow Robin. They drew to themselves a soul that was at its core firm as earth, deep roots and still water, and flung themselves into it. Annot felt as though the blood was rushing from her heart, flowing out her fingertips, out her mouth and eyes, all her heart spilling from her in a rush of silver wind. She couldn't have fought if she tried.

Korby fought something, but he fought it out of stillness, which she had never thought he had in him. He cooled the fires under snow and water until they could only smoulder, sullen and defeated, and then the baroness was coughing from smoke she had not breathed, smoke that was only scent on the wind. No glow lit the sky, and the fog had lifted save for a wavering smoke and steam where Lowater House stretched skeletally against the paling sky.

It seemed they rode for miles, though it could not have been, before the road opened up into the muddy street of a village. Women and children clustered in doorways, staring towards the house. There was no sound of battle. Was it over? Had it begun? Had there been no trap at all beyond the burning house?

She freed the dogs from their improvised leashes and rode ahead, heard Boots' heavy drumbeat of hooves breaking into a canter behind her. The village women stared and said nothing as she galloped by.

She almost rode down the Fenlander who stood guard, bill raised, the long-shafted blade designed for killing mounted enemies, but he recognized first a Talverdine horse and then her, and jumped back, shouting, "Oakhold! Here's Oakhold!"

They swarmed her, and she ignored them, frantic now. Fenlanders everywhere, guarding unhappy men sitting huddled with their hands on their heads and others, better dressed and armored, lying prone, bound or tumbled dead. King's men and House Keldyachi Talverdine shoved through the Fenlanders and someone took her bridle. Too many talking at once. Faces swam; she recognized no one, but dreamlike, knew she should know them, almost all of them.

"Maurey!" she shouted, standing in her stirrups. "Korby! Maurey!"

No one seemed to give any answers that made sense, though Robin and Fuallia were in urgent conversation with Mollie Moss'avver, one name come back to her anyway.

A knight kept talking to her, trying to take Moonpearl's reins, trying to lead her away so she could not see the ruined house. The mare reared, and he fell back. She sent Moonpearl leaping forward, scattering them all, not caring if they got out of the way. Boots swung in behind. A cluster of dark figures drew her, but he was not among them. Korby, helmet under one arm, leant with his back against Harrier's shoulder and his other hand on the hilt of his greatsword as though it were a walking stick, coughing. Romner and Aljess stood, arms about one another's shoulders, Aljess talking to a royal knight on horseback. They were all black and slimed and dripping, all shivering visibly. Romner saw them first and pulled away from the captain so that she almost fell. Harrier started to rear, seeing horses dashing at him out of the dawn twilight. Korby lurched away, sword raised, and sheathed it almost at once, quieting Harrier, who recognized his brother and whinnied at Boots. Fuallia slid off Boots as Korby, catching his bridle, said something like, "And a horse-thief as well?"

The silver-haired girl flung herself at Romner.

"You said you'd be careful! You promised! You're hurt! You're burned! Where's the prince?" She rapidly became as filthy as Romner, dragging her own Fen blanket around him. He rested his chin on the top of her head, hugging her close, looking over her to the baroness. Romner's face was blistered, livid.

"Oakhold!" Sir Jehan shouted. "Phaydos be thanked! I never thought to see you alive."

Aljess was at her bridle; Korby trudging around the black stallion.

"Hey," he said to the baroness. "I lost him. But he isn't dead." Korby seemed to look somewhere beside her. "Margo." He began coughing again so that he could not speak. The baroness opened her mouth to tell him Margo was dead, which he surely knew, but he waved his hand and croaked. "I'm sorry. Thank you. Go to Genehar. My blessing on your road. Forgive me, eh? Somehow?"

Awake and sane though the baroness thought she was, she saw Margo then, not carrying a sword or in her nightgown but the girl she had been a few years back, her hair dressed with a wreath of violets and a gift of silver pins for Fuallin-day, that borrowed velvet dress with the lace at the low-cut neck. Korby had been there that festival, and Maurey, and they'd danced all the village dances...Margo flung arms of light and air around her and kissed her, a touch of mist. "My lady," she said. "Annot. Be well. Take my farewells to my father and brother."

She had seen Margo's brother somewhere among those guarding the prisoners. The baroness looked around at the crowd that had followed her but could not spot him. Margo darted at Korby, who stood as if expecting a blow, making no move to defend himself. She kissed him on the lips and then her eyes widened, looking back at Annot.

"My lady, run!" she said, and was gone, into the warm embracing darkness that opened for her. For a moment, all Annot's heart leaned after her. So easy to slip to that road; her head hurt so and she was tired...Korby gripped her arm painfully in a steel gauntlet.

Blaze, who had been sitting where he could watch the baroness, suddenly bounced to his feet, barking and snarling, his ruff bristling. He leapt at Moonpearl's head and sent the horse shying back. Korby spun away, grabbing for the dog. Other dogs began to bark and howl and whine, and Moonpearl, who had never done such a thing in her life, bolted. The baroness heard Korby cursing behind her and fought Moonpearl back to some sort of control, circling around. Blaze and Taddie passed her, running flat out with their tails tucked low.

They were all ahorse and following her: Jehan, Aljess, Robin on Boots, Fuallia mounted before Romner. Even Korby had fled, though he turned beside her, fighting his horse's will to flee, to face what was coming. Maurey's warhorse, Lightning, tied to a cherry tree, screamed and fought his bridle. The branch snapped too late, and the white stallion was engulfed by darkness, becoming mere flickers of silver, strangely distorted, like reflections of a horse flung up by a churning stream.

The ruins of Lowater House swam and flowed inside a roiling mass of liquid black glass. That was the only way the baroness could think to describe it, later. Korby said it was a tear in the world, a place where the fabric of nature went wrong, black and oily, gleaming, and something else welled up through. She saw charred beams snap and fly away into fragments, water rise into the sky, burning. They were deafened by a noise almost too deep to hear. It ate silence, ate sound, and she felt it in her bones, felt Moonpearl stagger with it. In her deaf ear, she heard Lightning's screams abruptly stilled, though the corner of her eye still caught flashes of silver as he galloped madly, fleeing along a road of water between earth and sky. The house was in the wrong place, as if it or she had feet in the sky, hanging downwards.

In her deaf ear, Maurey whistled for Lightning. Clouds poured down, a racing storm-sky. Real lightning blazed in sheets, thundering through the glassy black folds that were all the wall between them and the destruction raging through Lowater House.

She could see him, a flicker of dull steel by the horse, a flash of green surcoat in the sky, an eye, a hand enveloped in lightning, sparks running over his skin. "Maurey!" she screamed, her words lost in the thunder of the twisted sky. He looked around, but he was in the sky, then, and he stared up into alien stars. She kicked Moonpearl, but the poor beast shied away, trembling, legs braced, so she slid down and ran.

She felt rather than heard the hooves pounding behind her and dodged like a hare, screaming, "No, don't! Let me go, he's in there!" and other foolishness that her pursuer would not hear, but she was snatched up and heaved over the horse, cutting her lip between teeth and an armored thigh.

Then they hit the barrier of black light and ripped a way through, into madness. No up nor down, no ground, no sky: only jagged fissures where stars showed through. They were awash in a sea of cold lightning and thunder.

"Where is he?" Korby demanded, hauling her upright, relative to the horse at least. So he had heard after all. She struggled to get a leg over Harrier's neck.

She felt herself being torn by wind, spreading out into tendrils of flame and thought, and yet she could see herself, see Korby and Harrier.

The sheets of lightning were beginning to be less random in their shooting passage. They caught together, swirled, forming a whirlwind. It did not burn, but she could feel it dissolving her away, pulling threads from her soul, leaching strength and will and self. She was fuel for that fire, nothing more. All life was: she and Korby, Lightning and Harrier, the roots of the grass and the gooseberry bushes from the garden, the carp in the moat... all dissolving into the light of stars, she thought. Even Maurey had stopped fighting it. Korby's grip on her slackened. The place was folding about them, growing smaller, more enclosed, more a tunnel stretching away into a void of chaos. A whirlpool, sucking them down to some other, unknowable depth. Like a whirlpool, it was going to turn to eddies and ripples, the walls of the world would close and heal, and they would be lost, for the little thought that remained to them. It hardly seemed to matter. It would certainly hurt less.

She thought her deaf ear heard Blaze howling, far in the distance. The baroness rammed an elbow back into Korby's ribs, which hurt her but at least jarred him.

"Ride," she ordered. He grunted, and with nothing beneath his hooves, Harrier ran, down the long throat of the storm.

The baroness shut her eyes and reached into the dreams that always seemed to be there now. That was the way to him. "Maurey!" she shouted, and in her mind's eye she saw him. He had caught Lightning, but now he sat motionless in the saddle, head bowed. Man and horse were hazy, like grass and saplings in the halfworld, like the shade of Margo. At her call he looked up, sparks floating in his hair, sparks crawling slowly up Lightning's legs, dissolving into the storm, into the void it fed. Drying blood from a clotted cut over one eyebrow stained half his face dark. "Don't stand there! Ride!"

He wheeled alongside. Korby hadn't seen him. Harrier didn't react. She leaned and caught Maurey, flinging arms around his neck. Korby yelled and grabbed her waist. The horses snapped at one another. When she opened her eyes, Maurey was really there and insanely trying to kiss her, which smeared them both with her bleeding lip. She was as eager, as mad. The horses were really trying to bite.

"Idiot," she said, in tears, while Korby growled at Harrier. She kept hold of Maurey by the hand. He gripped her as if he would never let go. "We've got to get back."

Korby and Maurey both reined in, slowed the horses to a trot. "Back where?" Korby asked.

"The way we came."

"It's the same all ways," Maurey said. He sounded inutterably weary, elation burnt out. "Oh Powers, Annot, he said you were dead. You shouldn't have done this. Not you. Not both of you."

"And it's going to eat us," Korby said. "Can you feel it? We're burning slowly away. This isn't Fescor's road. Not meant to be like this." His voice was growing dull. "Just ashes. Not even lost shades…"

Time for another elbow in the ribs. "Don't *look* at it, witch." She was drunk with the touch of Maurey's hand in hers. "Sweet Mayn, when Linnet hears I have to teach you your business— *feel* your way home. Can you hear Blaze?"

"No."

"Someone must want you back."

"Don't know why she would." But he seemed himself again, blinking and looking around, looking annoyed, head tilted as though he listened for something. He reached out a grasping hand, closed it over emptiness, she thought. "Don't let m'lord go," he told her, so she leaned and clung to Maurey again, an arm around his waist, one hand knotted in his belt and the other in Lightning's dark mane.

Korby pulled, and Annot felt the black-glass world rip and part around them.

They fell every which way, horses and arms and legs. Robin leaned back in the saddle, Korby's reaching hand in both her own. He overbalanced and pitched onto her, the first time the baroness had ever seen him fall off a horse, but maybe that was deliberate, because he was certainly laughing insanely, as Harrier, insulted but still on his feet, unlike Lightning, trampled away.

"Don't keep doing that," Robin said and started laughing herself, terrible and choking, a breath from tears. Leaning on Boots, Korby thumped Robin on the back with his fist as if she were one of his Moss'avvers, until she stopped.

The baroness and Maurey, struggling to their feet, trying not to let go, failed and ended up in a knot around one another on the sodden ground. Lightning, by some miracle, had not fallen on them. The white stallion sorted out his legs, lurched upright and backed away, teeth bared at Harrier, the obvious villain of the affair. Blaze hurled himself atop the heap. Annot was never getting out of his sight again. Well, she felt like that about Maurey.

"You bloody fool," Aljess snarled at her prince. "You should have waited."

"Probably."

"And she wasn't even there!"

"I know."

"And what in Veyros' name was I supposed to tell the queen if you just disappeared and didn't come back?"

"Probably won't do it again," Maurey offered.

"Where's Alberick?" Romner interrupted.

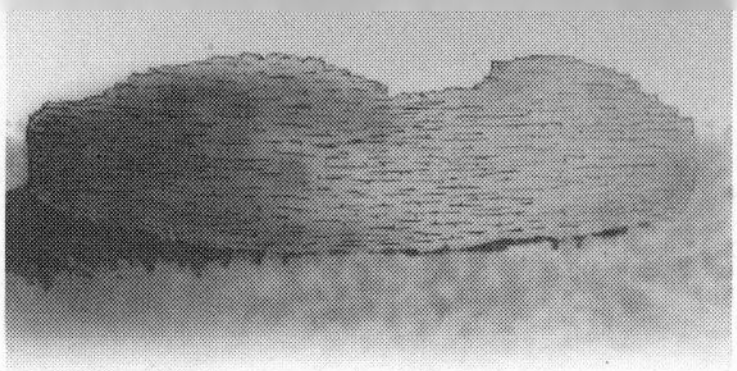

CHAPTER THIRTEEN
MAUREY: PRINCE OF THE YEHILLON

"The body was a man's; it wasn't Annot," Romner kept telling me, and though I knew he was right, it made no difference. We had broken open a door to find the charred corpse of the prisoner huddled by a narrow slit of a window even a slender woman could not have crawled through. It had not been Annot, but I was convinced Annot was still in that burning house, by some miracle alive. I couldn't face the alternative. Being able to survive the flames and the smoke in the halfworld myself made it hard to realize how bad it truly was, when I wanted to believe it was possible she could survive.

Romner dragged me away, in the end. I fell from the halfworld trying to escape him, but he followed and grabbed me again and never let go, despite the heat and smoke. We were both wheezing and choking, blinded, as we stumbled through the gatehouse towards the bridge. We had found it lowered and the door standing open when we arrived, as if the inhabitants had fled in a hurry. The few rooms beside and above the passage had been the first we had searched, and all had been unlocked and empty. The gatehouse was still the only part of the big house not ablaze, but the passageway through it was thick with smoke now. I seized the latchhandle of the door to give myself leverage and twisted away from Romner again, trying to go back. He actually punched the side of my head and dragged me onto the bridge while I was, for a moment, stunned. I thought I heard someone call me, then. It was not Annot, which was all I cared about. The words did not sink in at the time, but they had been, "*Warlock!*"

"They've gone. They may have taken her with them," Romner bellowed in my ear, but some other thought was trying to find a rational shape and there was no room for his desperate hope.

That door I had just grabbed...We had left it standing open when we searched the gatehouse on our way in.

"Go back!" I yelled in his ear. "Someone's in there!"

"She's not there!"

"A man! I heard him!"

What with the roaring and the coughing, neither of us was really understanding the other. Romner kept dragging me and I kept fighting him, growing more and more angry. I knew it was dangerous and I had stopped caring. All through our desperate search of the house I had held some core of myself still and distant, even as I fought Romner and screamed Annot's name into rooms that had become cages of flame. There had still been some inner fastness where that power, which had grown and grown the more I exercised my skills as a Maker, lay coiled: something I tapped only cautiously, trying never to let the full flood of it rise up to burst the walls I had learned to build around it. Those walls had cracked before, when I was angry, when I was hurt or afraid, and I had learned better, each time, to hold onto stillness, because of the consequences when I did not.

I had discovered in my reading of ancient histories that the old strong Makers, the ones like me, had more often than not ended as hermits, retreating into the wilderness like holy men and women, called upon by the rulers of Nightwalker Eswiland at need, but living apart. In solitude, I supposed, they could more easily cultivate that quietness that made them safe. I hadn't told Romner, or even Annot and Korby, what I had learned. I needed Annot and, yes, Korby. I didn't want to be alone. I had been alone too long, and I feared it. And now

Annot was taken from me. Behind that closed door lay my last hope of finding her.

I struck Romner away. I punched him, I think, but the walls about my rage shattered, if only for a moment, and the air ignited. I know I saw Romner recoil from me, shouting, caught in the burning air, but at that moment he meant nothing and I flung myself back into the gatehouse, into the halfworld, the deeper halfworld, and through the thick oak planks of that newly closed door.

There were two men beyond. They were human. They were in the halfworld, waiting for me, one back a little, one to the side of the door, presumably to attack me as I went for the one they assumed I would see first.

And beyond, on the stairs, Alberick was waiting. He had to be Alberick, and I had no time to be shocked. But—he was a Nightwalker. I shouldn't have been surprised. Dying, Margo had told Korby a Nightwalker killed her.

The spell practically formed itself, fast as thought, no need to shape and bind the power. I dropped to the normal layer of the halfworld and as the two startled Yehillon came at me, aware of me for the first time, I struck the first with my left hand wrapped in a smouldering knot of red light. He hit the wall and dropped out of the halfworld, limp and already dead. I'd lost my shield somewhere in the house, but the red light was as good a defence for the second man's lunge at me. He was terrified of me, panicking; he left himself open to two swift cuts that put him out of the fight for good.

I went back to the deeper halfworld to find Alberick moving slowly down the stairs towards me. I had thought I was the only one who could reach this place. He obviously thought so too. Though his eyes were fixed on me, he didn't seem to feel he was in any danger. He was a fool though. He could have been right there on top of me, could have dropped on me unseen as I'd dropped on his men. He stalked like a cat but, unlike a cat, didn't know when to pounce.

Bodyguards, I thought. He was raised by the High Circle, guarded all his life as their precious prince. He had never had to fight without a shield of other men about him; he dealt in murder and shadows.

I saw a tall young man, dressed in the latest fashions of Rona. Even his brigandine was velvet and ribbon-trimmed. He wore a fine black veil draped over his head, held in place by a velvet cap. He had folded it back over the cap, secure in his invisibility. His black hair was cut short, as no Nightwalker would wear it. Dark eyes were usual among Ronishmen, but his were black as ink, and his skin was like snow. There was no doubt my first impression had been right: Alberick was a Nightwalker.

Or someone like me. Was that why he could reach this deeper halfworld I thought I alone had found? I knew others of mixed blood. It couldn't be that. The Governor of Dralla, Aljess's grandmother, had a human father, and she wasn't even a Maker.

Alberick held his sword too low and had no shield. He still thought I couldn't see him. Swaying back and forth, he began to sing.

I couldn't tell what he was singing. The sounds and patterns were Talverdine. I recognized it the way one can, if one knows languages, say someone is speaking a Hallsianish language without understanding it or even knowing which of the Hallsianish tongues, Hallian or Hallsian or Eswyn, it is. He swayed back and forth as he sang, like a boy chanting his Old Ronish verb declensions in grammar school. He didn't have more than a vague idea what his words meant himself, only what they were supposed to do.

"Where's Annot?" I demanded. My voice croaked, hoarse

from the smoke, sounding more troll than human. He lost his place and leapt backwards, raising his blade. "What have you done with the baroness?"

He grinned. "You're too late, Night-eyes," he said, speaking Ronish. "She was up there." He gave a sideways shrug of arm towards the rest of the house. "Geneh has called her for punishment, as she calls you now too. Your harlot may find forgiveness after a long time in Geneh's purifying fires, but there's no such hope for the likes of you. *You filthy monster.*"

He put such passion into the words, as though they were old and familiar to him. Strangely, what I felt then was not rage, but a great, grey weariness. I had known it, of course. Annot could not be alive in this inferno. They would not have taken her to safety when her only usefulness was to draw me here away from Kanifglin.

"You don't have a hope of getting scouts through Kanifglin," I told him. Let him know that he had failed as well, before I killed him. "It's guarded at both ends. By the time the snows melt, the knights of Talverdin will be waiting for your men at the western end of the pass."

"Kanifglin?" he asked, and I saw that he did not understand. He didn't speak Eswyn. I repeated myself in Ronish.

"Scouts?" Alberick asked. "My scouts mapped Kanifglin months ago. My army will be crossing Kanifglin already. Hundreds of men, all blessed with the Lesser Gift of the Powers, many magisters of the philosopher's arts. They will disappear into the hills and forests of Talverdin, and in the spring, on the appointed day, as I ride from Kanifglin myself, Talverdin will burn. Your queen will burn. This weeping island will be cleansed of warlocks and the *wallachim* who lick their feet. The counts of Hallaland and Hallsia will come at my call as they came at Blessed King Hallow's; Eswy will throw off its Dunmorran yoke and Eswiland will be renewed and made clean again."

He was boasting, lying. With Alberick facing me and the tale of *Iarakullanar* and *Iahillalana*, the Yerku princes and Prince Iahilla, in my mind, I knew Romner was right. No Yehillon with the Lesser Gift was going to be making philosopher's fire. Many of them must be ordinary humans, if he planned to use the fire at all. And he could not possibly have moved an entire army, even a small one of a couple of thousand men, through the Westwood without Greyrock hearing of it, or without my small company catching some whisper of it. But I feared, with the same grey weariness, that he had nonetheless moved far greater numbers than I had expected. I had prepared for scouts seeking their way, or a handful of furtive assassins, nothing even a vainglorious, deluded braggart could call an army.

I failed twice over, betrayed two trusts. I lost Annot, and I lost Talverdin.

"Once you're dead, prince of warlocks, the one they talk about even in Rona, the greatest weapon of the Nightwalkers is gone. I have the Great Gifts. Without you, Talverdin has nothing that can stop me razing its cities and temples of sacrifice to the ground. Nightwalkers will be wiped from the face of the earth."

"No cities," I said. Even the port of Dralla was hardly more than a large town, by continental standards. "No temples. No sacrifices. And you know, don't you, that even killing every last soul in Talverdin is not going to obliterate Nightwalkers from this world. Look at yourself."

"I'm no half-breed! I'm not like you. The curse on me is a sign of my blessing!" His voice went shrill as he came down to the last step.

The door opened. Korby and Romner rushed in, dripping water. They circled the room, checked the bodies, dashed upstairs. They were pale and distant as shades, their voices meaningless. I hadn't killed Romner after all, I thought. That was, in some remote way, a relief. My attention didn't leave Alberick, or his me, even as they rushed through the Yehillon prince again and then through me on their way out, shouting my name.

"You're not Talverdine, no."

I began to see it. A thread of truth ran through many old stories, Romner always said. "And you're neither cursed nor blessed. You've been taught that, but I don't think you believe it anymore." I moved slowly towards Alberick. "You already knew the story of *Iarakullanar and Iahillalana* from some other source, didn't you? When that unhappy bookseller was told it held secrets of the Yehillon, when Master Arvol wanted to use the secret to win admission to your cult, you killed everyone who had contact with that copy, just in case they really did understand it—because you must have been brooding on whatever histories of the Yehillon origins you could find for years, trying to understand yourself. You *know*. Your High Circle doesn't. You *are* Nightwalkers, you Yehillon. All of you. What were you, centuries and centuries ago? Soldiers sent to bring the Yerku twins and their followers back to be judged for some crime? The other side in a civil war? I don't know where my father's people came from or how they came here, but none of them ever found their way home, did they?"

I was almost to the foot of the stairs. I didn't care that this gave him the advantage of height. I just wanted within striking distance. "And while the Nightwalkers settled on Eswiland and built a kingdom," I went on, "the Yehillon wandered, and married humans, and whispered their secrets until those secrets were so warped and distorted you believed you were some Powers-chosen instrument of retribution for a crime you don't even remember. You made our existence the crime. Maybe there wasn't a crime at all. Your Great Gift merely means those of you who have it are throwbacks to your ancestral blood, warlocks. *Nightwalkers*. That's all you are. Humans with a drop of Nightwalker blood.

No more blessed or cursed by the Powers than I am. Are you
going to let the High Circle raise your child to be as mad and
self-hating as you, or did you leave Katerina to burn as well?"

He stared. "What do you know of that? You don't have the
Hallalander woman. She's well out of your reach by now."

I didn't bother with spells. For Annot's sake I was going to
cut off his head, as coldly and efficiently as Korby would have
done.

Alberick saw my shift of weight, realized his danger, and
sang out a short high phrase, the conclusion to whatever spell he
had started before. The power in it rocked me, and the air grew
cold, though it is always cold in the deeper halfworld. Even as
the stroke hissed towards him my sword twisted in my hand.
The blade shattered. Shards flew outwards. Alberick yelped
as one pierced his coat and stuck, quivering; another sliced
my forehead before it left the halfworld. That shouldn't have
happened. Neither of us had bothered to dodge. Objects didn't
remain in the halfworld on their own.

Were we so far in that the flying shards took time to fall into
reality? Romner would be asking questions. I didn't care.

Even the hilt of my sword was twisted, the tang of the blade
split, forcing the grip apart. I didn't bother drawing my dagger.
As he fled up the stairs, I whipped the broken sword at him and
sent a short spell with it, to keep it in the deep halfworld over that
greater distance. I'd never have thought of trying such a thing if
those shards had not lingered long enough to cut. It worked. The
jagged stump of the blade struck home in Alberick's calf, and he
stumbled, recovered, gave me a look of almost comical outrage,
and went on, limping, singing to himself under his breath as he
passed out of sight around the spiral. I wiped away the blood
that dripped over my eye and followed. Something hit me as
I rounded the curve. I hadn't released the spell of force enclosing
my left arm, though I hadn't consciously maintained it either.

I slapped the unseen blow away. Lath and plaster exploded from the wall opposite. Alberick, on the far side of the room, sent another invisible blow with a phrase and a gesture, and when I parried that too, he tried something different. His voice rose clear and confident. I felt the spell reaching for me, clawing into my chest to still my heart. I shattered that as he had my blade, with a brief intense spell of my own.

He was reciting memorized spells, not building new structures as he needed them. He didn't even know what the words he used meant. That could be a weakness, when the expected didn't work. It could be a strength, when one didn't have to think about one's next move, or so my uncle Gelskorey, the queen's Consort, had taught me, back when they still thought there was anything to teach me.

Alberick started something else that closed my throat, had my lungs dragging as though the air had been sucked from the room, and at the same time he lunged across the room at me. His blade skittered over my hauberk. I caught it in my left hand, shielded by the red light of the spell, and snapped it. I called air back to my lungs. Another word of his sent my spell of force blowing away in lurid red smoke. Didn't matter. I had my hands around his throat by then.

The terrible thing was that since the moment when I had nearly incinerated Romner, I had been perfectly calm and cold, drawing the power of my Making out as I needed it, no more. That was what I had struggled so long to achieve: a cold control over the emotions that let a storm of fire and magic loose on those around me. That was what the old strong Makers had cultivated in their wilderness retreats. I had stopped feeling anything except weary acceptance. Annot was dead. I would kill Alberick. He might kill me. It didn't matter. I was dead inside.

The first Nightwalker I ever saw was Aljess, or maybe her twin Jessmyn, leaning over me in a summer snowstorm.

It was an eerie experience, to be nose to nose with my own black eyes and a face as white as that snow. Alberick had never seen a Nightwalker until me. Even with Fescor reaching for him, there was something hungry and desperate in his staring, which brought that first encounter back to me. My own face, my own eyes. Alberick and I shared more than a shallow resemblance of skin color. He walked the deeper halfworld that I thought no one but myself had ever found. He was a powerful warlock, even if he had only learned his spells syllable by syllable from some ancient manuscript of the Yehillon and could not truly be called a Maker. Eye to eye with him, I should have realized he was more like me than anyone I had ever met. He had simply never been frightened before. Angry, yes, but a cool, arrogant anger. Filled with hatred, as much for himself as for everyone else, yes, but he had lived with that all his life.

I hadn't scared him before. All his life, whatever else they called him in contempt and loathing when he was a boy in need of discipline, he had known he was the High Circle's sacred Powers-blessed prince. All his life there had been others to kill for him and die for him. And all his life he had been able to run away, where no one could reach him.

I saw terror start to bloom in his eyes. We were already in the deeper halfworld. Maybe he hadn't realized what that meant before. If either of us willed it, we would drop through the timbers of the floor as if they were tissue. We could plunge out through the bricks of the wall. There was no place for him to run that I could not follow. He could not get breath to shape a spell. He could not pry my fingers from his throat.

Lightning sparks flared over my hands as the air around him crackled with power, flinging me off, through the painted plaster and into the bricks of the outer wall. A bad place to lose one's hold on the deep halfworld. I almost ended up a fly in amber, encased in brick, but I pulled myself back.

He had lost his cap and veil. Sparks wreathed his hair, traveled over his arms. "Kill me! It doesn't matter. It's too late. Talverdin is doomed. I'll be a Lesser Power, a saint of Eswiland, if I don't live to be its king. Your own brother is tainted with your mother's sin, unfit to rule because of you. There are warlocks at court in Cragroyal, mixing with innocent human girls, dancing with them—touching them. You've spread your poison to Eswy, you've poisoned the king so your *wallachim* brother can take the crown in his wife's name. How long till you kill him and take his place and his wife, as your father took King Burrage's wife? You're sending spies and assassins throughout the continent, creeping and sneaking like a plague, waiting to break out. You warlocks destroy everything you touch, and you're the worst of them because you think you're human. You destroyed Oakhold yourself! You corrupted that beautiful lady! You made her unfit to live among humans any longer! She *had* to burn."

He snatched up the hilt of his broken sword with its foot of jagged blade and launched himself at me, no spell shaped, but by then I was lost. It wasn't that I failed to keep the walls up. I tore them down myself and let the fires engulf us both. I meant for us both to die.

"They treat *you* like you're a human, and you're only a filthy Night-eyes," he was screaming, and then he was merely screaming when his own mad fury met mine and they flared together. The world shattered around us. I felt earth and air and the halfworld itself fly into brittle shards one moment, the cracks between a void of cold, and the next it was like silk tearing and the weight of the world leaving us behind as we fell through it, if that makes any sense. The words for it don't exist.

Lightning sheeted on all sides, and beyond was darkness. Stars passed and lurched beyond cracks in the sky, which stretched over our heads and rolled beneath our feet. A great storm surged around us, the sort of thing that breaks and remakes the small islands of the sea. We had dragged Lowater House with us, or the storm was swallowing it through the path we had made.

Alberick yelled, "This is the true shadow road, Night-Eyes! This is the road to Geneh's damnation for us both!" He lunged at me once more with his broken sword. I stepped aside and came back within his over-extended arm. My dagger bit between the plates of his brigandine, into his side under the ribs. He grunted and his eyes went wide and startled. I flung him away before he could bring his blade around at me, but he had dropped it anyway. The edge of one of the sheets of lightning caught him and drew him under.

Then I was alone and not yet dead. I supposed it was only a matter of time.

I suppose I walked, waiting. It seemed as though hours of thoughtless time passed, while the black void roared and seethed around me like the waves of a maelstrom or the sands of a desert storm, but from what I've been told, it could not have been so long at all. The lightning never touched me. Fragments of Lowater whirled by, disintegrating as they went. A brick passed through my head. Even here, in this hell I had made, I was in some layer of existence set apart. I tried to leave the halfworld, or wherever I was. I tried to draw the lightning to me, to let it end the empty weariness that was all I seemed to be anymore, but it flowed around me. Water flowed into what would be the sky, if there were any up and down. There were stars beneath my feet.

I heard screaming, not human, but an animal in terror. I whistled, enough life left in me to feel some fellow pity for the beast, whatever it was, and Lightning galloped at me from an impossible direction, his trailing reins still knotted to a broken branch. I reached for him and felt a shock, a fistful of black mane, and swung myself into the saddle. I got him slowed to a nervous sweating walk and managed to gather up the reins, petting and soothing him without hearing my own words.

He calmed almost too quickly, as if my own dull hopelessness had spread to him.

After a while we just stood, while the void closed in around us.

When I heard Annot shouting my name, I thought I had died without noticing it and felt only a fierce exultation that Alberick had been wrong; we were together and I was not damned after all.

Annot, looking like one of Korby's hearthsworn after a brawl, her lips soft and warm and tasting of salt blood, was most definitely not dead.

❄ CHAPTER FOURTEEN ❄
KORBY: GLACIER AND MOUNTAIN-FOX

Robin wouldn't meet my eyes, but that was all right. The little horse-thief sat Boots like she owned him. She looked good there.

My lord and Annot were getting positively indecent. I was thinking about a well-applied fistful of snow when Aljess started into him with such a torrent of Talverdine that I couldn't follow.

"Where's Alberick?" Romner asked.

Sir Jehan nodded. "We don't have him here dead or alive, if the others are telling the truth."

"He's dead," said Maurey. He looked to where Lowater House had stood. The earth was a scarred pit, neither stock nor stone remaining. "Or gone." He turned back to Annot, but she pushed him to arm's length and said, "Kanifglin!"

"Phaydos and Mayn, yes. He told me. His scouts already found the way. They're going through soon, he thinks. I don't know how much he was lying." He took my arm to get to his feet and pulled Annot up, clinging to him.

"They're already there," Annot said. "I saw them. Maurey, they've killed the men and women in that new watchtower. There're two hundred of them, on skis, and a lot of them can enter the halfworld."

"Lowrison was left to build the watchtower after we set out," Aljess said slowly. "How do you know of it?"

"I saw it," Annot said. "Ask Robin. She knows. She saw it too. The Yehillon burned it."

"When?"

"Now. Last night, at the Sanctuary. But it was dawn there—then." She seemed to fold up into herself, looking a huddled child. Maurey drew her onto his lap, wrapped his arms around her, her head on his shoulder. "I don't know," she whispered into his neck. "Maybe it wasn't real. I thought it was. I think I'm having visions. But I thought Margo was there too, with me in Lowater. I don't know what's wrong with me. I keep dreaming things."

I knelt down and took Annot's hands. "Look at me."

"The lady's a witch," Robin murmured above my shoulder. "Didn't she know?"

"She didn't use t'be," Mollie said beside her. "People don't just—just catch witchery. Do they?"

Annot was exhausted. Her eyes, when she obeyed me, were so shadowed and sunken they looked bruised.

"It's all right," I told her. "Margo's shade *was* with you. You're not mad. I sent her to guard you. She's free now. She's gone to Genehar and is at peace. She told me how you dreamed. I saw some of the dreams you drew her into. Don't doubt yourself. If you see things, they're real."

"Why?" she asked. "How? How can this happen to me?" Her gaze sharpened and a bit of her old spark came back. "Powers, Korby, you're contagious."

"I am not."

"Well, what's your explanation then?"

"Don't have one. Old witch-blood, sleeping. Your great-grandmother was a Fenwoman, sister to my great-grandfather. It's an awfully distant inheritance, but something woke it up."

"Old witch-blood," Romner muttered. "Hah. I want to talk to you about that later, Moss'avver." He was swaying where he stood, cracked and oozing blisters standing out livid against his white skin, which had gone an unhealthy skim-milk color.

Fuallia, now holding his mare's bridle, reached out a cautious
hand, drew it back, looked up at her sister, bit her lip, took his
arm anyway and said, "Sit down."

Romner sat, a shoulder against the mare's foreleg. After a
moment he leaned the less burned side of his face on Fuallia's
thigh. A hand on his head, she was dulling the pain for him,
nudging his body into beginning to heal already.

She's grown strong again, let her go, I would have told
Robin, who was looking down at Fuallia as though she had lost
something—maybe time you let someone hold *you* up, for a
change—but that wasn't going to help anyone just now.

Maurey brushed tangled curls out of Annot's face. "Could
you tell, was this attack in Kanifglin something that had
already happened, or is it just happening now? Or has it not
happened yet?"

"Nobody was shouting, 'Huzzah, it's the twelfth of
Pepsmahin, let's all invade.' Or whatever today is."

"Time is always difficult," I said. "Hardly anyone ever knows
if what they're seeing has happened or will or only might."

Annot held out a hand and I helped her up. Maurey unfolded
beside her. She stood, rubbing Blaze's ear, comforting herself as
much as the dog, watching me. "Those people at the new tower,
then. We can't warn them?"

"They may already be dead." Mollie kicked the back of my
heel, but I don't know what else I was supposed to say. Annot
wouldn't thank me for lying to spare her feelings.

"Korby—," Maurey said.

"Ah, no, my lord." But it was a protest for form's sake. We
both knew what he was about to ask. We both knew I'd do it.

"I need to know."

"Not here," I protested, which was merely negotiating the terms
of surrender. "Dawn, she said, and the sun's already up. It's either
too late, or it's yet to come. An hour or two now won't matter."

"Two hours," he said. "We all need to rest. But then I want you to see Kanifglin."

Some may have rested. Nobody I know did. The names of the men of Lowater, ordered in the king's name by "some man of Sir Ervin's" to take part in the ambush against the evil Nightwalker horde, were taken down, in case Dugald wanted to summon them to bear witness later. Nearly all had surrendered as soon as they saw king's men among their supposed enemies. The surviving Yehillon, of which there were few—they had mostly tried to fight to the death—were put in chains, since I had Faa with me and Lowater had a forge. Romner and a couple of other warlocks among the Nightwalkers put spells on their chains, just in case any of them had the Lesser Gift or other skills. Even Aljess didn't argue with Sir Jehan over the fact that they were the king's prisoners, taken by the king's warden of Greyrock in Dunmorra for crimes of abduction and imprisonment and murder committed on Dunmorran soil. But the Yehillon ought to have thanked the Powers that was so. She had a grim look in her eyes.

Korharbour was the nearest town with a royal garrison; they would be taken there for imprisonment, to await the king's pleasure, just as soon as we were able. Maybe in Korharbour we would be able to find whatever High Circle types had carried Katerina off as well, or young Gerhardt, whom Annot said was somewhere about, looking for his niece. I wasn't hopeful. I couldn't send my Fenlanders out very far quartering the countryside without stirring up trouble; the same went for Nightwalkers, and my lord couldn't spare any of Jehan's men, who were the only ones with royal insignia to make the lot of us respectable.

Maybe we should have tried harder to find the girl. Katerina had made her choice to stand by Annot and deny the Yehillon. She was a fickle friend, not someone whose loyalties I would ever trust, but she didn't deserve to be abandoned to the High Circle's mercies, she and her unborn baby. We did search around Lowater; Alun tracked Gerhardt and his two horses as far as the next village east, where he and his little sister Mathilda were run off by the reeve and a dozen village men with bows. By the time we got back to it, days later, Gerhardt's trail had vanished. Maurey's agents did eventually track down the small smuggler-vessel that had taken five foreign men and a lady over to Hallaland. But that was all later.

That morning, none of us got the baths and bed and fussing-over some at least deserved. Annot though, made my lord hold still long enough for someone to stitch his forehead. Once Fuallia and the physicians of the Sanctuary of Mayn were done with Romner, he was more bandage than face.

"Half of my beard," he told my lord, "has burned off."

"Shave the rest. It made you look old anyway," was all Maurey said.

"That was the general idea," Romner retorted, which was the end of it. Neither of them ever mentioned again how close my lord had come to killing his friend, and when people ask and he thinks it isn't any of their business, Romner says the puckered scars splashed across his face are due to an alchemical explosion in his workshop. He claims he's still prettier than me. I point out he never was, but it's an honorable quarrel— I never sink so low as to mention the way his ears stick out.

By noon, my lord finally sent a courier riding to his brother in Cragroyal with a report of events, including Sir Ervin's probable death. We couldn't know for certain, but it seemed likely his was the body Maurey and Romner had found. Whether he was a witting and willing traitor betrayed in turn, or just a duped fool, we would probably never discover.

And Powers with me, Dugald would send back word

I wasn't to be taken and beheaded for carrying my banner out of the Fens.

To seek out a vision when the power is already there, pressing and pounding on you, is a simple and natural thing. To slide through your own dreams into that fluid shifting world where soul touches soul and the dreaming Powers shape time and fate is just as natural. But to force yourself into vision, when the gate is not unlatched to invite you, is a bad idea. There are some few witches who seek out waking visions. The brew of herbs it takes can snare you if you turn to it too often, leave you hungering for more, and more, till the dreaming world takes all that you are and leaves you a husk, eats you up and you don't eat, don't wash, don't speak, and you die that way, a foul and wretched creature, barely human. The tea's not that different from the one that'll chase the hangover of vision away though, a matter of adding a few common medical herbs; so Linnet and I raided the supplies of the Sanctuary's apothecary.

The brew is sickeningly bitter too. I was feeling ill before I'd drained the cup. Possibly it's best not taken on an empty stomach, but on the other hand, less to be sick with afterwards.

We took over Senior Sister Rowena's private cell, though it wasn't going to be private enough. I'd rather it had been just me and my lord, but I was going to need Annot, I thought, and Linnet had no intention of letting me do this to myself without some guardian who knew what was going on. Aljess wasn't letting her prince out of her sight again...and my little horse-thief installed herself grimly in a corner, arms folded. She glowered at my lord so that he shrugged and didn't even bother trying to chase her out.

I didn't want her there. Maybe I did. I didn't want the fight it was clearly going to take to get rid of her.

"Quite a show," I muttered, my words already slurring. "I should charge for this."

Romner opened the door and came in, followed by, of course, Fuallia, followed by, of course, her hound. Two more Nightwalkers came in on their heels, a man and a woman.

"Romner," I started to snarl. I didn't try to get up from where I sat cross-legged on the floor. The room was tilting badly. He put a hand on my shoulder a moment, looking, for Romner, sincerely apologetic.

"Maurey'lana asked for them," he said. "Sorry. There's something we're going to try, if there are Yehillon in the Kanifglin Pass already."

My lord gave me a rueful smile and didn't apologize. I'd met those two before, briefly, around the time of Dugald's wedding. Both were warlocks of Aljess's level of talent and skill—meaning they were nothing exceptional, regarded themselves primarily as warriors, not Makers, and hadn't honed their skills beyond basic competence. They were House Keldyachi knights of Maurey's bodyguard though. My lord didn't need to tell me they would never speak a word of what went on.

Maurey had been through this sort of vision-seeking with me at least once before. He made sure the windows were covered. There was no fireplace, so the only light came from a single candle. It was far too bright, a small sun in the center of my sight.

I think I'd started to mutter to myself by then. Important not to get lost, important to remember what I was seeking. I sensed rather than heard or saw when my lord came to settle beside me, an arm around me, anchoring me. Those walls of ice he carried, they were changed. They ran all through him, like water, great deep rivers. Whatever he was planning, he had a quiet certainty in it. His calm calmed and steadied me.

"What did Korby want me here for?" Annot whispered to Maurey or Linnet. She was like a dancing hearthfire behind me.

"It's your vision we're starting from," Linnet said, speaking softly, but not whispering, so that her sibilants did not go shooting and banging around my head. "Sit down by him."

Annot did so, at right angles to me so she could watch Maurey too. She was sickly nervous. Never wanted to make Annot afraid. I reached out and caught her hand.

"Still with us, coz?" she asked. "Never seen you drunk, you know. It's educational. A warning to us all."

"Not drunk. Don't get smart." But I was speaking Fen by then, and she was miserably angry inside at the way her thoughts and tongue skittered around so childishly. Some injury there. If I could find the place...

"Kanifglin," Annot said abruptly. "Pay attention, Korby." She'd been following me, even if she didn't realize it. Awakened witch-blood indeed.

"Kanifglin," I agreed hazily and fell into the flaring sun that the single steady flame of the candle had become. It expanded until it filled the world, sparking on the snow. With Annot's hand in mine, I pulled from her what she had seen of the pass: the sun-glitter on the snow of the narrow rising ledges, the swelling, swooping, breaking waves of the heights. She had counted accurately when she made them about two hundred. I drew almost the same conclusion she had: The roped-together groups were led by those either capable of entering the halfworld or experienced in mountain winters. If not both.

I skimmed back towards Kanifglin. I had hoped there would be signs that someone had escaped—would escape? might escape?—the burning tower. I had been hoping that after the initial encounter, when they realized themselves outnumbered, they had fled up into the crags. It didn't look or feel that way. Their shades were gone with Fescor.

I turned Annot loose. I didn't need her now that I had the place, the time. A vision sought with drugs is easier, in some ways, to control. It isn't the whim of the Powers or mere eddies in the tide of fate. There's a price for that, of course. You're taking by force what's meant to be given. I didn't want that to touch Annot. I twisted the shape of it, holding fast both to Kanifglin and to my sense of *now*, the warm weight of my lord's arm across my back, his fingers digging a little into my shoulder, as though he felt I might fly away if he didn't hold me down. Doing this is fighting the weight of how things are meant to be and it *hurts*. It's far more sickening than normal visions are. Kanifglin, this bright-skied noon, was a lonely place.

Ravens—wild scavengers, not message-birds—claw and flap over the unburied dead. The ruins of the new watchtower stand cold and black. Night's hoarfrost silvers the lee-side of a Nightwalker woman in armor, as yet untouched by sun. It wasn't this past night that the tower burned and she died. It was yesterday's dawn when the Yehillon passed this way. The ravens have been busy. I fly among them like a storm, denying the birds, warding the forlorn dead, who are gone and can't care. The men and women coming from Greyrock will care though—their friends and comrades. A troop of horsemen is coming up from Greyrock, far too late, but it was probably too late when the message-ravens arrived yesterday. Too late, and this isn't what I'm here for. I fly along the valley, a raven myself, Genehar's bird. I rise along the knife-scar cut, scree covered in snow, into the confusion of cliffs and crags and frozen twisting streams, the narrow way that always continues, along ledge and ridge, right into Talverdin.

All is white, holding the blue of the sky, the blue of my mountain-fox horse-thief's eyes, in the shadows. Curves rise and break like waves. Jagged edges show where a hillside of snow has plunged away, softened in the sun. Their tracks appear suddenly. They had traveled in the halfworld, leaving none, till now. Then I am on them.

The Yehillon approach a valley like a giant's moat dug between peaks. Cliffs drop into it from either side, overhanging lips of snow break and fall, scattering like plumes of water. Beyond, the mountains still rise. They have not yet reached the watershed, where the brooks plunge west to the hidden kingdom instead of east to the Westwood. They travel slowly, warily, but with confidence. They know their way. Then a deceptive, narrow fissure rises up, an apparent dead end that is not, and then their route will take them along the next ridge...Before that fissure though, another valley pours down. It is a fold between a double peak: ice-filled, a frozen river. Here there are no trees; no summer green ever spreads over the rocks. Even in Melkinas the flowers grow small and woolly-pale between the stones.

"There," my lord says. "We stop them there. I can see how. Simpler than I hoped."

I did not realize, but my lord has been with me the whole time. I don't understand how he has done it. Warlocks don't go walking dreams in their minds. But his arm is around me, there in the Sanctuary of Holy Dragica, and a part of his awareness is tied to mine in the vision. He has made himself a bridge. He is not lost and dreaming as I am.

"Just follow," he says, and he begins to sing.

Romner's voice, not quite so deep, joins in at once. They have discussed this, obviously, while Linnet and I were hunting drugs. When they moved the stones in the Westwood circle, each sang as if alone, using the same spell but working it separately. This time they sing together. Aljess joins in, high and sweet, a little hesitant, and the two other warlock knights, plain but pleasant voices. The five singers don't keep to the same line, but like a choir take parts, weave under and over each other, pause and return. The words flow by me, meaningless, some ancient form of the Talverdine tongue. I can feel the strength of them. The air thrums with the shaping of power. And Maurey still holds me, quiet and deep. I am the *footing of his bridge, the far end of the span arcing down into the mountains. He shapes, he is the Maker, and the others follow. Their words strengthen his, and the force that feels its way into stone and ice and the shape of the land is not Maurey's wild and angry power. He has buried that behind the walls that are both icy adamant and flowing river; whatever he is shaping now, he could do in a moment of will and thought if he opened himself up, but he might leave Holy Dragica's a crater like Lowater Manor, and us with it. Only a fraction of his strength goes into this, but with the others, all in concert, it is enough.*

Rock shifts. Ice moves. The mountains shrug.

The glacier that hangs above this valley grows, or flows, and spreads. No mere avalanche, to melt with advancing spring. Ice groans and creaks. It grinds and squeals.

Gehtish voices yell of avalanche, but it is the valley above them moving, or its ice, not in the sudden rush and thunder of falling snowfields but with the ponderous slowness of some great beast turning in its sleep.

Ice flows into the narrow valley. A mountain of it, a wall, grinding rocks. Above, it is furrowed with cracks and fissures. Even if it could somehow be scaled, to try to cross it above would be death in a fall and a long, slow entombment. The Yehillon have no way out but back, and Lord Lowrison has come to Kanifglin.

The song ends. My lord is still with me. The glacier still creaks. Rocks crack and fracture. The earth groans. The mountains thunder, and snow sheets down the cliff, a great waterfall. When they cry avalanche this time they are right, and there is no outrunning it. A few survive, beyond the edges of the fall. The deputy warden will collect them as they struggle back through Kanifglin.

Did my lord do that as well as move the glacier? Did I? Is it the mountains themselves, defending Talverdin? Or just the great disturbance of the land, an unavoidable imbalance of natural forces?

I circle higher, a raven seeking the sun.
"That's enough," my lord says. "We're finished. It's over. Korby,
Moss'avver, come back."

Coming back was no gentle waking. I curled on the floor, eyes and teeth clenched, cold and sweating. The room rose and crashed in storm-waves. My lord murmured some spell over me, a hand on the back of my neck, but it didn't do much.

"Did it work?" Aljess asked. "What did we do?"

"We sang a glacier down," Romner said. "It probably won't seal the pass forever, but for long enough. It won't melt in a single summer."

"Part of the cliff came down under it," my lord said. "Who knows, maybe the way will be blocked even when the ice melts. If it ever does. An avalanche took most of the Yehillon. None of the rest will get any farther west. Lowrison should be able to take them."

Aljess shook her head. "Powers, Maurey'lana, how?"

"It felt a bit like when we helped the Moss'avver put the fire out," Fuallia said.

"It was," Romner said in Eswyn, not letting Maurey answer. I could feel him and the girl smirking at each other. I wasn't being fair. They were fairly glowing though, when their eyes met. "I've been thinking a great deal about the old warlocks, as you would say, Fu. In the oldest accounts I can find, there are Master Makers, and they seem to collect schools of disciples around them. The records hardly ever speak of Master Makers working on their own. But then once these powerful Makers like Maurey start to appear, the masters and their schools stop being mentioned, as if they're not important anymore. But I started thinking, perhaps Makers like Aljess and me are the normal ones, not Maurey'lana. Perhaps we're meant to work together, not alone, and when these abnormally strong Makers started being born, people forgot that. They started believing our magic was failing, when it was only that we were forgetting the proper way to use it." Romner, once he started lecturing, was hard to stop. "Of course, all the surviving Makers were called together to seal the Greyrock Pass when we fled into Talverdin, but that was seen as an exceptional event, whereas in the earliest days it would have been the usual way to…"

I could tell he had a lot more to say and would be quite happy to go on for another hour telling Fuallia how clever he was for figuring it out.

And poor besotted child, she would be quite happy to listen, for twice that long.

"Go away," I muttered. "I'm going to be sick."

They did, and I was. That's what comes of willfully poisoning yourself in pursuit of visions you weren't meant to have. But my lord stayed by me all that night. It was almost as bad as the aftermath of that foul storm of Alberick's I was caught in, though it didn't last so long. When you bear in mind that he hadn't seen Annot in months and had mere hours ago thought she was dead and lost to him forever…Of course, she'd been asleep on her feet, almost literally, and Linnet had swept her off to bed among the holy sisters someplace, into which probably even Maurey couldn't have charmed his way.

My lord did tuck me up in clean sheets and leave me, eventually, about dawn, when the worst of it was over and I was mostly just exhausted and headachy and feeling like a kitten too young to get up on its legs. I felt I could sleep for a week, but the Senior Sister might want her bed back before then.

The presence sitting by me on that narrow bed when I woke again an hour or so later wasn't my lord, but the mountain-witch. Maurey might be willing to hold my hand when I needed it—the halfworld being so awkward that way—but he wouldn't be trying to comb the knots out of my hair.

I opened my eyes.

The former outlaw fled as if I were some bear she'd been contemplating, skinning knife in hand, only to discover the arrow hadn't been fatal after all. This was a trifle insulting, given that I was quite clean and relatively respectable, wearing a nightshirt and everything.

She didn't say a word. After a moment she came back and sat down beside me, handing me the comb. Sitting up against the Senior Sister's thin pillow, and glad to discover I could without my head pounding—it was her heart I was feeling, not my head—I unravelled the second braid and started raking out snarls myself. Someone obviously thought I needed grooming.

"You need to stop calling me a horse-thief, my lord," she said at last. "I'm not. The only horse I ever stole was Lord Romner's, and Queen Eleanor stole it right back."

"I don't. I didn't. I only said it once."

"You're thinking it. You're laughing at me every time I see you and thinking it."

"Outlaw."

"Not that either."

"Mountain-fox?"

That brought a smile to her, like someone had handed her flowers. Wildflowers, of course. Dog-tooth violets and spring beauties and little prickly roses with petals like pale silk.

"You're doing it again, my lord."

"Korby's good enough," I told her. I got the comb stuck in a particularly bad knot.

She snorted. "What kind of a name is that?"

"A Fen name. My name."

"It just means a crow. Vepris, let me do that before you break it. It was my mother's." She took the bone comb from my hand and started on the knot. Her hand shook a bit.

"So? What kind of a name's Robin?"

"The only one I've got."

"Can't help you there. In the Fens you're stuck with the name you're born with, no matter who you marry."

"What's that got to do with anything? There. That looks better." She moved farther away but watched as I started redoing my braids.

"Nothing, really. I just thought I'd mention it. What are you doing here?"

"I came up to see…I kept knowing how sick you were, all night, and it scared me. I couldn't sleep." She sighed and leaned forward, hugging her knees. "They let me in, Tam and the others out there. I don't know why. I suppose they think…" She flushed. "They're not very good guards, are they? Or do they let girls in a lot?"

"They are. They do not. And Tam's a witch. He knew you weren't intending to chop me into bits." She did have an eight-inch knife in her belt, after all. I'd bet Aljess wouldn't have let her sneak up on my lord sleeping with that. "Or were you plotting some other wickedness he approved of?" Her cheek darkened. I grinned. "I'm sure my honor's safe with you."

"I hate the way you're in my head all the time. Like you're so bright, you blind everything else."

"You don't have to let me. Linnet's not rolling over you that way, is she? She's just as powerful a witch as me. So are you, and you're not getting into Tam's and Mollie's dreams."

"I saw the baroness's vision of Kanifglin, when I was sitting with her."

"Sitting right beside her holding her hand, trying to heal the scars in her head a little, I would guess. That's different. You were trying to connect with her. But this—you've gotten into my head too, you know. Ever since last summer. I saw you then, when I was trying to find the princess and you'd captured her. But since then, it's not one of us doing it to the other. It takes both to get this tangled together. We're going to have to put effort into stopping it. Or not."

"Yes, but I'm just…a shepherd. A peasant."

"One doesn't exclude the other." She looked blank. "One doesn't mean you can't be t'other."

Robin shrugged, looking at her hands, still red-faced. "Anyway. You're not."

"Not?" Not a peasant, ah. "No, but I have a lot of sheep, and I keep a fair number of them in the house. And you're the lady of Kanifglin. That evens things out a bit, for those that care."

That made her laugh and look up. "I'm not! And I don't even know you."

"What are you doing in my bed then? For all you know, I don't have any drawers on."

She scrambled down, crimson-faced and indignant. I wasn't going to follow, because I really didn't.

"You'd better marry me t' save my reputation. Why didn't you bring your sister along as a chaperone anyway?"

"Because she's with Lord Romner," she snapped, her good humor gone.

"Ah. Well, he's a good man. A bit sharp, but he's kind under it." And Powers help Fuallia if he took her home as his bride, I thought, though I knew the ancient castle in the fells of Talverdin's South Quartering was Romner's from his mother, nothing his grandfather actually had any claim on. A human bride or a mistress? Powers knew what Romner intended or what the head of House Rukiar might think of the matter, though Maurey, as the girls' overlord, wasn't exactly in a position to get self-righteous about their virtue in the eyes of the world. Anyway, Fuallia might be the excuse Romner needed to throw the hateful old man out.

Robin saw something was worrying me. "They'll be all right," I said, and I wanted to believe it, remembering how Romner and the girl had burned for each other last night. He surely wasn't going to let her take any harm, and Romner, if anyone, knew how his grandfather's words could scar. "He can't help his ears sticking out."

Robin frowned at me, a small huddle of loneliness who'd come here to find me half against her will, because I was the only thing that seemed to belong to her, with Fu claimed by another. Half expecting whatever fate did come upon willful peasant lasses who went crawling into baron's beds and not sure if she was relieved or disappointed I hadn't obliged. "You're obviously feeling fine now. Sir Jehan is looking for someone in charge, and I know His Highness has gone to Baroness Oakhold and Captain Aljess is sleeping. I'll send Sir Jehan to you. You'd better get dressed, my lord."

"My lady." I did crawl out of bed, the blanket wrapped about me.

"Don't make fun of me."

"My mountain-fox, my eagle, my lady, I wasn't. *This* is making fun of you." I bowed her grandly out. "And serve you right for threatening me with Jehan before breakfast."

At least she was smiling again when she left. She'd be back. It didn't seem to me we were very likely to get away from one another, ever.

Yerku help me, did that mean I was going to end up with Romner as marriage kin?

❄ CHAPTER FIFTEEN ❄
MAUREY: ANNOT

Annot had been put to bed in the librarian's cell, more private and quiet than the infirmary, which held our few seriously wounded. Various Moss'avvers and Nightwalker women kept a guard beside her, nobody on duty more than an hour, because we were all so exhausted by then. I left Korby a few times, when he seemed to be sleeping quietly and neither being violently ill nor shouting in equally violent nightmares of the witch-troll. In those quiet moments, I went to check on Annot, trailed by whichever one of my own guard was spending that hour yawning and propping up the wall in the passageway outside. There were always a couple of the Moss'avver's hearthsworn there too, sleeping like dogs on the floor, rolled up in their blankets.

The tight tense lines of Annot's face eased as the night passed. Her hand kept slipping down to find Blaze's fur on the floor beside her, and then she would settle again, never waking but reassured.

By dawn Korby was finally over the worst of it and sleeping soundly. He didn't lack for people within shouting distance if he did wake; the problem had been keeping the swarm of Moss'avvers out. He'd be all right now. I shut the door of the librarian's cell on Elwinn'den and the Moss'avver swordswoman who'd been sitting with Annot, shed my boots and belt, and crawled in with her myself. I think she woke up and said something, laughing, but I was so weary by then I only wrapped myself around her and went to sleep, soundly and without fear for the first time in nearly two months, with her breath warm on my cheek.

Annot and I were to be married on Fuallin-day in Cragroyal, in the eyes of the court and the world. Forcing my aunt to accept her as my wife did not seem so important anymore. I sent a message by the ambassador's ravens announcing my intention. I asked, once more, her blessing on our marriage but said that with or without it, we would be wed. No reply came back. Annot was more hurt by that than I, though maybe she always had been. She had trouble hiding her feelings now, a legacy of the injuries she had taken. She was recovering some…mental strength, I suppose you could call it. It seemed she had to train her mind all over again, she said, and called it a strong and willful dog, which she had to keep scolding, jerking the leash or searching for, lost in dense woodland. I surprised her in tears far too often, and there was nothing I could do to help but hold her. No Maker-craft or witchery or physician's skill could do much to repair a wound already healed or change the scars already there. If we had been there when she was first injured…but we weren't. Though the force of the sick headaches was lessening over time, and her ability to concentrate and to remember things continued slowly to improve, she still had dizzy spells. She never recovered her hearing in one ear.

Worse were the dreams. She woke me, whispering and muttering of dark skies and summer snows, of being stalked through a labyrinth of cold lightning, lost in a desert of glassy black sand, a rain of stone, a burning horizon…She never knew I was there when she stared empty into the night, talking to herself as she had once talked to the shade of Margo. Sometimes she said she saw our faces among the fur-bundled travelers on the dark road. Sometimes she called them the Yerku and talked of the Yehillon and the stone circles and the shadow road. None of the witches—the *other* witches—could give her any advice but to let the dreams wash over her and not worry about them, waking. They seemed very far away, was the best Korby could tell us. Past or to come, a vision of the forgotten history of the Nightwalkers and the Yehillon we had begun to uncover, or merely a dream-melding of Romner's research, my guesses and an old wonder-tale. Whatever they might be, they were beyond our reach. Annot could not shrug them off and let them go, but at least her determination to find the truth in them gave her a focus, as she grimly set out to relearn languages she had once read with ease, planning a new scholarly assault on the most ancient histories of the Nightwalkers, pillaging the libraries of the colleges of Cragroyal and taking over a vast table in Dugald's private library for her own use and Romner's, when he could be prized away from Fuallia.

My message to assure Lowrison that all was well, and his telling me of the destruction of the Kanifglin watchtower, the deaths of the outpost there and the search for the enemy in the mountains that ended with a few terrified prisoners and a wall of ice, passed one another in the Westwood. Lowrison's report also told of the imprisonment of a man claiming to be a messenger from Alberick, demanding a meeting to discuss Annot's fate. My lieutenant-warden was not inclined to honor the man's claim to have a herald's safe-conduct, though he was, he said, awaiting my pleasure regarding the man's doom.

That was a matter for the king and council to decide, I supposed, but the man need not expect to find mercy there. Dugald's displeasure was hardly less than mine.

In Cragroyal, the ambassador still had no raven-message from Talverdin. My aunt, I had to conclude, was not only withholding her blessing from our marriage, but was disappointed enough she would not even acknowledge it was taking place. But on the twenty-ninth of Ferrin-month, the eve of the wedding, my young cousin Prince Korian showed up, with a heavily armed escort of the grimmest and most Maker-skilled of the royal household knights. Our old friends Jessmyn and her husband, Lord Hullmor, came as the boy's guardians.

Korian charmed my brother, his wife Eleanor and the court. It's astonishing how quickly those who still looked at me or the Talverdine ambassador's household and felt uncomfortable, particularly the court ladies, were cooing over both his manners and his eyelashes. "Oh, isn't the little prince sweet," is not exactly admitting that someone is a person with as much right to exist as oneself—"As if I were a kitten," Korian later said in indignation. "Some fat baroness *patted* me!"—but perhaps it can be a step along the way.

Korian conveyed his mother's greetings to the king with adult gravity but was far less dignified once out of the king's presence and away from the eyes of the human court.

"Imurra's very annoyed because Mother wouldn't let her come as well," the boy announced cheerfully. "She says I'm a spoilt brat and she hopes the Moss'avver boxes my ears for me."

"Well, the queen could hardly allow her heir to face such dangers, Korian'lana," Korby said, straight-faced.

Korian missed it. "I know. I'm expendable. But I get to have all the fun that way. I'm going to sail to Rossmark and Gehtaland and even Berbarany someday. Maybe even Dravidara. And Imurra will be stuck at home forever. Annot'kiro, my mother sends you this, with her love."

With a flourishing bow he handed Annot a sealed letter. "For you, personally. Not for my cousin. There are some pearls or something too, from my parents, and a package all wrapped up from Imurra that she wouldn't let me see, but Jessmyn'den has them. I think the letter is probably the important part though." He made an impish and uncourtly face at me and put the final ruin to any illusion he was a staid and mature diplomat by adding, "There was a bit of a noisy breakfast. Lots of shouting. Imurra said Mother had to stop thinking you were a horse to be bred from." Jessmyn advanced on him, threatening to swat his royal behind, and he fled laughing to Aljess for protection.

Annot took the letter away to the window of Korian's chamber to read. When I joined her she was rubbing away tears with her sleeve. I took the letter from her hand and read it, with her in the circle of my arms. It was only a stiff, if honest, apology for withholding her blessing so long.

...But I see he is never going to choose another, and I must honor that. My objection was never to your race, nor to your person, my dear Baroness. You are one human for whom I and my Consort have always felt the greatest friendship and respect. I have perhaps thought too much on Maurey's great strength as a Maker and my belief that this talent must be passed on to another generation of our own people, and have not had enough respect for the other great strengths and virtues of you both, which have done as much for us. Talverdin owes its continued peace, and perhaps its continued existence, to you, Oakhold, and it may be that we have not considered enough what Talverdin owes you in return...

Ancrena could have said that years ago, I thought. But at last it was said.

The fact that she sent her youngest child as her representative to Cragroyal, where her brother had been executed not so many years ago, was as great a token of her welcome and blessing as any letter, and an even greater sign of her trust of Dugald. And of course, no one could fear this prince was about to elope with Eleanor. My parent's tragic history was not likely to repeat itself.

And so we were married, with Senior Sister Rowena of Holy Dragica's and a solemn priest of Phaydos and my brother the king to bless the wedding.

That night Annot dreamed. She woke me, shivering and staring open-eyed into nothing, talking of a straw-haired boy following the shadow road. I held her and soothed her back to sleep. In the morning, she said it was only a nightmare born of an earlier dream, nothing new. Nothing to worry about.

Even if she thought she believed her own words, her eyes said she lied to herself.

⚜ APPENDIX ⚜

THE POWERS AND THE CALENDAR

The Great Powers

The Seven Great Powers are each associated with a celestial body—the sun, the moon or one of the planets. The uneducated may regard them as actually being the same thing; philosophers and astrologers would say these are only symbols, their connection to the Powers being in human minds. Some would say that the Powers themselves are only symbols of principles or of human needs. Why the majority of the Great Powers are seen as female, even by humans, when in most human lands women are regarded as properly subordinate to men, is a matter of philosophical debate. Some even believe that each Power was originally represented by a pair of beings, male and female, and that the twin Lesser Powers, called the Yerku, and the dual nature of Viridys are a last remnant of this, although this still does not explain why only Phaydos and Ayas are consistently male.

Phaydos governs the sun. He is often regarded as the most important of the Powers and is associated with concepts of light and life. The Talverdine (Nightwalker) name for him is *Veyros*. Whether the Nightwalkers adopted human names for the Powers and merely kept the older forms when the Ronish names changed, or whether they knew the same Powers under similar names long ago, is a matter debated by scholars both human and Talverdine.

Mayn governs the moon. She is the wife of Phaydos in many, but not all, mythologies. She is regarded as a particular guardian of women, especially during perilous passages such as childbirth, but she is also invoked as the archetype of the mother and is associated with the fertility of all the animal world. In many lands, an aspect of Mayn, the Mother of Beasts or Mayn of the Swelling Udders, the guardian of cattle and other domestic animals, is celebrated on a feastday in the month of Melkinas. The Talverdine name for her is *Maynar*.

Ayas is the smith, patron of those who make things, whether with their hands or their minds: everyone from carpenters and smiths to painters and poets. In Talverdine, he is known as *Eyiss*.

Vepris is the Power associated with the wilderness and, by extension, with hunting. She is believed to have a special care for wild creatures and places, and for young creatures of every sort. Some put her in opposition to all the arts of civilization. It is possible that Jock Wildwood is a male aspect of Vepris, memory of whom has been lost outside of Eswiland. In Talverdine, she is *Vebris*.

Geneh, like Mayn, is a Power of birth, but she is also the Power whose realm is death. Many believe she receives the souls of the dead and is the guardian of all shades as they await the ending of time. Some lands regard her as the judge of the dead. She is *Genehar* in Talverdine and among the Fenlanders.

Viridys is the Power whose care is the natural growing world. Some regard Viridys as male, others as female. Different aspects of this Power are sometimes given different genders. He or she is particularly associated with festivals of sowing and harvest. In Talverdin this Power is usually female and is called *Viridir*.

Huvehla is the Weaver, a Power concerned with the destinies of men and women. She is also, like Ayas, a patron of those who make things. Among the Penitent sect, however, she is regarded as the supreme Power, a harsh and implacable judge of human souls. She is *Hevehr* in Talverdine, where she is regarded as only a Lesser Power, the seventh Great Power being *Luflara*, who is called "lord and lady of the seas." In some human lands as well, the seventh Great Power (and the fifth planet) is not Huvehla but *Luvlar*, a Power whose influence is over the ocean and all waters. Like Viridys, Luvlar is sometimes male, sometimes female, and is often portrayed as both within the same shrine. In some lands Luvlar is an androgyne, male and female in one body. Whether Huvehla became Luvlar or Luvlar Huvehla, whether there were once eight Great Powers or whether, as some assert, Huvehla is only a lesser Power, a personification of fate who has taken Luvlar's place, is a matter best left to the debates of philosophers. However, the fact that astronomers and most astrologers still call the fifth planet Luvlar is perhaps significant.

The Lesser Powers

The Lesser Powers are often said to be closer to the hearts of the common folk, who see them as more concerned with the day-to-day anxieties and trials of life. There are probably dozens, if not hundreds, of Lesser Powers, some worshipped across many nations, some known only to their own small region or group of adherents. The origins of many Lesser Powers can be traced to heroes or holy men of legend.

Anaskto is an embodiment of holiness, of sanctity. He is the power of kingship and is invoked for the protection of monarchs. Anaskto is widely honored in human lands but is not known among the Nightwalkers.

Sypat is another Power revered worldwide among humans but not in Talverdin. She is the embodiment of the forces of chance, luck or fortune.

Tanyati is the Power whose domain is violent upheaval. He is invoked as the Power influencing both storms and war, at least in Eswiland and the adjacent parts of the continent, including Rona and the north. It is suggested that the name is Talverdine in origin and that Tanyati displaced two earlier Lesser Powers.

Fescor is the escort of the shades of the dead. He is greatly revered by the Nightwalkers, and some claim he is in origin a Nightwalker hero; however, Fescor is found worldwide and in the most ancient writings of Dravidara under similar names, so this seems unlikely. Recently, the Talverdine scholar Lord Romner has suggested that many centuries ago, confusion arose between the Lesser Power Fescor, known to humans and Nightwalkers since most ancient times, and a Nightwalker Maker, musician and warrior who bore the same name and about whom many legends gathered. Fenlander mythology claims Fescor and Geneh (or Genehar) as the ancestor of all witches and says he was a mortal human man, beloved by the Great Power of the dead.

The Yerku are twins, invoked by warriors. They are Talverdine heroes, playing a role in many myths of Nightwalker origins. They are brother and sister, but in most human lands to which their worship has spread they are mistakenly believed to be brothers. The northern nations of Rossmark and Gehtaland, and the Fenlanders of Eswiland, still regard the twins as brother and sister. Although humans (save the Fenlanders, of course) hold them to be human, it is interesting to observe that in Gehtaland, where nearly all of the people are fair-haired, artists always portray the Yerku as dark-haired.

Good King Hallow, who conquered Eswiland and ended centuries of Nightwalker rule there, is a Lesser Power for the humans of Eswiland. He is also revered by those on the continent who fear the Nightwalkers.

Elinda, a minor princess of the royal houses of Hallaland and Hallsia, was the founder of the Penitent sect. She is revered by her followers, and some go so far as to offer her prayers and build her shrines, though this is not approved by most branches of the cult. The religious awe with which she is regarded entitles her to be regarded as a Power, though her own worshippers deny that any Power but Huvehla should be so honored.

Thalloa is an ancient Lesser Power associated with spring and with the flowering of the natural world. It is also a Talverdine woman's name, but they may have adopted it from human usage.

Asta was a scholar and astronomer of Gehtaland around whom many legends have gathered, some of the most fantastical nature: for instance, the tale of Asta's flight to the moon, although she was also the first (at least the first outside of Dravidara) to demonstrate that the earth circles the sun. In the north, she has become a Power invoked by scholars, particularly those whose study is the natural world; her cult has recently spread to Eswiland with the founding of Lady Asta College for women at the University of Cragroyal in Dunmorra.

Jock Wildwood is a folk hero of Dunmorra in Eswiland, an outlaw reputed to live or have lived in the Westwood. He is, perhaps, a spirit of the natural world, a male aspect of Vepris of the Wilds. Similar roguish men of the wilderness are found under other names throughout the northern lands.

Fuallin-Queen is the consort of Jock Wildwood in Dunmorran and Eswyn folk-belief. She is likely an aspect of Vepris, or possibly of Viridys or even Thalloa, in origin. Her name is far older than that of Jock Wildwood; scholars believe she may be an ancient Power who has dwindled into a mere folktale.

The Months

Pepsmahin is the first month of the year, the month of the spring equinox when, even in the frozen mountains between Gehtaland and Rossmark, the world begins to wake (31 days).

Ferrin, the second month, is sacred to Viridys and Thalloa (29 days).

Fuallin is sacred to Vepris and Viridys together, and to Thalloa as well. The first day of Fuallin is one of the major feastdays in the calendar (31 days).

Therminas is the month of the summer solstice. It is sacred to Phaydos (29 days).

Melkinas is sacred to Mayn, who has a feastday as Mayn of the Swelling Udders, when she is honored as Mother of Beasts. She is often depicted as a cow in association with this month. In most lands, no meat may be eaten during the month of Mayn, although fish is permitted. Exceptions are made for pregnant and nursing women, the ill, the elderly and so forth. Indeed, many ways are found around this fast (31 days).

Morronas is a month of growth and plenty (29 days).

Aramin is the month of the autumn equinox and of the grain harvest in Eswiland; as such Aramin is sacred to Viridys as Lord of the Harvest (29 days).

Mullin is the "crown of autumn" and is again sacred to Viridys and, in Dunmorra, to Jock Wildwood (31 days).

Theyin is the ninth month and is dedicated to Fescor in those lands where this Power has an important place (29 days).

Desmin is the month of the winter solstice, dedicated to Fescor and to Phaydos (29 days).

Darthanin begins the year in the calendar of Dravidara (29 days).

Brotin, the Month of Shades, is the final month of the year in the Ronish calendar. Brotin is sacred to Geneh and is the month when the dead are remembered. Families make offerings of bread and wine and sweet oil at tombs or household shrines to honor their ancestors (28 days).

Roughly every other year, at the end of Brotin-month, between twenty-one and twenty-three days are added in order to keep the calendar in step with the seasons and the cycle of the sun. Determining how many days to add and when to add them is the preserve (and indeed the primary function) of the College of Astrologers in Rona. Some philosophers have advocated adopting the calendar of Dravidara, which is more accurate, but the College continues to be vehemently opposed to this idea.

"If one book has shaped what I think a book should do and what literature should be," K.V. Johansen says, "it is *Lord of the Rings*." As Tolkien was, she is thorough in her research as she creates other worlds for her stories. Readers will find themselves richly rewarded. Johansen, who has a master's degree in Medieval Studies, lives in a bit of another world herself; she grows exotic trees indoors and seedling oaks and apples outdoors in what used to be the vegetable garden, and hopes some day to have her very own forest, because both the house and the yard are getting rather crowded.

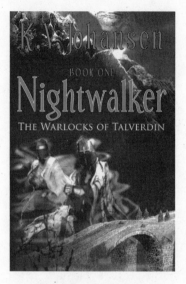

Book One

Nightwalker

The Warlocks of Talverdin

978-1-55143-481-0   PB $9.95 CDN • $8.95 US

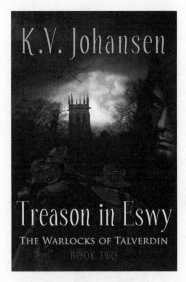

Book Two

Treason in Eswy

The Warlocks of Talverdin

978-1-55143-888-7   PB $9.95

Also by K.V. Johansen

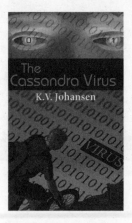

The Cassandra Virus

978-1-55143-497-1   PB $8.95 CDN • $7.95 US